Life comes a Full Circle!

Renuka Nair
& Mahesh Naulakha

BLUEROSE PUBLISHERS
India | U.K.

Copyright © Renuka Nair and Mahesh Naulakha 2024

All rights reserved by author. No part of this publication may be reproduced, stored in a retrieval system or transmitted in any form or by any means, electronic, mechanical, photocopying, recording or otherwise, without the prior permission of the author. Although every precaution has been taken to verify the accuracy of the information contained herein, the publisher assumes no responsibility for any errors or omissions. No liability is assumed for damages that may result from the use of information contained within.

BlueRose Publishers takes no responsibility for any damages, losses, or liabilities that may arise from the use or misuse of the information, products, or services provided in this publication.

For permissions requests or inquiries regarding this publication, please contact:

BLUEROSE PUBLISHERS
www.BlueRoseONE.com
info@bluerosepublishers.com
+91 8882 898 898
+4407342408967

ISBN: 978-93-5989-389-1

Cover design: Shivam
Typesetting: Namrata Saini

First Edition: March 2024

Dedications

Renuka Nair

I would like to dedicate this book to
my late sister Rekha Pillai.

Mahesh Naulakha

This book is dedicated to my parents who have always
encouraged me to achieve my dreams.

Acknowledgements

"Life is a full circle" suggests the cyclical nature of the often-testing circumstances that shape our eventful lives. This book is an amalgamation of real-life facts and fiction.

The support of my family and friends was a constant source of encouragement during this journey. My wise and dependable dad, Shri Rupendra, and my loving mother Smt. Saroj have inculcated strong values in me, especially respecting women.

Arti, the love of my life is my rock, my motivation to work hard and achieve my dreams. Divya, our daughter has truly lit up our lives. I feel so encouraged by her adoring smile. Not to forget the energy levels of my nephew Advitey. He probably gets it from his dad Amol, my wife's brother, a fashion designer, as his mother, is the kind soul who makes sure to cook all our favourite dishes when we meet.

So does my sister Richa, who has certainly passed on her calm nature to my niece Gopika. Her husband, Hemendra is considered as the 'Mr Dependable' of our family, the 'go to' person for all our issues.

Another very significant person in my life is my mentor Mr Amit Raina who reshaped my professional life.

My heartfelt gratitude to my past colleagues and family, who appear in the spruced-up chronicles that make up this book, and a special mention to my co-author Renuka, a former banker and colleague, for bringing this book to life.

I am sure book lovers will find it a gripping read.

Mahesh Naulakha

Acknowledgements

I was introduced to my co-author Mahesh during my stint at ICICI, but the pressure levels were so high then, that it was just his name that registered in my mind, not his face. In fact, for a very long time, I kept confusing Mahesh with another sales manager.

Well, we re-connected several decades later, after I quit the banking sector to start my own training institute, and I happened to mention it to him that I had published a novel centred around the RPOs (Recruitment Process Outsourcing) in Vadodara. I was really surprised when, after reading my book, he suggested we should pen a book together.

This happened three years ago, and I am grateful to him for urging me on through the often-frustrating journey, with our fair share of disagreements and verbal wars, to complete this book.

Then of course came the next step I always take before I submit a book to a publisher, that is run it by my "punctuation obsessed" husband, Paraman, and narrate the arguments we had over sentence constructions on the phone with our US based daughter, Vaidehi. She tutored me on the nuances of creative writing, and never hesitates to vocalise her dry humorous comments on my maverick ventures. This time around, my nephew, Tridib, also joined the literary cacophony from Singapore.

My non-judgemental sister-in-law, Mala, deserves a special mention for always appreciating my crazy endeavours. So do my best friends Brenda and Saswati.

There is another lady I have been blessed to become friends with, Priyanka, the prime mover of Manthan, the book lovers' club at Vadodara. Her passion for books and stories is exemplary, so is her dedication to whatever venture she undertakes.

Last but not the least, my friend, philosopher, and guide of 29 years, Pankaj, my first boss at NIIT in the 1990s. His positivity and sense of humour is truly inspiring, so is his vast knowledge.

My heartfelt gratitude to all of you.

Renuka Nair

Prologue

People who have spent more than a decade in sales have this incredible belief that they can talk themselves out of any sticky situation, immaterial of the fact that their world is crashing around them.

Adivteya knocked and entered his super boss Priyansh's cabin, holding onto that thought. He was confident Priyansh didn't summon him from Ahmedabad to Mumbai just to fire him. Human Resources (HR) would have done that or maybe would have politely asked him to resign as they did with his sales manager.

"Hey, Adivteya, come in. Have a seat. Did you have a good flight?" Priyansh rose from his chair to give him a friendly hug and a thump on his back.

"Yes, boss."

"So, that's quite a pickle you and Tony have got yourselves into, huh?'

"Boss, I'm being framed…"

"Save your breath son. I didn't ask you to come to Mumbai to repeat the details. You've already updated me in Ahmedabad. I summoned you to convey something else. Well, you must be aware of the cutthroat competition in Retail Banking, but you may not know an underlying fact. No one rises in this industry on their own merit. Everyone needs a godfather. You probably feel Tony's yours but he's about to throw you under the bus, Adivteya, as I've told him the only way, he can save his ass is to ensure you take the fall for what happened. HR wants heads to roll for the Rs 5 crore fraud that took place under your nose. They are not satisfied with asking your sales manager to leave. They want either yours or Tony's scalp."

Priyansh deliberately paused to gauge Adivteya's reaction and was disappointed with just a flicker of fear reflecting in Adivteya's eyes.

"Why am I here, boss?"

"I'll be your godfather and get both you and Tony out, provided you do something for me."

Adivteya listened, stupefied, to what the Vice President and National Head of Personal Loans at *TCI, The Credit Bank of India* wanted him to do.

"If don't, your nemesis will, but then you're out," Priyansh concluded callously, and opened his laptop; an indication that Adivteya should leave.

"Let me mull over it during my flight back to Ahmedabad," Adivteya stated, hoping the disgust spewing through his being didn't reflect on his face. He hurried out of the room, haunted by the words uttered a decade ago by the person he was being asked to betray now: *You cannot succeed in sales with that straightforward attitude of yours, Adi.*

Contents

Chapter 1: A hold over his boss 1
Chapter 2: Mettle 4
Chapter 3: Taming the Dork 8
Chapter 4: The son of his soil 13
Chapter 5: Poor little rich girl 17
Chapter 6: Change is the only constant! 22
Chapter 7: The Complexities of Retail Banking 25
Chapter 8: Survival of the Fittest 28
Chapter 9: A force to reckon with 33
Chapter 10: Internal Dynamics 38
Chapter 11: 'New High' 40
Chapter 12: Family Ritual 42
Chapter 13: Village Politics 45
Chapter 14: The horrors of his past 48
Chapter 15: Vanity 51
Chapter 16: Occupational hazards 54
Chapter 17: The Mountain has come to Mohamad! 57
Chapter 18: Arranged marriage 60
Chapter 19: Golden Goose 65
Chapter 20: I play smart! 69
Chapter 21: Alcohol virgin 73
Chapter 22: Catch-22 76
Chapter 23: The much-needed x-ray machine 80
Chapter 24: Wine, beer, and an escort in Rajkot 82
Chapter 25: A personal thing 87
Chapter 26: Alarm bells 91
Chapter 27: Anti-climax 94

Chapter 28: 'Seeing the girl'	97
Chapter 29: Tradition	100
Chapter 30: Skip tracing	103
Chapter 31: Love or lust?	106
Chapter 32: The alleged perpetrator	110
Chapter 33: Dark side	113
Chapter 34: Corruption	116
Chapter 35: The tide would turn	119
Chapter 36: Housewarming	122
Chapter 37: Déjà vu	125
Chapter 38: Insane Connections	128
Chapter 39: Fate	132
Chapter 40: Shattered Dreams!	135
Chapter 41: Work-life balance	138
Chapter 42: The Food Chain	141
Chapter 43: The Elephant in the Room	145
Chapter 44: A gut feeling	150
Chapter 45: From Cloud 9 to Cloud 0	154
Chapter 46: The horrors he had been living with	158
Chapter 47: Benched	162
Chapter 48: Blackmail?	166
Chapter 49: Bunty aur Babli	170
Chapter 50: Guilty until proven innocent	174
Chapter 51: A pattern	177
Chapter 52: A murky aspect	180
Chapter 53: And the plot thickens	185
Chapter 54: The Mastermind	189
Chapter 55: Aukaat	192
Chapter 56: Just another day at work	196
Chapter 57: Contempt for bankers	201
Chapter 58: The Crime Scene	204

Chapter 59: Dilemmas 207
Chapter 60: A time bomb 211
Chapter 61: If a criminal lawyer wants to commit
murder, he will cover his tracks. 215
Chapter 62: What might have transpired? 218
Chapter 63: Gimmick 220
Chapter 64: Quid Pro Quo 225
Chapter 65: Just Lucky 228
Chapter 66: A Convenient Label 233
Chapter 67: Nonchalant revelation 238
Chapter 68: Practical Logic 243
Chapter 69: The two alpha males 246
Chapter 70: It takes a crook… 251
Chapter 71: Needle in a haystack 255
Chapter 72: Beating the System 258
Chapter 73: Digging his own grave. 261
Chapter 74: All in a day's work 264
Chapter 75: Lacunae 268
Epilogue 272

Chapter 1

A Hold over His Boss

The very first day of the new financial year, April 2002 was an exceedingly hot and humid one in Mumbai. Adivteya, a.k.a. Adi was all sweaty and clammy when he set foot in the opulent lobby of the elite publication *Mumbai Xclusive (MX)*. It functioned not only as a Mumbai guidebook, but also featured advertisements of offbeat eateries, fashion houses, jewellery stores, and so on.

The job offer of a Management Trainee from *MX* had been one of the several, he had received during campus placements at FMS Delhi. He had accepted it mainly because the publication had the backing of a prestigious Indian conglomerate. Of course, the clinching factor was Mumbai, Bollywood's heartland. Having lived most of his life in the North of India, Adi couldn't wait to experience the city's glamour.

The receptionist, who appeared to have just stepped out of the cover pages of *Vogue India*, informed him he could find his new boss Tony Braganza seated at the second last workstation at the far end of the hall. So, Adi pushed open yet another glass door and was hit by a cacophony of sounds. Weaving his way through smartly dressed men and women scuttling about, shouting, chatting, or simply greeting each other, he suddenly froze; his wandering eyes zeroing in on a tall, thin girl dressed in black trousers, a white shirt with diaphanous sleeves, and 6" black heels.

'Is she an alien?' the bizarre thought popped up in his mind on meeting her eyes heavily eyeshadowed in a shade of blue that matched the colour of her straight silky hair. It didn't take her even a fraction of a second to roll her eyes away in disgust. Embarrassed, Adi shifted his gaze to the man she was standing beside; a short, plump guy, seated at the corner workstation. Clearing his throat, Adi mumbled, "Er, excuse me, Sir. I'm Adivteya Ahlavat, the Management Trainee, and I'm here to report to Mr Tony Braganza."

"Who? What the hell?" the man probably would have turned to Adi, had it not been for a projectile landing smack in the middle of his workstation.

"Who threw this?" he bellowed, rising from his seat.

"I did."

"What now, Tony?"

Adi stared in amazement at the plump man's resigned demeanour on seeing a six-foot, 2-inch guy with silky black hair and a stocky physique saunter up to him, declaring, "That's the pre-press layout for this month without Z Boutique's advertisement, Saurabh. Mona's not willing to bulge. Your call, boss. We'll lose our biggest money spinner if Z's full-page ad isn't featured in this month's issue."

"Mona!"

Saurabh's thunderous roar almost made Adi wet his pants. He turned to survey the pin-drop silence that suddenly shrouded the office. A diminutive, full-figured lady dressed in blue jeans and an olive shirt walked unhurriedly towards them. "You summoned, Saurabh?" she enquired softly, halting a foot to the left of the haggard man with rumpled salt and pepper hair.

"Mona, please rearrange the pre-press layout. We can't lose Z's account," Saurabh pleaded.

"No can do. This is the third month wherein *Z's* cheque came in after the deadline. I accommodated them last month only for your sake S, but I can't anymore. Jatin's new restaurant *Gypsy Rose* in Versova takes precedence this month because their cheque for the same amount as *Z's* was cleared a week before the deadline. Now if you'll excuse me," Mona informed calmly, making a move to return to her workstation.

Adi couldn't help sneaking a glance at Tony and gawked for a second at the sight of Tony chatting, totally unfazed, with the blue-haired beauty. He quickly turned his attention back to Saurabh on hearing him plead, "Please, Mona, for last time, darling. *Z's* after all one of our oldest clients. Tony will ensure their cheque is cleared way before the deadline next month."

"Yeah, sure!" Mona snorted, ambling back to her workstation, ignoring Saurabh's ardent, "Thank you, sweetheart. I love you."

Darling, sweetheart, I love you?

"Who are you?"

Realising Saurabh was addressing him, Adi spluttered, "Adivteya Ahlavat. The Management Trainee."

"Tony, kindly get started with this recruit," Saurabh requested.

"Yes, boss. Anything for you, you're the best," Tony responded, turning to Adi, "come I'll introduce you to HR."

A strange sense of security descended over Adi as he followed the man who obviously had a hold over his boss.

Chapter 2

Mettle

August is probably one of the worst months in Mumbai, with its sweltering humidity. A tad happy to be back in the air-conditioned confines of *MX's* main hall, Adi tried to imitate Tony's swagger while walking to his workstation at the farthest end. He was about to saunter past a meeting room which appeared to be occupied, when Tony shouted from within, "Ahlavat, come in."

He didn't want to go in. It was 3 pm. He was tired and hungry as he had been pounding the streets of Juhu since morning, hoping to convince some new vendors to advertise in their publication. None of the ones he approached wanted to. After working at *MX* for four months, he had only managed to land a few Rs. 10K adverts. So, right now, he just wanted to drown his failure in the parathas he had cooked and sit for a while at his workstation, doing nothing.

Unfortunately, boss had summoned, so he hastened inside the room, trying not to cringe at the anger spewing from Tony's eyes. A quick glance at Mohit's smug face made him realise he was in hot water.

"How come Mohit picked up *Z Boutique's* cheque this month, and not you?" Tony snarled.

"I asked him why he did it, and he said territories are just a formality. Anyone can pick up a cheque from any customer because after all the business comes to *MX*."

"You imbecile! Is that what they taught you at FMS Delhi, to bend over so that another smart Management Trainee can screw you? Go and get me a 5-lakh cheque to compensate for what I lost to Jatin. I have been the top sales manager for the entire year. Today, your stupidity will result in Jatin's monthly revenue exceeding mine. Get me a cheque for more than 5 lakhs before the day ends. Prove the mettle of your MBA tag else I'll demote you and make sure you report to Mohit."

Thoughts of his favourite lentil parathas and his mom's red chilli pickle were replaced with the bitter taste of office politics. For some bizarre reason, *MX's* hierarchy, as narrated by HR on his first day started playing in his mind: *Saurabh's the Western Zonal Head of Sales. Tony, Jatin, Leila (the blue-haired girl), and two other men are the sales managers who are responsible for ensuring the publication gets sufficient advertisements to keep it profitable. Each of the salespersons had their own Management Trainees who scout for new clients.*

Three months before Adi's arrival, Mohit Patil, a trainee, was assigned to Jatin. Andheri was to be looked after by Mohit, while Adi had to handle Juhu, which was only eight km away. Adi's task was to approach and persuade small company owners, restaurants, and shops who hadn't yet advertised in *MX* to do so. Prior to the publication deadline, he also needed to pick up the monthly advertisement checks from Tony's clients in Juhu, but sadly, Mohit had been shrewd and had already picked up Z Boutique's check before him. Now he had to do something fast.

Recollecting Mona's disclosure on his first day about Jatin's new client, *Gypsy Rose*, a restaurant in Andheri, Adi hailed a cab, determined to turn the tables on Mohit.

His agitation increased in the crawling traffic, and he lost his nerve by the time he reached his destination. The exteriors looked so quaint and elegant with black wrought iron tables and chairs, a candy-striped awning, and red velvet ropes on gold stands separating it from the other establishments. The sheer urge to repair the damage he had done to his new idol Tony's position, gave him the courage to push open the closed doors of the restaurant and approach an impeccably dressed lady manning the cash counter.

"Hello, ma'am. I'm here to collect this month's cheque for *Mumbai Xclusive.*"

"Oh, are you in Jatin's team because he said we must hand over the cheque only to his team members," the lady enquired, trying hard not to hide her distaste as she appraised him from head to toe.

"Yes."

"What's your name?" she questioned, reaching for the phone.

"Er, Ronak. Jatin won't answer your call. He's in a meeting," Adi blurted, praying there was a Ronak in Jatin's team.

"Hey, Jatin! Sorry to disturb you. Ronak's here to collect this month's cheque. Shall I give it to him? What? Oh, okay."

Adi wiped his sweaty palms on his polyester trousers, trying to gauge what was being spoken at the other end.

"Why don't you have a seat, Ronak? Can I get you some tea, coffee, or maybe something to eat while my accounts department prepares the cheque?" she surprised him with her suggestion.

"Er, no," Adi replied nervously, pulling out the nearest chair.

He enviously surveyed the plush interiors, realising he needed a client like this to shine in Tony's eyes.

It might have been 15 minutes later when the wooden front doors opened. Adi's heart sank on seeing Mohit stride in and proclaim, "You can leave Ronak, I'll pick up the cheque."

"No, boss told me to collect it," Adi insisted.

"What's going on here?" the lady behind the counter enquired.

"Ma'am anyone from *Mumbai Xclusive* can pick up a cheque from a client. Since I was here first, it would be good if you could give me the cheque," Adi spoke first, praying she would agree.

"No this is my territory. Ma'am, my sales manager Jatin Sir, and I closed the deal with you. So, request you to please hand over the cheque to me," Mohit objected.

"You guys better get your house in order before you harass your clients for cheques. I'm not giving the cheque to either of you. I think I'll go with *CitiLights*, your competitor. Now, please, both of you, leave my restaurant," the lady instructed coldly.

Chapter 3

Taming the Dork

"Are you like retarded or something?"

Adi winced on hearing the sultry voice that matched Leila's personality.

She was the last person he had expected to approach him after the blasting Saurabh had doled out to Tony and Jatin for poor leadership skills. Adi had thought Tony would fire him. Tony, on the contrary, hadn't said a word. The whole floor, unfortunately, had heard Saurabh's tirade about losing a new account. Although Mohit had started it, everyone was throwing vile glances at Adi, slumped now at his workstation, wondering if he should go out and search for a new client, or just hop onto the next train back home. 'No, I can't admit defeat after merely four months of work. I need to hang on for two more months to be confirmed as a Sales Manager. Damn, will they extend my probation...'

"You are a dork!" Leila declared, unrelentingly.

"Sure, salt my wounds," Adi murmured, turning away from the only lady in the man's world of sales at *Mumbai Xclusive*. "What's a dork?" he added, curious.

"Come. I need a fag," she proclaimed, clutching his arm to drag him, when he refused to budge.

"I'm not gay," he responded, scandalized, marvelling at the strength in her skinny body as she had managed to drag him with his chair for a few feet.

"What! Obviously, you wouldn't know the other meaning of fag 'cus you're a dork! Come on idiot, I didn't call you a fag, I said I want to smoke. Yeah, you don't smoke, just come with me," she clarified, rolling her eyes. As uncanny as it may seem, Adi had been Leila's passive smoking partner on several occasions before, mainly when she needed someone to listen to her rant on a deal gone wrong or missed targets.

"A dork is an odd, socially awkward, unstylish person. Your smelly, oily hair, flowery polyester shirts, shiny pants, and the plastic bag you keep carrying around makes you look like a low-grade politician's sidekick. You're the face of our publication in one of the most up-market territories in Mumbai. You need to look well groomed." She bluntly came to the point, after lighting a cigarette in the parking lot outside their office, eyeing him through the smoke she was deliberately blowing at his face, despite him trying to dodge it.

"That's ridiculous! I use a hair oil brand promoted by Amitabh Bachchan. Even Manish Malhotra oils his hair."

"Manish GELS his hair. Which village are you from?" Her question punctuated by another eye roll.

"Bulandshahr. It's not a village, it's a proper city. I hail from a wealthy family of zamindars, landowners. We are *Jats*," he protested, but she cut him off, "no wonder you went barging into *Gypsy Rose*, demanding a cheque. Save your story for later. I hope your family hasn't disowned you and you're still rich because I'm taking you shopping after work. 'The Taming of the Dork' is about to begin. First, I'll get you dressed, then I'll teach you how to become an effective salesperson. Let's head back now. Oh, I'll pour a whole bottle of water on your head if you dare use that stinking hair oil with your new clothes. Use gel on your unruly hair."

She had turned her back to him after her declaration, so she didn't see him mimicking her under his breath, 'Use gel, chemicals instead of herbal oil. Damn, these big city snobs.'

*

'Mom will freak if she knows I paid 500 bucks for a haircut, but it's worth it. I do look good,' Adi thought, staring at his reflection in the *Jawed Habib Hair and Beauty* salon's mirror.

"Stop preening. We've got a long way to go. Come on," Leila chided, grabbing his arm.

Gritting his teeth at her bossy tone, he allowed himself to be led into an Allen Solly store.

"What size?" she questioned before the immaculately dressed salesperson could.

"I don't know."

"Mama gets all your clothes tailored for you?" she mocked, while the salesperson rushed forward with a measuring tape.

"Yes, so what?"

"Nothing. So, tell me, apart from the inherent testosterone gushing through the bodies of *Jats*, what made you think you could just barge into *Gypsy Rose* and pick up the cheque?" she inquired, shifting through the formal shirts the salesperson laid out in front of her.

"Tit-for-tat. They played dirty so why shouldn't I? Tony asked me to make up for the business he lost, so I tried to poach Mohit's territory just like he did mine. The thing is, I've always been straightforward. Once, when I was a kid, my mom bought 3 kilos of mangoes, but she forgot about it after getting into a fight with dad. I love mangoes and I wanted her to cut some for me, but she was angry that day, so, I waited for a while before asking her what I should do with the mangoes. Well, her anger hadn't subsided yet and she told me to throw them in the dustbin. I did it. She was so furious when she remembered the next day that she didn't allow me to eat a single slice of mango that summer," he confessed, innocently, earning himself another of her eye rolls.

"Okay, mama's boy. Save your pompous declarations of your lineage and cloying stories for your girlfriend. They are not going to help you succeed in sales nor will your straightforwardness. You need to dress smartly, be worldly-wise, and charm the pants off your clients. You must also portray you're trustworthy but not by flashing your education or job title. Now try these on," she counselled sarcastically, shoving a handful of clothes against his chest.

"I want to see how each combination looks on you," she called out, following him to the trial room.

'And she calls me a mama's boy. Thank God, she didn't follow me into the cubicle,' Adi chuckled inwardly, trying on the first set of clothes.

He dutifully modelled each item she had selected and smirked inwardly when she casually trailed her fingers down his arm or subtly caressed his chiselled jaw while adjusting a collar. She had been brushing and pressing herself against him since they had hailed a cab post work for his makeover. Fortunately, he hadn't responded like a sex-starved 'country boy', her latest nickname for him. Being in the proximity of girls for three years at B school had taught him that not every touch or hug was sexual. So, while he was amused by Leila's sudden touchy-feely attitude, he was deliberately not reacting, waiting to see where or how far she would go with it.

"You owe me a dinner," she declared when he finally paid the bill for his new wardrobe.

"Sure," he agreed and followed her into a *Hard Rock Café*.

"I'll order country boy because they don't serve parathas here." She took over once again, brushing her knee against his under the table.

"Where do you live?" he enquired as they waited for their food.

"Bandra. No more personal questions. Now if you want to become a performer, you need to know what the competition is offering. You must also smother the potential client with statistics regarding how a Rs 2 lakh or a Rs 5 lakh advert in our publication will increase their visibility 10-fold because our publications are placed in shops and strategic locations frequented by tourists, especially foreigners......"

Her monologue continued all through dinner as she downed four martinis. They finally stepped out of the mall at 10 pm and she promptly lit a cigarette.

"Are you a virgin?"

He had to fight hard to stop his lips from curving upwards on hearing the question he was sure she had hoped would unnerve him. Adopting a 'man of the world' attitude like she had advised him to, he quipped, "I thought we had decided not to ask personal questions."

"You can't but I can. So, are you?"

"Why do you want to know?"

"Because I want to get laid, but I don't want to sleep with a virgin," she retorted, stubbing out her cigarette.

He closed the distance between them, slipped his arm around her waist, and pulled her hard against him.

"It's just a random thing. Don't get attached," she gasped, clearly 'turned-on' by his 'macho' move.

'You wanted to 'Tame the Dork'. Looks like I'll be 'Taming the Shrew',' he smirked inwardly, hailing a cab.

Chapter 4

The Son of His Soil

The elegant yet understated lobby may have overwhelmed any man setting foot in a five-star hotel for the first time, except Adi. It had been an exhausting year, with him working for 14-16 hours a day and through most weekends to retain his position as the 'Star' performer of the year at *Mumbai Xclusive.* Having managed to help Tony beat Jatin who was neck-to-neck in the race to log in the highest annual advert revenue, he had just wanted to curl up on his bed in his bachelor pad and sleep, instead of being at JW Juhu that night. But Leila wouldn't hear of it.

"Adi, you're committing career suicide by not attending your very first 'Corporate' party at *Mumbai Exclusive.* Everyone from Eshwar the Business Head, right down to the new Trainees will be there, so you, the 'Outstanding Performer' cannot be absent. Get dressed, I'm coming to pick you up in 15," Leila had insisted over the phone.

So, he had donned his newest pair of Killer blue jeans, a black and blue plaid shirt, and a pair of old, scuffed Nikes. Since Leila was his senior, he had assumed the 'pick you up' would at least be in a Maruti 800. It had been a nerve-wracking 20-minute pillion ride on her 'Scooty' from his pad in Andheri East to JW Marriot, Juhu, with him clinging onto the bar behind him. It had bruised his 'Jat' ego when she had refused his offer to drive, so he had been determined not to clutch her slim shoulders, as she wove through the traffic.

"Hey, I forgot to tell you, the Bollywood stars love this hotel. Look, there's Sunny Deol in the lobby beside Mahesh Bhatt!"

Leila's casual declaration on entering the lobby snapped Adi out of his lassitude. A glance in the direction she was indicating, confirmed that the famous Bollywood actor was indeed in conversation with the popular director who had shot to fame with his 'true to life' scandalous films.

"Wait here. I'm going to get his autograph," Adi stated, heading towards them.

"No, you're not, country boy. Eshwar's about to address our team," she objected, grabbing his arm and dragged him down a winding stairway to the Emerald Room.

"How are you guys doing tonight?" Eshwar's voice boomed over the microphone the moment they pushed open the massive doors.

"We're doing great."

The entire room with 230 employees from Eshwar's vertical pan India, who had assembled for the party that night responded.

"Awesome. You guys rock! What's our mantra?" Eshwar questioned.

"Work hard, party harder," the room resonated again.

"Spot on. Let the party begin."

The lights dimmed as the strobe lights turned on and hard rock spewed from the speakers.

"Come on, let's get a drink," Leila suggested, grabbing his arm.

He complied, knowing he would be rewarded later. No matter how much she bossed around him and her team during the week, she was his docile partner during the weekends, responding eagerly to his lovemaking and giving him as much as she received. Adi was quite happy with their 'no strings attached' relationship. She was good company and had seriously taught him the ropes of sales including doling out gaalis, so his team would fear him. She had also introduced him to Hollywood and high fashion, simultaneously helping him to polish his English.

"Let's dance," she declared, downing half her drink in one massive swig. She sashayed up to the section left vacant for dancing, with him in tow, swaying with her glass to the thumping bass.

Adi was in his element on the dance floor. While he was still partial to Bollywood remixes, spending almost a year with Leila had given him enough practice at swaying to Western music. Probably an hour had passed when Leila whispered in his ear, "I want to smoke, come with me."

She extracted a pack of Marlboro Lights from her clutch purse before they could reach the hotel parking, and lit a stick, inhaling like her life depended on it.

"Looks like you're having the time of your life, country boy," she stated, eyeing him over the cloud of smoke she exhaled.

"Yeah, I get my kicks from dancing," he agreed.

"Who's your favourite Bollywood star?" she enquired.

"Amitabh Bachchan."

"Cool. Turn around and you'll see him."

"You're drunk," he responded, complying reflexively, only to find the tall, strapping actor striding across the parking lot.

"You've got to be kidding me!" he exclaimed, as he watched the silver screen legend walk towards a Lexus, with his son, Abhishek, at the wheel.

Ignoring Leila's restraining arm, he rushed towards his idol, frantically searching the pockets of his clothes for a piece of paper. Finding a visiting card of *Mumbai Xclusive* proclaiming him to be a Sales Manager, he held it out as he approached his idol, "Bachchan sir, may I have your autograph, please?"

"Sure, young man," he responded in his signature baritone, scrawling his name across the rectangular card that had been a source of pride and joy to Adi till now.

Amitabh then slid into the car, and Adi watched the Bachchans drive away for a few seconds before he floated back to a nonchalant Leila. Having grown up in Bandra, the preferred locale of Bollywood stars, Leila never got excited on seeing an actor in flesh and blood.

They returned to the party and Adi was called onto the makeshift stage with a flourish after a while, to receive the award for the 'Star Performer' of the financial year 2002-2003 at *Mumbai Xclu*sive from Eshwar. Adi, however, couldn't help feeling that the bigger win was the autograph of the illustrious son of his soil, the Bollywood legend who had been raised in Prayagraj (formerly known as Allahabad), a city just 700 kilometres from his hometown.

Chapter 5

Poor Little Rich Girl

It was probably because he was raised in a joint family and then had to share a hostel room with three boys during his MBA days that Adi decided he would live alone in Mumbai, immaterial of the bomb he had to pay for his tiny studio apartment. The room only had enough space for a 6 x 4 feet bed and a cupboard. The bed facilitated snuggling though, and that's precisely what Adi did that Sunday morning. He tightened his arm around Leila and drew her closer; her sweet fragrance stirring up desires he had thought would remain dormant for a while, post their frenzied sessions last night.

Realising she was in deep sleep; he buried his face in her silky hair, which was blonde now with black tips. Unable to ignore the rumbling in his stomach any longer, he gently eased her head from his arm, tucked the covers around her and got out of bed. Heading for the kitchen, he munched on some biscuits while going through the motions of preparing Aloo Parathas for breakfast.

"Come back to bed, country boy." He smiled on hearing her call out sleepily and removed the last paratha from the iron skillet. Turning off the flame, he neatly stacked the parathas on a plate and carried them to the bedroom along with some curd and mango pickle.

"Sit up, my lady, your breakfast is ready," he announced jovially, settling both himself and the food on the bed.

"Breakfast in bed, huh? Are you trying to make me fall in love with you?" she murmured, surfacing from beneath the cotton sheet.

"Why would I do that when it would ruin a perfectly good friendship?" Adi responded honestly. He was immensely contented with their casual 'Friends with occasional benefits' relationship. Although she was Tony's rival, and he reported to Tony, Leila had become his confidant. She was a very good listener and never hesitated to guide him. Most importantly, she kept his straightforward nature in check. He knew she was dating other guys because she never hid them from him. She encouraged him also to date other girls, but he was happy with his life; not interested or ready to let a new lady in.

"So, tell me, did you adopt this 'hard as nails' persona after you joined *MX*?" Adi couldn't help enquiring.

"Hey, I thought we decided, no personal questions," she objected, frowning.

"Aw, come on. We've been friends for more than a year now. Tell me something about yourself."

"Why? So, you can pity me? I don't want your sympathy or protection. Save your Jat chivalry for another girl," she retorted, placing a piece of paratha she was about to eat, back on the plate, while he continued to wolf down his.

Lighting a cigarette, she opened the only window in the room and took a long drag.

"Hey, sorry. Forget I asked. It's just that I often find you speaking tensely over the phone or looking dejected," Adi apologised, pushing aside the plate with only a solitary paratha remaining from the stack of six he had prepared.

"The reason why I have a 'no strings attached' relationship with random men is because I don't want to make the same mistake my mom did. She was only 16 when she fell in love with my dad, her schoolmate. My mom is much more beautiful than me, that's why my dad was probably insecure, and insisted they get married immediately after she completed her BA in Psychology.

"He was still in his final year of Engineering then, but they didn't have to worry about money because he hailed from a very wealthy family. Dad's parents bought a flat for them and what I remember from my mom's stories, they were happy. Being bigwigs in advertising, Dad's family often threw lavish parties for their clients, so Mom eventually became his hostess. I was conceived two years later much to their disappointment because they wanted a male heir. Dad had already taken over the family business by then.

"So, my parents kept trying, but for some reason, mom kept miscarrying. I guess her obsession with my dad set in around that time because his business was growing, and he couldn't spend much time with her. She used to attend their parties but was always suspicious of the beautiful women who talked and laughed with Dad. They had bitter fights about it later. As far as I could remember, Dad would always come to my room and talk to me after each fight. He would tell me how much he loved me and Mom, and that he was faithful to her. Anyway, she conceived again when I was seven and was confined to bed rest. That was also fine because I used to spend most of my time after school with her.

"Everything changed when my brother Noel was born. Mum's obsession shifted to him. She stopped caring for anything else, including Dad and his parties. She even insisted they sleep in different rooms. Dad had become my best friend by then but unfortunately, we stopped doing things together as a family. Dad cooked for him and me while Mom took care of Noel's meals. Noel started objecting to the smothering on turning 14. He had also drifted so far apart from me and Dad too, that he practically ignored us.

"Well, I enrolled for MBA in Marketing in NMIMS the following year and was amid a class presentation when dad came to my college to get me. Noel had overdosed on heroin. We had moved to a swanky 6-bedroom penthouse on Bandstand by then, with a bedroom for each family member. We were all living under one roof, but we didn't know Noel was an addict, or when he became one.

"Mom couldn't take it. She had a nervous breakdown and never recovered from it. She's highly delusional now and under heavy medication. Dad checked Noel into a rehab centre nearby and moved him to my paternal grandparent's house. They are very loving and supportive. They never blamed my mum for what happened. My grandma taught me grooming and social etiquette. In fact, she's been doing all the things my mom should have done for me, instead of neglecting me after Noel's birth.

"I started hosting parties for my dad when I turned 16. They were fun. However, my dad and grandparents wanted me to join the family business after I completed my MBA, but I wanted to get a taste of the outside world, so I took up this job with *MX*. Let's see, maybe later when I've gained sufficient experience, I may take over the reins," Leila shrugged, concluding her 'Poor little rich girl' saga.

She stubbed out what was probably her fifth cigarette since she had started speaking and turned from the window to sit beside Adi. He put an arm around her and drew her close. They sat in silence for a while, each lost in their own mind space. He couldn't help thinking how lucky he was to have a balanced, yet loving and doting mom. Sure, she's unsophisticated, having spent all her life in a small village, but she's a highly respected English teacher there.

"Hey, let's not make this a depressing Sunday. How about we go to Essel World? You've never been there, right?" Leila suddenly declared, disengaging herself from his embrace and bounding off the bed.

A broad smile spread over Adi's face at her mention of India's largest amusement theme park located close to Borivali. "You're amazing! How about a quick shower before we leave?" he suggested, impishly.

Chapter 6

Change is the Only Constant!

Adi felt ancient on concluding his meeting with the new Management Trainee assigned to him. 'Almost everyone who was here when I joined *MX* five years ago, has moved on,' he thought, walking dejectedly towards his workstation. He sat down on his chair and reached into his backpack to extract two thick bond envelopes. One had been handed over to him by Jatin, the new Zonal Business head; promoted when Saurabh took up *Pepsi India*'s National Head role. Jatin had personally walked over to his workstation yesterday morning to give him the envelope, congratulating him heartily for becoming the only Area Sales Manager in Mumbai.

Both Jatin and Tony had this job title till January 2007. Then Saurabh had suddenly submitted his resignation and Jatin had been promoted over Tony. It had taken Tony only a week to clinch an Area Sales Manager's job with *TCI, The Credit Bank of India*. He had immediately submitted his resignation and had been relieved the very next month after serving the notice period.

Adi had been devastated, especially because Tony's posting was in Ahmedabad, not Mumbai. It was not as though he and Tony were bosom pals or anything; it was just that Tony had become his idol over the past 5 years. Tony certainly pushed his team to the brink, only to reward them magnanimously with parties in some of Mumbai's most coveted discos and nightclubs. While he was harsh with the underperformers, he also supported them and fought hard with HR for salary increments for the deserving ones.

Confident Tony had a soft corner for him, Adi had rushed out after Tony on his last day at *MX*, questioning bluntly, "Why are you letting your ego force you to settle for something less when you're capable of much more?"

"Saale, if it had been anyone but you to ask me this question, I would have punched him in the face. You may have grown in these five years, Adi, but you're still a kid. There's no future at *MX*. *TCI* on the other hand is a leading private sector MNC bank in India today. I'm joining their Personal Loans (PL) vertical. So, what if it's the same job title I have here, it's with a bigger and better organization with a global and pan India presence. Hey, what if I get you a job at *TCI*, will you join me?" Tony had responded in his usual confident, go-getter style.

"Of course, I would boss. You'll succeed at anything you put your mind in," Adi had responded reflexively.

Well, the aftermath of his response was in the second bond envelope; an offer from *TCI*, for a Senior Sales Manager's role in the Personal Loans segment. Lowering his eyes to the CTC (Cost to the Company) portion, he held both the letters in each hand and started comparing the salaries each was offering.

"There's no way you're taking *TCI*'s job as long as I'm here at *MX*."

Guilt tugged at his heart as he allowed Leila to pluck *TCI*'s letter from his hands. The net salary was nearly double what *MX* was offering and so were the perks. The only catch was that the job was in Ahmedabad, yet another unfamiliar city. Further, it was kind of a demotion.

"Shall I tear it, or do you want to preserve it for posterity?" Leila enquired, flippantly.

"Leila, I hate Mumbai," he tried to reason, snatching the letter back.

"No, you don't. It's your *'bromance'* with Tony, that's confusing you," she retorted, walking away.

'Damn,' Adi cursed inwardly, acknowledging the fact that the *'bromance'* would have never developed had Leila not taken the trouble to teach him the ropes of sales in the first place. Their physical chemistry had fizzled out around four years ago, but they had continued to remain buddies.

*

"How about a Saturday night out at *Blue Frog* with your new boyfriend?" Adi suggested a week later, knowing she loved that nightclub.

"I broke up with him," she responded impassively.

"Okay, then it's just the two of us," Adi pressed on.

"Are you trying to placate my hurt at the fact that you chose Tony over me, so, you'll be relieved at the end of this month?" she questioned candidly.

"Yes. Leila, you'll always be the best lady friend in my life. Please try to understand, I didn't choose Tony over you, I chose a better life. Please don't let me leave knowing that you're so angry, you'll never forgive me," Adi pleaded.

"On one condition, I may want to get laid so be prepared," she declared unabashedly.

"I'll never say no to a chance to sleep with the sexiest lady I've ever known," he tried to joke, grateful they could part ways amicably. Change after all is the only constant in life!

Chapter 7

The Complexities of Retail Banking

Two months into *TCI*, Adi managed to gain some insight into the banking industry. On one hand, there were the Indian public sector banking giants like State Bank of India, Bank of Baroda and so on. Then there were the private players like ICICI, HDFC bank, etcetera. Although foreign or MNC banks had their presence in India for quite a while, by the time Adi joined *TCI* in 2007, MNC banks were considered 'The Banks' to work for, mainly for their lucrative pay packets.

They were also extremely aggressive in Retail Banking, an important vertical of any bank, that assisted consumers in managing their money, have access to credit, and make secure investments. Services offered by retail banks include current and savings accounts, mortgages, personal loans, credit cards, and certificates of deposit (CDs). This department is also responsible for selling third-party products like insurance, mutual funds and so on, which brought in fee-based income for the bank.

Another incentive was their swanky offices. *TCI* had leased out a six-storied building on Navrangpura Main Road and revamped it with marble, glass, and chrome. There was a cafeteria on the fifth floor, and the entire top floor was allotted to the loans department, that is the staff involved in the processing of Home, Personal, Two-Wheeler and Auto loans. The sales teams sat on the left of the elevators and the operations and credit team occupied the space on the right.

Tony being an Area Sales Manager, had a cubical to the right of the entrance to the sales half, while his senior sales managers, Adi and Bharat were allotted workstations beside his cubicle.

Adi was seated at his workstation that morning when Tony suddenly bellowed, "Ahlavat, why isn't the Tallinn Chemicals' case approved yet?"

There were many ways through which loans were sourced by banks, and Adi's team alone logged in over 50 Personal Loan (PL) files in a day, so it was very difficult for him to keep track of each file. After a few initial slip-ups, he started maintaining his own Excel sheet with details of his files. He didn't need to consult his sheet though, on hearing Tony's query regarding the sanction, as Tallinn Chemicals Pvt Ltd was his first big-ticket PL case of Rs 20 lakhs, the maximum permitted limit for an unsecured loan. Unfortunately, it had been forced on him by the Small and Medium Enterprises (SME) division of the bank.

They were in the process of sanctioning a Cash Credit facility to the company and they had convinced the promotor to avail a personal loan so he could pay for a term plan insurance with them. Tony had fought tooth and nail to get the term plan to be booked in Adi's name so that the fee-based income from it would be reflected in the PL department, but the SME sales manager had used his clout in the bank to get the insurance booked in his name. This case only added to Adi's confusion as to why entities within the Retail Assets vertical were at war with each other.

That wasn't the only issue though. To make matters worse, Trisha, the PL Area Credit Manager had declined the case yesterday, citing the client's financials weren't strong enough. SME had stepped in once again and Adi had baulked on hearing the SME credit manager tear her apart in front of the Branch Head, him, and Tony. The Branch Head had put her boss Swamy on speaker phone and Swamy had demanded she recommend the case for approval. She had stood firm declaring the case was a sure shot NPA (nonperforming asset). That was when Adi had childishly coined the 'Iron Lady' moniker for her. Out of sheer exasperation, Swamy had ordered her to email the case to him.

"Will do, boss," she had politely agreed, thanked everyone, and had excused herself from the room as though they had just shared a cup of tea.

No one knew whether she had even forwarded the email as she hadn't kept anyone in the loop, nor did anyone have the guts to ask her, as she was renowned for her ability to ignore people who tried to push her.

"I'll check with the 'Iron Lady', boss," Adi responded, shaking his head at the complexities of Retail Banking.

Rising from his workstation, he exited the main glass door, crossed the three feet wide corridor, held his magnetic *TCI* identity card against the card reader mounted on the wall beside another glass door, and pushed it open, scowling at the prospect of interacting with Trisha Mishra, the 'Iron Lady.'

Chapter 8

Survival of the Fittest

His scowl deepened as he approached her corner workstation, because the suave Bharat Mohan, his arch-rival, was perched on the space meant for her files. Bharat had been recruited from a competitor, *Oakland Bank*, so had Tony's boss, Priyansh, the regional head of Gujarat and Rajasthan. In fact, a few months prior to Adi joining *TCI*, several senior personnel had been poached from *Oakland Bank*, with offers of coveted positions in Operations, Product, Sales, Risk, and other departments in the loans division.

Adi's eyes shifted between Bharat and Trisha. She was a stunningly beautiful lady. Bharat too didn't lack in the looks department. His branded clothes enhanced his 5 feet 9" sturdy physique, chiselled face, and tousled wavy hair. To top it all, he had magnetic light brown eyes with a devilish glint that Adi was sure made women swoon over him, including Trisha, probably, for Bharat's approval rate was much higher than his. That was until he had stumbled upon one of Bharat's files. It was a Rs 2 lakh PL sanctioned to a person who operated an auto repair shop from a makeshift handcart. Adi had been stunned to see that it hadn't been Trisha who had approved the case. It had been escalated all the way up to the head of the risk unit who had accorded the sanction.

He had immediately taken up the matter with Tony, "Boss, you knew Bharat's escalating the cases Trisha declines and getting them approved by the seniors. Why didn't you tell me about it?"

"Because you are too straightforward for it. You don't have the cut-throat mentality Bharat does," Tony had candidly replied.

Adi had instantly learnt two valuable lessons. A good leader should never force his subordinate to confront his weakness. He must point it out at the right moment and either guide him if necessary or leave him to learn how to overcome it. The second lesson was that aggression is always necessary to survive in sales, irrespective of the industry.

This didn't stop Adi from turning green each time he spotted Bharat hovering around Trisha though, whenever he wanted his files to be approved on priority. Almost all the other members of the PL sales team including Adi were wary of approaching her when Bharat was around as Bharat had demonstrated on several occasions that he could get away with physically removing a salesperson from the spot till his work was done. Much to Adi's chagrin, Trisha seemed to revel under Bharat's attention and Tony kept exemplifying him as a 'go-getter'.

Well, Adi had to get his first high-value PL case approved, so he ignored his apprehensions and confidently pulled up a chair beside her. "Hey, Trisha, how are you doing today?" he greeted casually.

"What do you want?" Bharat growled.

"Oh, just Tallinn Chemicals' approval. You know, Tony's Rs 20 lakh PL case. He made a commitment to the client that the sanction letter would be ready by 11 am, but it's almost 1 pm now, so Tony sent me to find out why it was held up," Adi informed nonchalantly.

"Is that so? Bharat, I'm sure you wouldn't mind me issuing your boss' sanction letter first, would you?" Trisha enquired, fluttering her eyelashes. Bharat descended from his perch and left the room.

Adi would have rolled his eyes at her pseudo coquettishness under normal circumstances, but not that day, because not only was SME pressing Tony for a sanction, but it was also their month end; nothing was normal during a month end at *TCI*. Every Sales Manager had to do what it took to ensure he/she emerged as the best; a feat that also reflected on their bosses. This made them cajole the credit team first to approve their cases fast by assuaging their doubts of a probable default, then appeal to the operations team to book their cases in the disbursement database, and finally get their cheques printed on priority if their clients were too persistent.

At the end of the month, it was the survival of the fittest salesperson. The ones not on the top would be taken to task not only by Tony but all the seniors in the food chain.

"I didn't know you had it in you?" Trisha winked, signing the sanction letter with a flourish before handing it to him.

"What?" Adi enquired, absentmindedly, snatching the letter from her hand before she changed her mind.

"Pulling a fast one over Bharat. Tallinn Chemicals is booked in your name, yet you led Bharat to believe it was Tony's," she declared, startling him with her astuteness.

"I didn't know you would do this for me too," Adi joked, smiling for the first time in the past 15 minutes.

"Do what?"

Adi looked up from his first 'big ticket' sanction letter to glance at her heart-shaped face with a flawless milky white complexion, a fact he had noticed the first time he had laid eyes on her. He had also noticed her silky black hair and perfect petite figure then and had contemplated flirting with her during his first week at *TCI*, but she had blasted him for logging in trashy files and bringing down her approval rate.

It was mandatory for credit managers to maintain an 80% approval rate and her team was constantly being reprimanded for accepting subpar files. However, the hint of a sultry overtone in her seemingly innocent question now had forced him to wonder if she maybe did see him as a person, a man, and she wasn't really the 'Iron Lady' he thought she was.

"Give me precedence over Bharat," he blurted candidly.

"What makes you think I favour Bharat?" she questioned coldly.

"Sorry, Iro…err…Trisha Madam, I…hum…"

"You assumed, just because Bharat chooses to stalk me that I favour him?" Trisha interrupted his attempt at a plausible explanation.

"No Madam,"

"Well, if you didn't assume so, then please leave, I have work to do," she declared, turning her perfect face to her PC.

*

"You nincompoop, don't tell me the case isn't approved?" Tony thundered, on seeing Adi walk past his workstation with a sour look on his face, ignorant of the fact that it was an aftermath of an encounter with 'The Iron Lady'.

"No, it is. Here's the sanction letter," Adi replied, holding out the precious piece of paper.

"What will I do with it? Go and give it to the SME manager, you imbecile."

"Yes, boss."

"Adi, wait, what's wrong?" Tony called out as Adi turned to walk out of their department again.

"I just insulted the 'Iron Lady's' err I mean Trisha's intelligence by suggesting she does what Bharat wants her to do," Adi mumbled.

"Oh my god, you have the hots for Trisha!" Tony exclaimed.

"What? No! She did a good thing for me today and I blew it with a stupid statement," Adi tried to object.

"You are so totally pining for her, dude" Tony persisted.

"And you are totally delirious because this case has clinched you the position of the best Area Sales Manager in the West," Adi pointed out bravely.

"That's true! Along with the fact that my Jat has a crush on his credit manager!"

"Please, leave it, boss."

"No, you pursue it before Bharat does."

After spending five years in Sales, in Mumbai, Adi, a polite and chivalrous 'Jat' was used to profanities and snide remarks by men when referring to 'hot' women. It didn't matter that he hailed from a small town in UP where women were meant only to cook, clean, bear children and take care of their in-laws. The scene in his house was different. While his mum, a much-revered English teacher in his town, did supervise the cooking and cleaning of the house, she had help and was immensely respected by his father. Hence, Adi never considered women as objects to be bedded at a man's whim. He respected them.

That's why, Tony's parting declaration before Adi left the room hit a nerve. Wanting to sleep with her just because he was attracted to her was not going to happen, thereby forcing him to question inwardly whether a beautiful, powerful lady like Trisha would ever be capable of truly loving a man, and if he was only infatuated with her beauty and power?

Chapter 9

A Force to Reckon With

Fed up with sleeping on her side, Trisha turned for the umpteenth time, flopped on her stomach and buried her head under an oversized, soft pillow. She was back on her left side in 10 seconds, hugging the pillow to her chest. "Damn it," she cursed a few seconds later, flung aside her bed covers and jumped out of the normally comfortable bed, that had suddenly turned oppressive that night.

"It's all because of that stupid Adi," she addressed her empty bedroom, lit softly by white fairy lights strung on the wall behind her bed. She loved fairy lights. They were meant to be comforting especially at night as she couldn't sleep in the dark, despite knowing her parents' bedroom was across the corridor. Tonight, though, she felt anything but comfort. In fact, she had been annoyed since the afternoon, when Adi had implied that she was partial to Bharat. It had been work pressure that had forcibly taken her mind off her bizarre irritation, and she had forgotten about it till she had laid down on her queen-sized bed.

"Everybody on the 6th floor speculates about Bharat and me. Many of the lechers have even openly asked me if Bharat and I are in a committed relationship. I mean, what the hell? How can everyone assume that having sex with a colleague is a part of every unattached working woman's portfolio? Maybe it's a given with the married ones too, who knows? These men! If a woman sleeps around like them because she enjoys sex, she's a slut. If she doesn't, she's frigid. What was that other thing that almost slipped from Adi's mouth, iro… something? Has he also coined a nickname for me?

"And here I thought he was different because he has never treated me like a brainless bimbo who is an Area Credit Manager only because of her good looks. Sure, we've fought over cases, but damn, he has always politely informed me before escalations. Maybe that's why I was annoyed when he also linked me with Bharat. Why the hell do I care what he thinks about me? He's just a man, a sales guy in a bank."

Trisha continued her monologue with her bedroom as she paced on the multi-coloured rug on the floor.

"I shouldn't have appreciated the fast one he pulled over Bharat. It was after all only a lie. Salespeople are liars. They'll say anything to close a deal," she finally concluded, flopping down on a rocking chair beside a window. She gently rocked herself while gazing at the moonlight reflecting off the trees outside.

'What am I doing with my life? I know, I'm only 26 years old and lucky to be an Assistant Manager with a reputed bank in India. I owe it to my parents for having permitted me to work instead of getting me married like the other girls in our community,' she wondered, her thoughts drifting to her father, Dr Madanmohan Mishra. He had done his PhD in Textile Engineering and had relocated from Bihar to Ahmedabad because he had received a job as a scientist with ATIRA, Ahmedabad Textile Industry's Research Association.

Both her parents hailed from the Brahmin community of Bihar with staunch social norms. Every family had to have a son, and as far as Trisha could remember, her mother had always been subjected to snide jabs from both sides of the family for having given birth to two daughters. But neither parent had ever cursed Trisha or her sister, unlike some uncles and aunts she knew.

Tears welled up in her eyes upon recollecting the events preceding her older sister's wedding. It had been fixed at the appropriate (according to their community) marriageable age of 22 with a dentist residing in Bihar. She was even more beautiful than Trisha, so she could have her pick of the man she wanted to marry, but her father had to pay dowry.

He however worked with an autonomous non-profit R&D institution established in 1947 by the textile mills of Ahmedabad and was incorruptible. He spent his life catering to all his family's needs with his modest salary while trying to save as much money as he could for at least his older daughter's wedding. It hadn't been enough though and he had been forced to accept money from his wealthy father-in-law, who was a civil contractor in Bihar.

That had been a humiliating moment for her dad because his father-in-law had already paid a hefty dowry for his daughter's wedding, that had been used to buy the house Trisha and her family lived in now, but her maternal grandfather refused to acknowledge it. He constantly berated Trisha's dad for being a loser because he couldn't make money despite his education and had insisted Trisha's dad should take his granddaughter's dowry money from him, so at least she would have a good life.

Trisha, only 18 then, remembered her mother objecting to her father's insulting statements in vain and vowed she would never allow her father to pay dowry for her wedding.

Well, her beautiful sister had married that dentist at the age of 22. Having turned 30 now, her life revolved around her husband, two sons, kitchen, maid, and the vegetable market.

Fortunately for Trisha, her parents had permitted her to do her MBA in Finance from NIRMA University, after graduating in Commerce. She had studied hard and was the top ranker, so she was selected by *TCI* during campus placements. Since she already had a cynical view of life, it didn't take her long to understand she had to rise above her God-gifted beauty and prove she was a force to reckon with. She had also learnt to use her good looks for her advantage, by dressing impeccably for work, often in ridiculously high formal heels, and had used the right amount of flirtatiousness to get hardcore players like Tony on her side while ignoring his subtle hints at something more than a professional relationship. She had also worked diligently to ensure she received a near-perfect appraisal in the three years she worked at *TCI*.

Everything had been fine until Adi had joined the bank. He was like a babe in the woods initially, totally crushed when she declined his cases. It was probably the street-smart Tony who provoked Adi to become aggressive and fight for his cases, but that too was done apologetically. It didn't melt her though, on the contrary, it provoked her to be cold with him, especially since she had often caught him staring at her. The only difference was she had never seen his eyes lowered below her face, unlike other men who felt they only had to make eye contact with a woman's breasts as her eyes were just placed on her face for decoration.

"Oh my God! I like Adi!" she suddenly declared to her beautiful bedroom awash in the twinkling of the fairy lights.

"But like in what sense? Like as in I feel attracted to him? I don't know, 'cus I've never considered him in that way?" she questioned her declaration, conjuring up an image of his 5 feet 8 inch, moderately flabby body, with a round face, and full head of curly hair.

Something stirred in her as she recollected the way their fingers grazed when he requested her to reconsider some file or how he placed his hand on her chair to avoid contact as he bent to point out something on her computer screen, unwittingly giving her a whiff of his subtle cologne.

Feeling restless, she glanced at the digital clock on her bedside indicating 2:38 am, meaning she had only 4 hours and 22 minutes to sleep if she wanted to wake up at 7 am, so she could reach work by 9 am.

Chapter 10

Internal Dynamics

The air conditioner was on, and a ceiling fan was rotating, yet the moderately sized rectangular room with sliding windows on one side felt stuffy. They had been shut and the blinds had been drawn to prevent the noisy traffic on the main road from disturbing the ongoing meeting.

Adi had been staring at the ceiling fan for a while now, willing it to do a better job at distributing the air in the stifling room. Resisting the urge to tug at his tie which seemed to be tightening like a noose around his neck as each minute passed, he shifted his gaze to Hrian Patel looking impeccable in a powder blue shirt, with the Arrow logo prominently displayed on the cuffs and breast pocket. A sliver of a smile tugged the corners of Adi's mouth at the quicksilver transformation in the appearance of the owner of his biggest DSA (Direct Sales Agency) in Ahmedabad, Saccaritra Financial Services (SFS).

DSAs were another sourcing avenue for loan files in banks. They were businessmen who had their own office setup and used their resources to log in loan files in banks, in lieu of an incentive that varied from 0.2 to 0.5 or 1 percent of the personal loan amount disbursed to the client.

TCI wanted to increase their market share in the retail business so Priyansh, the Regional Head of PL had visited Ahmedabad that morning. He had started the day at the Direct Sales Team's (DST's) office, praising Bharat's team for their exemplary performance before dropping the bomb of doubling their targets for the rest of the year. A plethora of the choicest

Hindi cuss words had been spewed on Adi's new Team Leader (TL) because his performance was way below Bharat's TL. Priyansh had also threatened to transfer Adi from Sales to Collections if he didn't improve his performance. This had triggered a migraine, but Adi had held on, knowing he would be repeating the same words to his TL the following day. 'Passing the buck.' That had to be done in sales to ensure you retained your job while you brought out the best in your team.

The entire day passed in meetings with other bank officials, and DSAs, lunch with the credit and operations managers, and finally a visit to Hrian's DSA. Adi knew Tony had deliberately scheduled it as the last meeting of the day because Hrian's conference room opened to a spacious terrace. Tony, Adi, and Hrian had spent many month-ends celebrating their highs or drowning their sorrows in bottles of Black Label, Tony's favourite whiskey, and Pepsi for Adi. Tony never mooched off Hrian. On the contrary, he had several bottles of the bootlegged brand stashed in Hrian's office and didn't mind if Hrian indulged in a few.

Obviously, there was a party planned for that night as Priyansh was a lush. There were also rumours that he had a 'thing' for the fair sex. Adi dutifully swallowed a pill for his migraine when he rushed home after the meeting, to change for the party, as he was curious to experience his first internal dynamics and witness how Tony and Hrian would charm their boss for future favours that night.

Chapter 11

'New High'

"Mujhko Pehchaan Lo... Main Hoon Don!"

Adi sang along with Shaan, Bollywood's male golden voice as he raced his new black *Opel Astra Club Accent* on NH34 (National Highway 34). He had purchased the car a week ago, on receiving an email from HR stating that he had been promoted as North Gujarat's Area Sales Manager (ASM). It had been a well-deserved and timely one, that happened exactly two years after he joined *TCI*. Naturally, it came with a huge salary hike and a hefty performance bonus. While he hadn't yet been paid the new salary nor the bonus, he had been able to avail a car loan at the staff rate of 6% simple interest, so he had immediately fulfilled his passion for cars by purchasing the swanky machine.

Tony too had been promoted as the Regional Head of Gujarat and Rajasthan, after Priyansh was made the Western Zonal Head. Technically, Tony had to move to Mumbai after his promotion, but he hated Mumbai, so the bank made a special provision for him to continue to operate from Ahmedabad.

Adi hadn't informed his family about his promotion. Instead, he had applied for leave yesterday, after he picked up his new car from the showroom, and had embarked on the 1000-odd km, 16-hour journey from Ahmedabad to his hometown Bhulandshahr this morning at 5.30 am. It was almost 10 pm now and he was just a few kilometres away from his ancestral home in the outskirts of the prominent city in Uttar Pradesh.

Nostalgia hit hard as he braked his car outside the massive wooden gates of his ancestral home.

"Kaun?"

A window slid open and a face with an intimidating bar-handled moustache enquired who he was in Hindi.

"It's me, Adivteya," Adi responded, lowering his window.

"Forgive me, young sir, I didn't recognise you in the dark," the guard apologised, hurriedly opening the door.

"Please come in. I'll inform your mother," the guard bowed in welcome.

"No," Adi objected, looking forward to surprising his mother, and he drove past the opened gates.

The ferocious barking of his father's German Shepherds could be heard over the roar of the car's engines, and he was a bit perturbed by the heightened security, since his last visit two years ago. 'It could be due to the impending village council (Panchayat) elections, he thought. The political atmosphere of India had changed considerably, so had the divide between the upper and lower cast; it had intensified, forcing the upper cast to resort to hiring private security; especially at his home because his grandfather was the chief contender this time.

That was the main reason behind this impromptu trip. It was a matter of pride for him that his grandfather, who always had political aspirations, was finally taking the first step. The election was a week away, and Adi felt compelled to be there for his grandfather. He was sure he would experience a 'new high' as he campaigned hard in the final leg, something akin to what he felt while pushing his sales team to perform!

Chapter 12

Family Ritual

The familiar sight beneath the sprawling mango tree spurred Adi to accelerate. He swerved the car inches before the chair his older brother Veer was seated on and braked, kicking up dust.

"Sala, harami," Veer cursed, jumping to his feet. He flung his glass to the ground and whipped out a gun from his Kurta's pocket.

Adi quickly exited the car and raised his joined palms above his head, shouting out his greeting, "Pranam, bade bhaiya," the car shielding his body, in case his 'short-fused' brother decided to fire. Goosebumps broke over his arms feeling the cold metal of another gun pressed on his temple.

"Sab bandooke neeche karo. Yeh kya mazak hai, Adivteya?" his father thundered, commanding everyone to lower their guns before reprimanding Adi.

It didn't matter that Adi was the most educated person in his family or the only one who had an actual job and wasn't living off his rich grandfather, pretending to contribute to his highly lucrative farms. His father's disapproving baritone had the same effect on the 28-year-old Adi that it had on the 5-year-old boy who wanted to read books instead of learning how to wrestle in the village akhada (wrestling arena) like the other boys.

Adi immediately rushed to touch the feet of his grandfather, his father's older brother, his father, Veer, and cousins in the order demanded by age.

"Mumbai ka herogiri dhika raha tha kya, shehar ka launda? Aa, hamare pass bait," Veer taunted Adi lovingly for displaying Mumbai's heroism, before hugging him warmly and leading him to an empty chair beside his.

"Adi ke liye peg banao," their uncle commanded a manservant who was hovering nearby to make a drink.

"Nahi, mein maa se milkar aata hu," Adi objected, saying he would like to meet his mother first.

"Maa apne ladle se milne khud aayegi. Baito aur hame baatao, kitane shahar ke ladakiyon ke saath sahavaas kiya ab tak?" Veer countered, saying that their mother would come on her own to meet her son, and he wanted to hear about Adi's conquests with the feminine sex.

Adi reluctantly sat down, cringing at both his elder brother's unveiled animosity towards the special bond Adi had with their mom, and Veer's crude reference to the lack of inhibitions amongst city girls. He accepted the drink, knowing it would be pointless to try to explain to Veer that he still didn't drink.

"Ha, ha. If you have sown your wild oats, let's get you married after your grandfather wins the elections," his uncle stated, chuckling. Adi groaned inwardly, accepting a plate laden with food from the manservant. He pretended to take a sip of his drink before stuffing his mother's delicious biryani into his mouth, grateful that no one expected him to answer to his uncle's gaffe.

His cousins unfortunately picked on it and they started suggesting prospective brides, along with the dowry Adi would fetch, courtesy his educational qualifications and bank job.

Satiated with the food and having managed to surreptitiously pour his drink on the ground, Adi sat back and listened to the boisterous talk of the semi-inebriated male members of his joint family. Gathering beneath the mango tree on Saturday night for booze and good food was their family ritual. They were often accompanied by their male Jat neighbours.

The aromas of freshly barbequed meat wafted around them as they smoked from giant hookahs placed beside the chairs while sipping Royal Challenge. The gurgling sounds of water in the hookahs were drowned by the heated political discussions that were always the focal point of their gatherings.

Adi had expected half the village men to be at his house that night, considering the impending elections and had been surprised to find only the ten male members of his family. A casual question about it to Veer enlightened him about the village politics! His village was divided because his grandfather was standing against the current panchayat leader who also happened to be the richest zamindar in the village.

The sight of a statuesque lady walking towards them distracted him. He bolted from his chair and ran into her embrace, grateful for her timing as Veer hadn't realised his glass was empty. Adi hugged his mom tight, proud of the fact that she cared two hoots for the male chauvinistic rules that existed in Jat households, one being that the women of the house weren't supposed to be seen when the men were enjoying their mehfil (party). She did as she pleased and not a single male member in her household, including her husband, objected. Adi knew this was because they secretly respected her. She too was very careful never to hurt the male ego.

Chapter 13

Village Politics

The following morning, Adi stood for a moment at the threshold of the massive kitchen, taking in the sights, sounds and aromas. He had been away from home for ten years, three of which had been spent in hostels. Eating boiled potatoes and eggplant for five nights a week in his undergrad days had toughened him. He had taken all of it in his stride though as he had known he would be fed like a king on returning home.

Entering the room, he headed straight for his grandmother perched at her vantage point, at the head of a massive wooden table that lined one wall of the kitchen. She not only supervised her two daughters-in-law, and their myriad helpers but also dispensed garlic, almonds, cashew nuts and saffron that went into the dishes being prepared for the day; the condiments that were stored in a wooden box with an ornate brass lock in front of her.

"Pranam dadi maa," Adi greeted, touching her feet.

"My child, what a pleasant surprise. Look at you, how thin you have become! Come sit, have some hot halwa," she hugged him.

"Er, daadi maa, can I take ma to the temple first?"

"Look at my grandson. The city hasn't changed him at all. Yes, my child, please take your mother to the temple. I will serve you a hot breakfast after that. Bless you, my child," she beamed, kissing his forehead.

Adi dutifully moved on to touch his aunt's feet and just smiled at her taunt, "You have definitely learnt the art of fooling people."

His mother gladly allowed him to lead her out of the kitchen. She squealed when he suddenly covered her eyes with his palms as they approached the courtyard in front of the house, "what are you doing?"

"I have a surprise for you ma," he replied, removing his palm when they reached his car.

"Oh my god! Have you got it blessed in a temple?"

"We're going to do that now," Adi grinned, opening the passenger side door for her, ignoring the twinge of guilt at the truth in his aunt's taunt.

The temple was a ruse. Some palpable tensions were going on at home and he knew he could get his mother to reveal them under the right circumstances.

Post the 15-minute blessing ritual by the temple priest which lightened his wallet by 1000 bucks, his mum literally let her veil down when Adi opened the sunroof of the car and she stood, enjoying the cool morning breeze as her son drove down a tractor track in the middle of their sugarcane farms.

Adi finally voiced the issue that had been troubling him after he parked the car beside a canal running parallel to their fields, "What exactly is going on mom? Why do I sense tension at home?"

"It's because your grandfather is running against his best friend, Kishor Pandey."

"I know that, and it has ruined their friendship of 60 years. So why did Dada decide to contest this year?"

"The villagers requested him to do so. He is the only one who has the slightest chance of winning against Pandey ji. Bansi, Pandey ji's grandson has gone totally out of control,

Adi. He and his friends just keep shooting and molesting the lower caste. It was when they attempted to rape a Jat girl six months ago that the villagers requested your grandfather to stand for elections. Forget about Bansi's parents and grandparents, even the police are doing his bidding, so the villagers hope that if your grandfather wins, then maybe the police will shift their allegiance.

A chill ran down Adi's spine at the mention of Bansi's name and the village politics that accompanied it. They were of the same age and had gone to the same public school. Adi understood the villagers' anguish as he had often been at the receiving end of Bansi's bullying. Brushing aside a particularly brutal episode that had been the cause of several subsequent nightmares, Adi suggested, "Let's go home ma, I am starving."

Chapter 14

The Horrors of His Past

Adi seemed to be a part of Hercules, his favourite stallion, as they rode through the fields, towards a common goal; the lush verdant meadows bordering the river. Breeding thoroughbreds was one of his grandfather's passions, so they all had their own horses with typical names. Hercules was born when Adi had passed out of high school with flying colours, so his grandfather had indulged his request to name the newborn colt. Little had his grandfather known that it would be an unpronounceable one for the rest of their clan!

Hercules had turned out to be the star of his grandfather's stables, winning almost every race he had entered. He had retired at the age of six and was well taken care of. Adi rode him almost daily whenever he was home.

The first gunshot echoed through the fields like a thunderbolt. Hercules reflexively quickened his pace. Adi hung on for his dear life while trying hard to calm the frightened horse. He heard the second shot just as Hercules buckled. Adi found himself flying and braced himself for a painful fall. He heard a few of the four feet tall sugarcane crops breaking as they bore the brunt of his 75 kg body. Bansi and three of his friends were looming over him, leaving him wondering if he had died and gone to hell. Their laughter seemed to ascertain he may have. He shut his eyes tight, just as he had done 12 years ago when they had all turned 16, realizing he had no choice but to relive the horrors of his past.

Hercules was present then too. Bansi and his friends had cornered Adi in the stables, just outside Hercules' stall. They beat him up first before clamping a hand on his mouth. Nothing registered much in his semi-conscious state except the pain searing through his body as something or someone thrust into him. "Stay away from my girl you faggot otherwise I'll cut off your balls and feed them to you next time," he had heard Bansi whisper in his ear before he was thrown to the ground.

The warning hadn't made any sense and he had focused his energies on limping home. He had lied to his mother that he had fallen off Hercules. It had taken him a week to recover from his ordeal and resume school. Apparently, his best friend Kamini had also stopped attending school a day after the ordeal and had just vanished. Rumours were rampant that she had left town because Bansi had raped her. That's when Bansi's message had made sense and he had realized that Bansi had a crush on the prettiest girl in their class, Kamini, and had been pursuing her relentlessly. Kamini unfortunately wasn't interested in Bansi and preferred hanging out with Adi. He had started feeling immensely guilty for what may have happened to Kamini.

Adi opened his eyes on feeling himself being lifted from the mangled sugarcane. Someone grabbed a fistful of his hair and tilted his head back. "You think you are a man just because you are strutting your grandfather around in your new car with that opening on the roof? You feel your city boy campaigning will help your grandfather win? This is my grandfather's village He will win the elections. It's time to blast your balls and make you the eunuch you were born to be, Adivteya," Bansi hissed into his face.

A shot rang out and Adi looked down, sure he would see blood flowing from his groin.

"Let go of my brother."

Veer's voice provoked a furry of motions with Bansi's cronies frantically trying to figure out how they were suddenly outnumbered.

"Tell your grandfather to step down first," Bansi retorted.

"We have recorded your last words, and we will send it to the Chief Minister and Prime Minister if you don't stop intimidating the people of this village. We can get you arrested right now, but we will not do it out of respect for your grandfather. Leave this village for some time and come back only if you can live like a civilized human being," Veer cautioned, holding out his cell phone with the video of Bansi's threat playing.

Chapter 15

Vanity

Trisha raised her eyes for the umpteenth time from the yellow files she had been scrutinizing all day, to the frosted glass entrance door of the credit and operations department, wondering why Adi hadn't walked in yet, despite her having rejected five of his files that day.

Tony suddenly entered and she buried her face under a file, hoping he didn't want to talk with her.

"Hey, Trisha, how are you?"

Her heart sank on hearing Tony's greeting.

"I'm good, Tony, how about you?" she responded, flashing a cursory smile at him.

"I'm great. So, why have you rejected so many of Adi's files?"

"A few have bad CIBIL scores, while the third-party verifications of some are negative," she clarified, referring to the external agencies who were appointed to verify whether a customer's residence, business and income documents like bank statements, salary slips, and income tax returns were genuine or not. Since Personal Loans was an unsecured loan segment, meaning money was disbursed without mortgaging property or taking Fixed Deposits as security, frauds were rampant.

There had been many instances in the past where customers had provided fake property or income documents and then vanished after availing personal loans. So, banks had a separate vertical, called Risk Containment Units (RCU). This department appointed agencies that scrutinized loan papers for fraudulent documents. Another third-party agency conducted field investigations (FIs) by visiting the customer's workplace and residence and submitted reports to the banks.

It was the responsibility of the credit managers to make pragmatic judgements to either approve a case or reject it based on the reports of the third-party verification agencies.

"May I see the files?" Tony requested politely.

"Sure," she replied, handing them over, biting back the question that had been churning in her mind the entire week, 'Where's Adi?' Vanity prevented her from doing so. In fact, it had been the same negative emotion that had stopped her from crossing the corridor to personally congratulate Adi on his promotion. Of course, she had also been upset as she was overdue for a promotion but had been passed on yet again. She had been so sure though, that Adi would come over to gloat like Bharat.

"Trisha, I did it, man. I'm ASM of South Gujarat now, so I won't be sitting on your head anymore," Bharat had announced, tossing a 10 rupees Dairy Milk chocolate on her desk, before sauntering off without even a thank you for all her support.

But Adi hadn't bothered to even come and meet her. She hadn't seen him at all since his promotion. This hurt her even more because she had foolishly let her guard down with him, as he had managed to win her over with his polite, conscientious attitude.

"Trisha, can you recommend these two cases for approval." Tony's request snapped her out of her musings.

"Sure," she responded, listlessly accepting the files.

'That's all I do, anyway. Recommend bad cases so that Sales can achieve their targets while I lose my promotion. Well, Swamy's retort on hearing my objections at not being promoted had been, 'You don't support Sales, Trisha, you only care about your approval ratio. Change your attitude, then maybe next year,' Trisha thought, angry and frustrated not only with the system but also with Adi for feigning friendship so she would support him.

Chapter 16

Occupational Hazards

Adi exited the elevator on the 6th floor and paused for a fraction of a second before turning left. Nodding in response to the security guard's warm greeting, he strode into the near-empty room, hoping Trisha had come in early like she usually did. His heart lurched on seeing her seated at her corner workstation beside a window, a lock of her silky black hair covering her face, as she bent over a ubiquitous yellow file, the colour distinguishing the Personal Loan files from the files of other retail loan products.

She raised her head and acknowledged his presence with an apathetic "Hey."

"Trish, I'm sorry I didn't return your phone calls last week. Things were crazy at home…" he tried to clarify, but she interrupted him, "It doesn't matter Adivteya. Congratulations on your promotion. I've submitted my resignation as I didn't get promoted, yet again, and I'll be relieved by the end of this month. I guess it's time to move on from everything. "

"Trish, please don't be mad. My not answering your calls wasn't deliberate. Despite my trip home being hellish, I should have spoken with you for a few minutes. Look I agree you should have been promoted, you deserved it. We wouldn't have overachieved our targets without you and the operation team's help. I too may have resigned and moved on, had I been in your shoes. I get it, but please don't let this ruin our friendship. How about a peace dinner?" Adi requested.

His heart sank when she turned her face towards the window. A longing he had been repressing for almost a year and a half, stirred on watching her graceful, slim hand reached out to tuck a silky lock of hair behind her ears. It wasn't a typical male reaction to her sensual good looks. It was something deeper that had developed especially over the past six months when they had worked tirelessly together for more than 18 hours a day. He had ignored it though, to achieve a common goal: ensure Ahmedabad had the highest PL disbursements amongst all the non-metro tier 1 cities.

Their professional relationship had been volatile till then, with him trying to politely cajole her into approving his files and her coldly declaring they were unfit for approval. Obviously, he had escalated her rejections and had bragged when her seniors approved them. She had generally ignored it but had occasionally voiced her reasons for rejecting files. They could barely tolerate each other until last September. He had stormed into her department at midnight, intending to blast her for rejecting a very important file but had suppressed his anger on seeing her spray a painkiller on her right wrist.

"Is something wrong?" he had enquired.

"No. Everything's perfect," she had replied, reaching out for a crepe bandage.

"What do you want?" she had enquired, clumsily trying to wrap the bandage around her wrist.

"Let me do it," he had insisted, grabbing her wrist, only to let go when she had winced.

"Sorry, I didn't mean to hurt you, but why is your wrist swollen?" he had questioned.

"Occupational hazards, I guess, I don't know, as I haven't had time to consult a doctor," she had replied, trying to affix the bandage again.

"Please, allow me to help you, Trish," he had coaxed.

"Okay," she had relented holding out her hand.

He had settled himself on a chair first before reaching for the bandage and had tried to be as gentle as possible while he wrapped it around her wrist, enquiring every few seconds if it was too tight. He had raised his eyes to meet hers only after affixing the metal clip. That's when he had accepted that he couldn't keep ignoring the fact that he was smitten and he could have sworn she too had felt the same because she had held his gaze for more than a few seconds before diverting her eyes to her PC and had spoken in a more mellow tone, "thanks. Er, did you want something?"

"Yes, I wanted to request you to approve Mr Milap's loan," he had stated, curbing the urge to tell her to go home and rest her hand. He had also wanted to insist she visit a doctor but had refrained from doing so for selfish reasons.

"Okay, send me an email with the mitigants and I'll do it."

Stunned by her calm request, he had rushed to his desk and had done so, thereby bringing about a 360° change in their interactions. They had started discussing dubious cases like adults, making mutually beneficial decisions, often seeking each other out for breaks or meals in the cafeteria whenever possible and sharing titbits about their lives. His respect for her commitment and tenacity had increased, so, it had been heart-wrenching to learn she had been bypassed for a promotion while he, Bharat and Tony had got theirs.

"Okay. We'll eat at '*The Fern*'. Pick me up at 7.30 in that swanky new car of yours." Her consent snapped him back to the present and he rose from the chair, confirming, "Done," hoping he didn't appear too pleased.

Holding onto the memory of the faint smile playing on her lips while agreeing to meet him for dinner, he sailed through the day. It was only when he was showering before their 'date' that it struck him, his swanky car was in Bulandshahr.

Chapter 17

The Mountain has come to Mohamad!

It was 8.30 p.m. when Adi's phone rang, interrupting his scrutiny of the Management Information System (MIS) report on *TCI's Universe*, that is their main server.

"It's a number's game Adivteya and you are not freaking logging in enough of cases. Your average ticket size is half of Bharat's. I'll transfer you to collections if you don't buck up," Priyansh yelled into the phone even before Adi could greet him. Adi held the squawking phone a few centimetres away from his ear and stared at Ahmedabad's performance. The comparison with Bharat was inevitable, as they were the only two PL sales managers in Ahmedabad.

Grateful that Bharat who occupied an adjacent workstation had left for the day, Adi stole a glance at Tony's cubicle and was relieved to find it empty. Adi hadn't realised they had left because he had been engrossed in analysing the MIS and preparing responses for Tony's dissection the following morning. He hadn't expected Priyansh's phone call though and was dismayed to realise Bharat had beaten him by Rs 50 lakhs this quarter.

'I bet Priyansh hasn't achieved his numbers, that's why he's going ballistic now,' Adi thought, scrolling down to check the West Zone's performance. His hunch was right, Priyansh was off his target by a couple of crores and Adi wasn't the only cause. Heaving a sigh of relief on finally hearing the dial tone, meaning Priyansh had hung up, Adi couldn't help smiling sadly as he applied filters on Bharat's cases.

"Good evening, sir, may I take a few minutes of your time?"

Adi turned his head on hearing the polite request, and was surprised to see a nattily dressed, handsome man standing a few feet away from his workstation, smiling beguilingly at him.

"Er, it's after office hours. How come the security guard let you in?" Adi enquired cautiously.

"Oh! he was a security guard at *Oakland Bank* before he was transferred to *TCI*, so he knows me well," the man dressed in a crisp white shirt with blue pinstripes, the Louis Phillip crest clearly visible on his pocket, navy blue Chinos and polished black shoes replied modestly, his engaging smile firmly in place.

"Who are you?" Adi blurted, his eyes narrowing.

"Sidanshu Gaur." The man stepped forward, extending his right arm.

'I'll be damned! The Mountain has come to Mohamed!' Adi thought, dumbfounded.

Realising he was both gawking and being rude, Adi clasped the outstretched hand and stammered, "Er…hi. So, what…I mean why….no, what are you doing here? Sorry, that came out the wrong way, how can I help you?"

"Would you like to talk here, or may I have the pleasure of dining with you?"

Adi thought he was hallucinating on hearing Sidanshu's question. He had been trying for two years to get *Pinnacle*, Sidanshu's DSA, to sign up with him. Unfortunately, the only phone number available had been of Sidanshu's private secretary Reva and she would only take messages, never connect him with her boss. Adi had even visited Sidanshu's office on several occasions, requesting a meeting with Sidanshu, in vain; Reva had always politely turned him down while making it seem she was doing him a favour. Now Sidanshu had sought him out and was inviting him for dinner, rendering Adi totally speechless.

Chapter 18

Arranged Marriage

The exhilaration Dhiraj felt during his morning run at Law Gardens plummeted when he stepped into his living room. He should have been used to the sight of his wife passed out on the black leather couch by now; unfortunately, guilt kicked in each time he saw her sprawled there with the aftermath of her nightly drinking binge strewed around her.

Sighing, he walked towards the staircase that led him up to their bedroom, the frown lines on his forehead deepening. 'It's my fault. I am responsible for the sorry state of our two-year-old marriage. But what could I have done differently?' he wondered, shedding his clothes in the bathroom, and stepping under the shower.

Theirs had been a typical arranged marriage with his middle-class parents feeling blessed on receiving a proposal from a wealthy man in their community, for their 'doctor' son, especially because the girl was beautiful. He had refused any dowry but had consented to an ostentatious wedding and an all-expenses paid honeymoon in Mauritius; an indulgent gift from a doting father to his only child, and her father would have felt offended if Dhiraj had refused. Complaints unfortunately started within the first year; "I don't want to live in a joint family. Why aren't you allowing my dad to buy us a bungalow in Law Gardens?"

Fed up with the constant whining, he had naively resigned from his job as an orthopaedic surgeon in Ahmedabad's civil hospital, to start his own clinic, set up by his father-in-law. Overheads had started mounting in the very first month as patients were scarce so, he had taken up a job as a visiting surgeon with a reputed private hospital. This not only gave him a steady income, but it also improved his private practice, enabling him to avail a housing loan for a bungalow in Law Gardens, close to his father-in-law's home. Obviously, his parents continued to stay in their modest flat in a middle-class society. His father-in-law had wanted to buy him a Toyota Lancer as a housewarming gift, but Dhiraj had stood firm, thereby provoking the next grouse, "Shouldn't an orthopaedic surgeon be driving a luxury car instead of a Maruti 800?'

This goaded him into working for eighteen hours a day and a Hyundai Accent, purchased with his own hard-earned money replaced the Maruti 800 in six months. Although his private practice was improving, he had to continue to work long hours as expenses, especially at home had started mounting, leading to a new complaint, "You don't have time for me anymore." He had ignored it and had continued to work hard.

Approximately, a month later, he had let himself into his house at around 11 pm, bone-tired, to find her gorging on a chicken leg while sipping from a glass of what looked like water in her hand.

"Welcome home, hubby! Happy anniversary. Come, join me for a drink," she had shifted her eyes from a Hindi soap playing on their 42" wall-mounted plasma TV to greet him.

"Drink? Er, sorry I forgot our anniversary. I had back-to-back surgeries for the past six hours. I'll make it up to you on Saturday. Tell me where you want to go for dinner?"

"My friends' husbands take them to Goa, Manali and so on for their anniversaries, so take me to Hawaii to make it up to me," she had replied.

"You know I'm saving up for an X-ray machine. Please let me buy it first then I promise I'll take you wherever you want," he had pleaded.

"I'll tell Daddy to pay for it. After all, it was he who wanted me to marry a middle-class doctor. Why should I not have fun because you are not rich like the other doctors?" she had retorted.

"No, I cannot take any more money from your dad. Please, I promise you I'll buy it soon and then take you wherever you want."

"You're a loser. Just get lost and let me enjoy my wedding anniversary on my own. Get out," she had screamed lighting a cigarette, and draining the glass in her hand in one gulp.

Totally stunned, Dhiraj had stumbled up the stairs to his bedroom and had fallen onto their bed, fully clothed. Being a stickler for routine, he had woken up at 5 am the following morning, donned his jogging tracks and had descended the stairs, shocked to find her passed out on the couch. He had thought it would be a passing phase.

Alarm bells rang when his full-time maid intercepted him two months later, the second he had returned from his run and demanded he pay her salary because his wife hadn't.

"How much does she drink?" he had enquired, reaching into his pocket for his wallet.

"Half a bottle a night," the maid had replied.

Dhiraj had opened his wallet and had been grateful to see enough money in it. Extracting a bunch of 100-rupee notes, he had asked, "What does she drink?"

"Vodka. One bottle costs Rs 800. Since madam drinks half a bottle a night, she needs 15 bottles a month, making it Rs 12,000 a month," the maid had astutely answered Dhiraj's unspoken question, adding, "It's her father's bootlegger."

"Oh my god. Does her father know?" Dhiraj had reeled in shock, both at the maid's knowledge of the cost of alcohol in Ahmedabad and the worry that his father-in-law knew his daughter was drinking heavily and it was only a matter of time before he would destroy him.

"Her father doesn't know. I requested the bootlegger not to tell him, but he has started charging her extra for a bottle. That's probably why she didn't have money to pay my salary for the past two months," the maid had shrewdly assuaged his worry.

"Here, this is Rs 20,000, 5000 more than your normal salary. Please take care of her and please don't let her father know about her condition. Also, make sure she doesn't burn this house down with her smoking. Does she go out to buy cigarettes?" Dhiraj had begged.

"No, the local paan shop owner delivers it home."

Totally baffled with the turn of events, Dhiraj continued to work hard to no avail. Expenses kept mounting and he couldn't afford a brand-new x-ray machine costing Rs 21 lakhs. His wife continued to drink till the wee hours of the night, in the living room, while watching some inane family dramas where the women dressed to their nines and plotted schemes to either swindle money from the family business or belittle a family member. There were generally more than one vamp and a couple of docile wives who took everything in their stride, be it a wicked mother-in-law or a straying husband.

Her unhealthy lifestyle had resulted in her bloating out of proportion. Her skin had lost its glow and hair its lustre.

It had become a common sight now for him to wake up in the morning, alone in the master bedroom, don his tracksuit and go for a run. Unfortunately, he had to pass the living room each morning on his way out and the sight of her sprawled body on the couch saddened him. It was the same sight that welcomed him when he returned from his run, and their cook too who came a few minutes later. He had started paying the cook more money with the hope that she wouldn't gossip about his wife's alcoholism in the neighbourhood.

Somehow, maybe because of his middle-class upbringing, he blamed himself for his wife's condition and didn't know how to get her out of it. His naivety never got him to question the flaws of the 'arranged marriage' system or why a rich man would want his beautiful daughter to marry a person like him when there were other eligible doctors from affluent families.

Chapter 19

Golden Goose

The email battle had been raging since 2.30 pm. It had started when Ahmedabad's new Area Credit Manager, Surbhi had rejected a Rs 20 lakh PL case of Dr Deepak Munshi, on the grounds that the doctor wanted the PL to buy a new medical device. There was no concept of loans for purchasing medical devices in 2008, so the banks had incorporated a new section into their existing PL policies, enabling doctors to avail PLs for the same, provided they submitted original invoices from the vendors of the medical devices and the loan amount was capped at Rs 20 lakhs. Adi had pointed this out to Surbhi via email.

It was 4 pm when she replied stating that the doctor was over-leveraged.

Refusing to give up so easily, Adi marched up to her and demanded the file.

"Sorry, files cannot leave the credit area once they are logged in," she replied coldly.

"At least tell me what his debt-equity ratio is. I'm sure it's within someone's approval powers," he requested.

"I have used my discretion in this case. Now, kindly leave, and stop disturbing me," she stated, dismissing him to bury her head in a yellow file.

'Damn, I miss Trish! No, I mustn't be selfish. She's moved to a much better profile, and we're in a good place in our relationship, although we haven't yet declared our love for each other. Do I love her? I don't know. Most of all, does she love me? Now, stop this nonsense and focus on Surbhi and your Rs 20 lakh case,' Adi channelled his wayward thoughts and walked remorsefully back to his workstation.

Logging onto *TCI's Universe*, he filtered his cases and cursed inwardly, 'Damn Surbhi, she's so freaking shrewd. It's almost month end. She's ensured her approval ratio is way above the stipulated rate, so she's rejecting my cases for no rhyme or reason. I need this goddamn case to be the top achiever in the West Zone.'

This triggered the competitive spirit he had developed since his first sales job at *Mumbai Xclusive*, and he shot an email to Surbhi's boss Swamy requesting him to instruct Surbhi to email the case details to him. His phone rang within seconds of sending the email.

"How can you call yourself a Sales Manager, Adivteya, if you cannot maintain a cordial relationship with your Credit Manager? This is not kindergarten where you complain to your teacher about a fellow student who is not allowing you to play with the toy she's playing with."

"With due respect, your statement is unfair," Adi started to speak only to hear the dial tone because Swamy had hung up on him.

Enraged, Adi clicked the compose button and started typing an email, 'Dear Priyansh, a Rs 20 lakh PL case to a cardiologist with an annual income of Rs 5 crores has been rejected by the local credit manager....".

His phone rang exactly 2 minutes after he hit the sent button.

"Adivteya, Swamy and Surbhi are on the line with me. What's the problem?" Priyansh stated.

"Sir, this is our new DSA *Pinnacle's* case. It has been declined on the grounds of overleverage, but I don't know what the debt-equity ratio is because despite requesting for the calculations, the same is not being shared," Adi declared.

"What's the debt-equity ratio, Surbhi?" Swamy demanded.

"It's 3.5," Surbhi answered defiantly.

"3.5? For a cardiologist with an annual income of Rs 5 crores? Are you deranged? Why the hell have you not recommended this case to me? Your approval ratio is way above the permissible limit. Don't expect a pat on the back for that," Swamy raged over the phone, causing Adi to cringe. Although cuss words were rampant in the bank, Adi was careful never to utter them around women.

"Sir, this case has been logged in *Oakland Bank* also for the same amount and the same reason, that's why I rejected it," Surbhi stunned everyone with her reply.

"How did you get this information? Is it mentioned in the FI report?" Swamy's tone became suspicious.

"No sir, I came to know from *Oakland's* credit manager."

"Did you ask her, or did she tell you herself?"

"I asked her."

"Why?"

The silence was so ominous, that Adi was sure he could hear his accelerated heartbeats.

"I'll recommend the case to you for approval right away sir," Surbhi responded.

"You better do and stop discussing our cases with credit managers of other banks. We hired you because we thought you would use your two years' experience with *Oakland* to improve our business, not hand it over to them on a platter," Swamy blasted her before ending the con-call.

Adi was ecstatic. Yet another big-ticket (high value) case of *Pinnacle's* was going to be approved. His figures were already way above Bharat's that month, but Dr Deepak Mushi's disbursement would put him at par with Mumbai's best performing PL Sales Manager. Grabbing his cell phone, he dialled Raghav, *Pinnacle's* PL executive who was handling this case and instructed him to process the disbursement.

"How are you doing boss?"

Adi looked up from his scrutiny of the MIS on hearing a familiar voice an hour later.

"I'm doing great, Sidanshu," he responded, rising from his seat to shake the hand of the man he started to consider as his 'Golden Goose'.

"Here's Dr Deepak Munshi's disbursement," Sidanshu stated, handing Adi a manila envelope.

"Why did you bring it?" Adi chided respectfully.

"Why not? It's my first high value disbursement at *TCI*," Sidanshu clarified, adding, "I also wanted to come over to personally invite you and Tony over to my place to celebrate this disbursement."

Chapter 20

I Play Smart!

Dhiraj flung his bloodied gloves and gown in the designated bin in the Operation Theatre and headed for the scrubbing area. He went through the motions of sterilizing his hands post a lower back surgery of an ace cricketer of the Indian cricket team, who happened to hail from Ahmedabad. He felt exhilarated by the surgery as his reputation as a sports surgeon would certainly go viral if the cricketer recovered well and could play in the upcoming World Cup. Drying his hands on a sterile towel, he walked towards the elevators.

Dr Dhiraj Mehta, MD Orthopaedics. Dhiraj paused for a moment to glance proudly at the gleaming brass plate outside the consulting rooms he shared with a paediatrician in the Outpatient Department (OPD) of the private hospital. Considering his success rate, the hospital had offered him a full-time position with a hefty salary and perks. He had been tempted to accept it as it would permit him to spend more time with his wife. The fear of being accused by her of failing at the private practice her father had set up for him, stopped him. Sighing, he entered the waiting area which was already full of patients and headed towards a wooden door to the left which had another brass plate proclaiming it was his.

Changing into a simple white shirt and dark blue pants in his private washroom, he sat down behind a glass and chrome desk and pressed the bell for his first patient. He finished with the hospital patients by 10:45 am and headed for his private practice. There were only five patients waiting for him there.

He chatted with them to prolong their presence but was done by 12:30 pm. Forcing the depressing awareness that he still couldn't afford an X-ray machine out of his mind, he picked up the latest medical journal on orthopaedics and proceeded to update himself.

The shrilled ringing of his landline phone distracted him, and he absentmindedly reached out for it.

"Good afternoon, sir. I'm Priya from *TCI*. I want to speak with you regarding a special offer of a Personal Loan for doctors to enable them to buy medical equipment. Please may I take a few minutes of your precious time?"

"Madam, I'm not interested in availing any high interest Personal Loans," Dhiraj responded curtly.

"Doctor, the rate of interest of the loan I'm referring to is even lower than that of a home loan. I can request my boss to personally visit you and share the details."

*

It was 2 pm when Dhiraj strode into the cafeteria on the 20th floor of the private hospital, as he had been doing for the past two years and ordered the usual lunch of four chapatis, steamed vegetables, a bowl of lentils and a bowl of fresh fruits. The cafeteria was huge, so he was able to eat his lunch peacefully, as always, on the corner table overlooking Ahmedabad's skyline. Thanks to this cafeteria, he was able to discontinue the services of his cook and pay his maid a few extra hundred rupees to only cook dinner for him. Post lunch, he spent the next four hours attending the continuous stream of patients, before leaving for his clinic at 6.30 pm.

Surprisingly, his clinic was full that evening and it was almost 9 pm when an extremely handsome man dressed suavely in a crisp Louis Phillipe white shirt, Indian Terrain black slacks and what Dhiraj assumed were Red Tape, polished shoes (courtesy his wife's knowledge of the appropriate brands men should wear, another thing he didn't comply with much to her chagrin) walked in.

"Good evening, Dr Dhiraj Mehta, I'm Sidanshu from *TCI*."

"Oh, yeah. Priya said you'd be coming at 8 pm. Sorry to have kept you waiting. but while I do need an x-ray machine for my clinic, I don't want to take a loan for it," Dhiraj got straight to the point, returning Sidanshu's handshake.

"Doctor, the fact that you operated on Shiven Patel, India's best all-rounder cricketer today, is on national news. You were able to do so only because you are a consulting surgeon at *Zeus*. Suppose he recovers well and plays in the upcoming World Cup in the next six months, wouldn't the number of patients in your clinic increase? They certainly will with the right publicity. But then, you will have to refer them to another radiologist for x-rays, as you don't have your own machine, so maybe they'll prefer an orthopaedic surgeon who has one?

"*TCI* will sanction a personal loan to you at 11%, 1.5% lower than your existing home loan. The only documents you must provide are copies of your last three years' Income Tax returns, your bank statement reflecting the payments to you from *Zeus Multi Specialty Hospital* and an invoice from the vendor of the x-ray machine, with the actual cost. If you know him well, you can escalate the cost so you can retain the extra amount for your personal use."

"How do you know I don't have an x-ray machine?" Dhiraj questioned, suspiciously.

"Doctor, I'm a businessman, a loan facilitator in a highly competitive market. The only difference between me and the other so called 'DSAs' is that I play smart! I research my customers and make a solid case before approaching them. You remember that young guy who came to your clinic last week, complaining of lower back pain and you sent him to a radiologist a few blocks away for an x-ray? Well, that young man works for me, and he was only scoping your practice to see if you could become our probable customer," Sidanshu responded, almost apologetically.

Chapter 21

Alcohol Virgin

"Where's Tony?" Adi enquired, entering Sidanshu's black Mercedes S class, wondering how a DSA could afford a Rs 1 crore car.

"Oh, he's already at my pad, being entertained by my staff," Sidanshu replied, flashing a charming smile.

'Your staff? At your pad? What about your family?'

"I'm a bachelor by choice. I enjoy life on my terms," Sidanshu declared mysteriously.

*

"Who's the man, guys?"

Adi's heartbeat accelerated on hearing Tony's slurred question, the second he and Sidanshu set foot into the latter's swanky penthouse in Bodekdev, one of the costliest localities of Ahmedabad. Knowing that Tony didn't get drunk fast, Adi couldn't help wondering if Sidanshu's team had deliberately been serving Tony triple pegs as it was only 10.30 pm.

"Adi's the guy," Sidanshu and his team of 20 responded, prompting Tony to insist, "Give my guy a drink, a vodka with orange juice and soda. Adi's an alcohol virgin, guys, let's make sure he loses his virginity tonight. He certainly deserves it," Tony declared.

Sidanshu promptly complied, and Adi found himself staring into a crystal glass filled with what looked like harmless orange juice and soda.

"Drink up Adi, cheers," Tony prompted, raising his glass.

'What the hell,' Adi thought, raising the glass to his lips. The first sip wasn't so bad, prompting a second.

The music in the opulent living room suddenly rose a few decibels and Adi found himself ogling the scantily dressed nubile beauties of the opposite sex gyrating to the beats of remixed Bollywood songs. An absolute stunner in black hot pants and a slashed top was engaged in a version of 'Dirty Dancing' with Tony. 'Wow, I didn't know Tony could dance this way,' Adi wondered, draining his first glass, only to have a second promptly thrust into his hands.

Three pegs down, he was also on the makeshift dance floor, oblivious to the fact that the lights in the living room had been dimmed and only blue laser beams and strobe lights were on. Unaware of how to move his body to the beats of the techno-remix of a popular Bollywood song, Adi started dancing to the original tune in his head. The ever-observant Sidanshu immediately requested the DJ he had hired for the night to switch from remixes to the actual songs.

An upbeat song 'koi kahe kehta rahe' from a famous Bollywood movie, 'Dil Chahta hai', started blasting from the bass speakers. A svelte girl dressed in a mini denim skirt with a mirror work halter top matched Adi move for move as a fresh glass of something brown was thrush in his hand. Adi downed his glass in one swallow and emulated the steps of the energetic song, prompting others to follow suit. Feeling nauseous halfway through, he stumbled away from the dance floor. Strong hands grabbed him and guided him to a washroom, where he promptly threw up. The same arms guided him upstairs and insisted he drink a glass of water before passing out.

He woke up the following morning and reached for his cell phone. Finding it beside his pillow, he was horrified to see it was almost noon on a Friday. Rising guiltily from the bed, he flopped back on the pillows as the room had started spinning. His head immediately started pounding and he felt nauseous.

"Good morning boss, here, have some water and aspirin."

"What, why?" Adi objected to Sidanshu's cheerful voice which had the effect of drums pounding in his head.

"It's the best cure for a hangover," Sidanshu declared, forcing two pills into Adi's gaping mouth while pressing a glass of water on his lips.

Adi swallowed the pills, unable to bear the pain in his head and drained the glass of water, before flopping back on the bed.

"Good, now slowly sip this orange juice while you eat," Sidanshu suggested, gesturing to a man who was standing beside him holding a bed tray, to place it on Adi's bed.

Ignoring the food, Adi closed his eyes, waiting for the pain in his head to subside. It was only when he woke up again at 5 pm that he realised that he was on a double bed that had the mussed-up look of more than slumber happening on it.

Chapter 22

Catch-22

The setting sun painted the sky in hues of blue, grey and orange. A cool breeze provided the much-needed respite from the sweltering heat. Adi leaned back on the wrought iron bench, savouring the minuscule wonders of nature in a concrete jungle. Tightening his arm around Trisha's shoulders, he silently thanked God for bringing such a beautiful lady into his life.

It was one of the rare Saturday evenings when they could leave work at 5.30 pm. Longing for some fresh air, they had decided to meet at their usual place, the Sabarmati Riverfront, a promenade built on the banks of the perennial river Sabarmati. They generally ate dinner first in different restaurants near the River Front, after which they strolled on the promenade. Since it was too early for dinner that evening, they had decided to just hangout for a while. It had been four months since they started dating, and their relationship had reached the point of comfortable silence.

Annoyed on hearing his phone ring, he retrieved it from his shirt pocket and stared at the unknown number for a few seconds before answering the call.

"What's up, country boy?"

"Leila!" Adi exclaimed reflexively on hearing the familiar voice, a broad grin spreading over his face.

"Yep. So, someone's become an ASM at *TCI* huh?"

"Yep! Who told you? How come this call after years of silence, and what happened to your old number?" Adi shot off the barrage of questions while trying to pull Trisha back into his embrace. She however brushed his arm aside and shifted so she had a full view of his face.

"You are speaking to *TCI*'s new PL ASM, South Mumbai, country boy. This is my official number."

"What? No! Why? When did you join?" Adi tried not to cringe on seeing Trisha raise her right eyebrow in response to further questions from his side. She reached out and pressed the speaker button. Adi froze, realising he was in a catch-22 situation because there was no guarantee what Leila would reply. Knowing her nature, she may flippantly say she missed him, and he didn't know how Trisha would react.

"*Mumbai Xclusive*'s parent company shut it down in January. We were laid off with three months' pay. I applied for several jobs and got offers too, but the one with *TCI* seemed to be more appealing, so I joined in April. Hey, it looks like you're outside, we'll talk later"

Stunned yet relieved by her sober reply, Adi agreed, muttered a quick goodbye, and disconnected the call.

"Old flame?" Trisha voiced the obvious question, her doe-shaped eyes narrowing.

"Er, sort of," Adi replied honestly.

She stood and walked to the railing. Adi followed and flung an arm around her shoulders. She shrugged it off, stating, "I want to hear every detail."

"Aw, come on, it was nothing, just a fling," he replied, trying to be nonchalant while narrating how their trust for each other evolved. Although their intimate moments were vivid in his mind, he downplayed them, emphasizing more on how Leila transformed him.

"I want to walk," she suddenly declared, turning away from the flowing water she was fixated on till now. Adi fell in step beside her.

"What's the guarantee your old passion will not rekindle when you and Leila meet at an offsite event in Goa or the Maldives?" Trisha questioned quietly.

The sky had darkened by then and although the lights were on, certain parts of the promenade were dark. Spotting one behind a Gulmohar Tree, Adi slipped an arm around her shoulder and guided her to it. Pressing her back gently against the tree trunk, he cupped her face and met her eyes before replying, "It won't because I will never do anything to demean our relationship, Trisha."

"Neither will I Adi," she answered softly.

Desire coursed through his body at her unexpected reply. While they had held hands or wrapped their arms around each other during their dates, they hadn't kissed yet, although there were enough dark places on the promenade for couples to lock lips. He wanted her so badly that he was waiting for the perfect moment for their first kiss. He had even contemplated inviting her home for dinner, many times, but had refrained from doing so as he wasn't sure he could trust himself to limit their physical contact to just kissing.

Unable to hold back anymore, he cupped her chin and lowered his lips, so they were centimetres away from hers.

"Adi," she whispered huskily. He closed the gap, pressing his lips against her slightly parted ones. Wrapping his arms around her, he deepened their kiss, coaxing her lips to part further. He thrust his tongue into her mouth and sought hers. She responded, pressing herself against him, her tongue entwined with his. Tightening his left arm around her waist, he moved his right palm over her back and shoulders to rest at the base of her neck. He caressed her neck with his thumb for a while before lowering his lips to the area between her ears and the base of her neck. "I feel like taking you home and making love to you right now, however, I want to wait because I want our relationship to be more than just lust. I love you Trish and I know it's too soon to say this, but I kind of want you to be my life partner," he whispered, hugging her tight.

"Oh really! In that case, you should propose to me with a huge diamond ring in a proper romantic setting. I'll decide based on the size of your ring as to whether you deserve me or not," she replied, trying to be flippant but her shaky tone betrayed her arousal.

Feeling guilty at her response, because he had impulsively used passion to divert her from the Leila debacle, he wrapped an arm around her shoulders and guided her back onto the promenade.

Chapter 23

The Much-Needed X-Ray Machine.

'Medial: deltoid ligament, Lateral: posterior talofibular, anterior talofibular and calcaneofibular ligaments, Syndesmotic ligament,' Dhiraj scribbled the x-ray positions on his prescription pad. He tore the page and handed it to his patient, instructing, "Please go to the radiology department of the clinic which is adjacent to the consulting room for an x-ray of the ankle. The receptionist will guide you."

Leaning back against his executive swivel chair, he rang the bell for his next patient. Seven months had passed since he had operated upon Shiven Patel, who had since recovered and had ensured Team India's place in the cricket World Cup semi-finals. This had increased Dhiraj's private consulting patients and had given him the courage to avail a PL from *TCI* to purchase the much-needed X-ray machine, a month ago.

The only saddening factor was that Dhiraj's wife refused to take help for her alcohol addiction which had persisted for a year now. Dhiraj didn't have the energy to deal with it as he had to continue with his consultancy with *Zeus* to pay for his recent PL EMI, along with his clinic's overheads and the exorbitant salary of his full-time maid cum cook who ensured his wife was fed and hydrated.

He was examining a patient with a severe case of spondyloses when his cell phone rang. He ignored the call and ended his examination by prescribing a cervical x-ray. It was only when he finished with his last patient for that morning that he checked his cell phone and realised Priya from *TCI* had phoned him as he had saved her number. He pressed the button to answer her missed call.

"Good afternoon, Doctor, how are you doing?" Priya responded on the first ring.

"I'm good, what can I do for you?"

"I am extremely sorry to inconvenience you, doctor, but may I come by in the evening to take some additional Post-Dated Cheques from you as TCI is requesting the same? Also, I need your signature on some documents," she requested.

"Sure, come at 7.30 pm. You may have to wait though if I have patients," he responded.

"That's not a problem," she assured, disconnecting the call.

Dhiraj headed for Zeus' cafeteria, silently blessing Priya for being instrumental in him finally getting that X-ray machine in his clinic.

Chapter 24

Wine, Beer, and An Escort in Rajkot

Adi forced himself to relax as Tony wove his Honda City between the trucks and cars on the highway connecting Ahmedabad and Rajkot. Tony rarely drove below 100 km/hour on a highway and Adi was used to it, but the purpose of this trip was worrying him.

"Slowdown, Tony, I'm sure you don't want me to die before I reach Rajkot and approve your rejected cases," Swamy, the cause of Adi's unease commented from the backseat.

"Chill man and enjoy the highway. This is the problem with you credit guys, you never trust the person at the steering wheel," Priyansh who was also seated behind, between Swamy and Surbhi, tried to joke.

"This is where you are wrong, my friend. Right now, both the steering and the brakes are in Tony's control, so I must submit myself to his instinct. But, in the bank, I won't be doing my job if I don't press the breaks," Swamy jibed, in his trademark South Indian accent, courtesy of him being educated mostly in Chennai.

Adi winced at Swamy's response. They were in March, the last month of the Indian Financial year. It had been the incessant battle between Surbhi and him that had resulted in the Zonal Sales Head-West, Priyansh, the Regional Sales head, Tony, and his counterpart, the Regional Credit Head – Swaminathan Iyengar, a.k.a. Swamy to visit Adi, the Area Sales

Manager's territories to assess why there were so many rejections and escalations. Swamy had insisted they start with Rajkot, the location with the highest declined cases.

They reached *Hotel Silver Palace*, Rajkot's sole Five-Star hotel at 8 p.m. on Sunday. Adi's cell phone rang the second he entered the plush room assigned to him. "All's well boss?" a grin spread across Adi's face on hearing Sidanshu's voice. Seven months had passed since he had appointed *Pinnacle* as a DSA, and man was he glad he had done so. His monthly figures had shot up by at least two crores, with Pinnacle logging in minimum 5, high value cases to doctors and other self-employed professionals each month.

Surbhi, unfortunately, didn't share Adi's enthusiasm. She kept rejecting Pinnacle's cases from day one stating CIBIL (credit agency verification report) defaults or negative field verification reports. This had frustrated Adi and he was so sure Surbhi had a grudge against *Pinnacle* because *TCI* had hired her from the same MNC bank *Pinnacle* had exclusivity with earlier.

"What happened? Did the debonaire Sidanshu reject your amorous advances at your former bank? Is that why you quit and now you are trying to get back at him by rejecting his cases here?" Adi winced upon recalling his childish accusation one evening, three months ago, when Surbhi had rejected 8 of the 15 cases Pinnacle had logged in that day.

"What a disgusting, typical male chauvinistic reaction to a woman who is doing her job instead of pleasing her male colleagues," she had retorted.

"You are not doing your job, you are blindly rejecting only Pinnacle's cases instead of recommending them if they don't fall within your powers because you're not able to handle the load," he had countered in frustration.

"That's not true. Out of the total 30 cases I rejected today, 8 are Pinnacles, 5 Hrian's, 7 of other DSAs, and 10 of your DST team. Why are you fighting only for Pinnacle, why not Hrian or your other DSAs or DSTs?"

Their yelling match had continued till Tony had entered the credit department 10 minutes later, and had bellowed, "That's enough. Adi, pick up the files you feel were wrongly rejected and send an email to her with the mitigants. Surbhi, I request you to please forward the emails Adi sends you with the reasons why you rejected them and the mitigants you feel are strong."

"Sure, Tony," she had agreed in an amicable tone, resulting in Adi hating her even more, forgetting the fact that she had to be polite with Tony because he was senior to her.

Things had changed dramatically since then. *Pinnacle* had opened offices in all the locations Adi was handling in North Gujarat. Further, Sidanshu somehow always knew when a senior from the Personal Loan vertical, especially Priyansh, was visiting Ahmedabad, and had started insisting he would entertain the senior if he/she wanted to. Hrian usually did it, in a sedate manner, which paled now, in front of Sidanshu's flamboyance.

'Sidanshu's so assiduous. He's really God sent,' Adi mentally thanked the Almighty before answering, "Yeah, the arrangements are impeccable."

"This is nothing, boss, the night's still young," Sidanshu chuckled, disconnecting the call.

"Yeah," Adi muttered to himself, smiling at Sidanshu's suggestive statement. Excited to experience whatever was in store for them, he flopped down contentedly on a recliner couch in his room for a quick nap.

As expected, he was summoned shortly into Priyansh's suite, where Swamy and Priyansh's favourite brands of whiskey, Black Dog and Antiquity respectively, were being served. What he hadn't accounted for, however, was that Surbhi had a glass of red wine in her hand and was in an animated conversation with an absolute hunk of a guy nursing a beer. 'Wine, beer, and an escort in Rajkot to placate the firebrand Surbhi! Sidanshu's outdone himself this time,' Adi wondered, extracting his vibrating cell phone from the breast pocket of his Polo T-shirt, after accepting a glass of Black Label from the waiter assigned to take care of them.

"Hey, Trish, what's up?" he answered the call.

"Yeah, we've reached."

"I won't, sweetheart, stop worrying. I ll be back in Ahmedabad on Thursday, after visiting Mehsana and Himmatnagar," he tried to assuage her concern about him getting drunk.

"I love you too, sweetheart," he responded dutifully before hanging up.

*

"The collection manager said it's too risky to lend to small business owners in this region as most of them are protected by the Bharwad (the cow herd) community. That's why I rejected the case," Surbhi objected.

"What the hell, Surbhi, we are talking about approving a Rs 2 lakh personal loan to a gear manufacturer in Jamnagar, not a dairy owner. Recommend this case right away," Swamy thundered, raising Adi's spirits.

He had Sidanshu to thank for it because it appeared as though Swamy was in sales this morning, finding flaws in Surbhi's judgement. She did put up a fight, but it was kind of half-hearted.

Ninety percent of her rejections were shredded to pieces in all the locations, before they reached Ahmedabad, leaving Adi with the hope that he may finally surpass Bharat's disbursement figures in this financial year. Further, not all the cases belonged to Pinnacle.

Chapter 25

A Personal Thing

It was that time of the year again when the future of a banker was decided by one email from the Central Office Operations Team. Well, the email was in Adi's inbox, but he was too nervous to open it. A year had passed since he was appointed as the Area Sales Manager (ASM) of North Gujarat and according to his personal MIS (Management Information System), he had achieved 140% of his annual target, to emerge as the top ASM in the Western Zone. He couldn't celebrate that fact though unless the Central Office Operations Team confirmed it.

"Ahlavat, my man, you have done it! Team, clap for my boy here who is the best ASM in the West."

Tony's declaration and the applause echoing in the sales department of *TCI* prompted him to finally click on the email from the Central Office Operations team and confirm the fact for himself.

"Thanks, boss, I couldn't have done it without your support," Adi acknowledged the applause and accepted the congratulations from his team of four sales managers in Ahmedabad. His phone rang and he answered the call from his sales manager in Rajkot, the second biggest location in his territory. It was while he was answering a call from the sales manager at Himmatnagar that he locked eyes with Hrian, his top performing DSA till Adi had signed on Pinnacle.

A stab of guilt pierced his heart as Hrian had warned him a few months ago about the files that *Pinnacle*, his star DSA in the past year, had been logging in not only in Ahmedabad but also in the entire Gujarat. So had Trisha, but he had dismissed it as professional jealousy in Hrian's case, and a bruised ego for Trisha because *TCI* was doing better in Personal Loans than the bank she had joined. Well, it was because of *Pinnacle* first and Hrian later that he had finally been declared as the Area Sales Manager with the highest Personal Loan Disbursements in the entire West, having surpassed his bitter rival, Bharat.

"I'm organising a party at *The Lotus Room* of *The Grand Bhagwati* tonight to celebrate Adivteya Ahlavat's success. Make sure all of you along with your DSAs and DSTs are present," Tony declared, plummeting Adi back to earth.

"Er, boss, I can't attend a party tonight, I have a personal thing," Adi informed sheepishly.

"Sorry team, party postponed to next Saturday because the guys from the other locations can't make it at such short notice," Tony announced, recollecting suddenly that Adi had consulted him about his 'personal thing' a week ago when he was sure he would surpass Bharat in his disbursements that year.

*

Adi reached the restaurant *360°*, the only revolving restaurant in Ahmedabad, atop a five-star hotel, *The Elite*. He had reserved a table a week ago and had arrived early in an autorickshaw because he wanted to confer with the maître d.

'Oh my God! She looks like a goddess. What have I done to deserve her?' Adi wondered inwardly, promptly jumping to his feet on seeing Trisha walk into the restaurant, dressed in a printed sea green skirt, clinched at her slim waist, and flowing over her hips and legs to rest just above her ankles. Her slim, smooth arms were emphasized by a light green sleeveless top tucked into the wide waistband of her skirt, and her exquisite silky black hair was unbound, flowing over her back.

The maître d greeted her, and she probably introduced herself, for he promptly grinned, and escorted her to the corner table reserved for Adi, besides the floor-to-ceiling windows of the restaurant. Living up to its name, this revolving restaurant did offer the diners, especially the ones seated next to the windows a 360° view of Ahmedabad city.

Adi couldn't help sneaking a glance at the other men in the restaurant. Heads turned, not only of the men but also of the women as Trisha sauntered towards him. Her skirt swayed as she walked on black, stiletto encased feet, displaying a seductive amount of shapely leg and mid-thigh, courtesy the discrete slit on the right.

"Hey," she greeted, sitting down on the chair the maître d' held out for her.

"Hey," Adi responded, resuming his seat, unable to take his eyes off her subtly made-up face, and the thin, delicate gold necklace around her neck, with a solitary diamond nestled in a hint of a cleavage.

"Looks like someone outperformed his rival this year," she winked, her face lighting up as she smiled.

"Hmm, what about you?" he enquired, ignoring the blood surging through his body, especially to a spot that hadn't yet calm down since she walked in.

"Yeah, I'm on the top in Gujarat but Mumbai's surpassed me," she responded modestly while the waiter placed a virgin Mojito in front of her and lemonade for him, along with some bites.

"I hope you don't mind, but I've pre-ordered our meal," he enquired nervously.

"No at all, as I know you've ordered all my favourite food to celebrate our first successful year-end in rival banks," she responded, flashing her killer smile.

He, fortunately, had done so, and they both tried to ensure the conversation steered clear from their work as they shared the delicious cheese nan with a roasted cashew nut curry, green salad, dum pukth biryani and pineapple raita.

"No, don't tell me it's a chocolate truffle pastry! I'm stuffed," she groaned when a waiter cleared their table and placed a plate with a cloche between them.

"How can it not be, madam?" Adi questioned, removing the cover with a flourish, after the waiter left the table.

"What's this? Adi don't tell me, you're going to, oh my god!" she exclaimed on seeing the sparkling diamond ring placed in a box at the centre of the triangular pastry.

"Yes, I am, my love," he declared, standing to pluck the ring from the box.

Getting down on his right knee beside her chair, he extended the ring to her, placed the palm of his right hand over his heart and declared, "I love you with my whole heart, soul and being. Trisha Mishra, will you marry me and share the rest of your life with me? I promise to do the best I can to ensure your smile will retain the same radiance it does today, for the entirety of our life together."

"Oh Adi, of course I'll marry you, I love you too from the bottom of my heart," she responded, extending her left hand.

The entire restaurant exploded as the guests and staff applauded and whistled while Adi slipped the ring onto her finger.

Chapter 26

Alarm Bells

Under normal circumstances, Nishant Sapre, Collection Manager of *TCI* Ahmedabad, would have been in the air-conditioned confines of his office, leaning back on his swivel chair that would have been creaking under the weight of his 86 kg frame, while he would have been on one phone call after another, taking updates from his team.

Not that afternoon, though. Desperate times called for desperate measures. Several high-value loans had turned into NPAs (non-performing assets) as the customers had not been paying their EMIs for over 6 months. So, here he was on the second floor of a derelict building, trying to ignore the muck lining both sides of the long, dingy corridor as he made his way to shop number 27. His heart sank on realising that the worn-out door beside shop number 26 appeared as though it had not been opened for a long time because there was a thick layer of dust and litter outside it.

Sure he may have read the address wrong, he looked at the copy of the employment field investigation (FI) report in his hand to confirm the shop number. It was right. Shop number 27 had been reported in the FI report as belonging to a Gaurang Shah, the owner of Gaurang Textile Trading. The executive had prepared this report, 7 months ago, before *TCI* had sanctioned a PL of Rs 5 lakhs to Gaurang Shah.

All the boxes pertaining to the presence of a board proclaiming the business, staff, verification from neighbours, etc, had been ticked. The business had been categorized as textile trading and well, generally only an office was required for the same as most of the traders were just middlemen, connecting wholesale buyers to sellers.

Seven months down the line, not only was the door of shop number 27 shut, but so were the ones before and after it.

Tracing his steps back, Nishant entered shop number 20 which was open and enquired from a thin man seated on a stool at the entrance, "How long has shop number 27 been closed?"

"Are you from a bank?" the man asked, triggering alarm bells in Nishant's mind.

"Yes, why, have other people from banks also asked about that office?" Nishant questioned.

"Hmm. Many have given me money to phone them just in case that office opens," the man replied, licking his lips, probably in anticipation.

"So, when was the last time the office had opened?" Nishant enquired, whipping out his wallet.

"I don't remember," the man quickly responded, eyeing the wallet.

"Was it three months ago?" Nishant tried again, extracting 100 bucks.

"Two months ago. Some girls came, opened the office, cleaned it, and put up a board. They took down the board after a few days and left. No one has opened it since then," the man informed after pocketing the money.

"What about your office? Why are you the only person here?"

"I don't know. My boss lives and works in Mumbai. He pays me to open the office daily at 10 am, clean it, and sit till 5 pm."

"What's your boss' name? Have any bank people visited your office?"

"Patel, sir. I don't know anything else, and no bank people have ever visited this office."

Nishant checked his records for any defaulters with an employment address in this office number 20. Not finding any, he thanked the man and walked away, as he had planned to visit at least 8 doctors who had availed multiple PLs of Rs 20 lakhs each that day. All the cases belonged to *Pinnacle*, the DSA appointed less than a year ago, despite his protests.

Chapter 27

Anti-Climax

Adi could barely keep his eyes open as the Lufthansa flight from Munich to Ahmedabad landed at the city's international airport in the wee hours of Saturday. Nudging Tony, who was still fast asleep on the seat beside him awake, they collected their hand baggage and deplaned. Customs clearance was a breeze. Sidanshu's driver was waiting at the arrival gate. He quickly relieved Tony of his trolley and led them to airport parking where Sidanshu's Mercedes was parked.

Tony and Adi promptly fell asleep in the car during the 45-minute drive to their respective homes. Their all-expense paid trip to Germany, *TCI*'s reward for the star performers of the PL sales team in the previous financial year, had been spectacular. This was the second time in a row that Adi and Tony had won an international trip after joining *TCI*.

"Adivteya sir, we have reached your house." The driver's polite tone managed to penetrate Adi's jetlagged stupor. He exited the car and allowed the driver to accompany him with his luggage right up to the elevator of a 20-storey apartment building in Navrangpura. Adi had rented a studio apartment on the 15th floor, which itself costed a bomb, considering the area. But it was within walking distance from *TCI*.

Managing to fit the right key in the lock, Adi opened his front door to find his living room lit up with candles and Trisha waiting for him. She knew his itinerary and had probably gotten a spare key from the neighbours. Adi didn't care. He shut the door behind him, dropped his bags and hugged her tight when she flew into his arms. He was ecstatic she had decided to reconcile after their horrible row regarding Leila just before his Germany trip, for she too had won it.

Shifting slightly when her lips sought his, he groaned apologetically, lowering his head to her shoulder, "Trish, babes, I'm sorry. I haven't brushed my teeth or bathed since I left the hotel on Friday.

"Ug. Okay, go freshen up while I whip up some fresh paneer parathas for you," she suggested, breaking away from their embrace. He dragged his bags to the foot of the bed, and collapsed on it, intending to rest for a minute. Not hearing any movement, she looked up from the kitchen counter after a while, to find him fast asleep. She woke him up after a few hours, forced him to eat a paratha, and drink some juice before he slid back into an exhausted slumber.

It was around 8 pm on Sunday when he was able to finally surface from nearly 14 hours of rest. Disappointed on not seeing Trisha around, he reached for his cell phone. 'Hey, I couldn't stay out for two nights in a row, so I've gone home. Phone me when you wake up,' her text message read. He was about to do so when his cell phone rang. Seeing 'Dad' flash on the screen, he rose from the bed, walked to a recliner, and answered the call. "Have you returned from Germany?" his father got straight to the point.

"Yes, Dad."

"Good. You must come home next month. We are finalizing your marriage with Mr Chaudary's daughter, but we must complete the formality of you meeting the girl before we proceed, so make sure you are home. Here talk to your mother," he commanded stoically.

"Beta, how are you? How was your trip? Have you eaten anything since you returned? What did you eat there because

I don't think you would have got any vegetarian food in Germany?"

It took him an hour to give his mother a blow-by-blow account of his trip wherein he had to conjure up a sob story of having mainly survived on bread, cheese, and fruit. Guilt rocked him though, as he had gorged on chicken, ham, and bacon, only drawing the line on beef, an almost staple in Germany. He wanted to talk to her about the 'arranged marriage' threat his father had sprung on him, but he knew his father would be hovering around his mother and she would have put the call on speaker.

Dragging himself to the tiny bathroom when the call finally ended, he stood under the hot shower for a long time, pondering over the anti-climax ending to a fabulous trip.

Chapter 28

'Seeing the Girl'

"What crap!" Adi exclaimed upon clicking on an email from Nishant Sapre, Ahmedabad's collection manager.

"What happened?" Bharat, who sat at an adjacent workstation enquired, trying to peer over Adi's shoulders.

"Mind your own business," Adi snapped, turning the screen away.

Taking a deep breath to calm his rising blood pressure, he re-read the email marked to him, with a copy to Tony, Priyansh, Surbhi and a bunch of seniors in the collection vertical:

'I recommend an immediate suspension of the cases logged in by the DSA *Pinnacle* in the entire North Gujarat as we have five skipped and untraceable cases and 14 defaults by the customers logged in by this DSA. Most of the new defaults in Ahmedabad are self-employed and a few are salaried cases, one being a scientist working with a reputed pharmaceutical company.'

A chill ran down Adi's spine as he logged onto *TCI's Universe* and extracted the details of the said cases. Comforted upon learning all the third-party verifications were positive and Surbhi had either approved the cases or recommended them without escalations from his side, he hit 'reply all' and pointed this out in his response email, including statistics on the total cases logged in by *Pinnace* in North Gujarat, their approval rate, and the percentage of NPA cases against the total approved, which was less than 10%.

They were in the first week of June and although his other DSAs and DSTs were doing a good job, Adi couldn't afford to stop *Pinnacle*'s business.

*

"Hey, we should do this more often," Adi greeted, hugging Trisha close, the second she settled down beside him in the autorickshaw.

"Do what? And why are we taking an auto? Where are we going?" she questioned, snuggling close.

"Meet during our lunch break," he replied, deliberately ignoring her question about their destination. Deciding to divert his mind from Nishant's email, he had impulsively phoned her and insisted they meet.

"Ha, as if our timings coincide! Today, I made sure I was free at 1 p.m. because you said it was urgent. So, where are we going?"

"Five more minutes."

*

"You bought a Honda City?" she squealed when the autorickshaw halted in front of a Honda showroom.

"Not yet. I wanted you to help me decide whether it should be a 'City' or an 'Accent'," Adi clarified, paying the driver before alighting.

"But you already have an auto loan going on for your Opel, then how can you buy another car," she objected, refusing to bulge from the pavement outside the Honda and Hyundai showrooms adjacent to each other.

"Veer bhaiya deposited a cheque of Rs 15 lakhs in my account last week for the Opel I left at home, in Bhulanshahr, so I thought I'll buy a car with this money and let the auto loan continue, at the simple interest staff rate of 6%."

"I don't know Adi. Maybe you should close that loan first and then apply for a fresh loan. What's the urgency for a car? You know you can always use mine," she continued to protest.

"Sweetheart, I cannot borrow your car to come to your house to ask your father for your hand in marriage, nor can I come in an autorickshaw, can I? We are already in the first week of June and my dad expects me to be home anytime to 'see' Chaudary uncle's daughter. What's there to 'see'? I 'saw' her last year when we visited Chaudary uncle's home to solicit his vote. I don't have time, Trish. I need to meet your dad soon and obtain his consent." Adi tried to clarify and emphasize his frustration with the English version of the age-old Indian marriage custom of 'ladki dekhna', 'seeing the girl' with air quotes.

"I'm not happy with this," she stated, reluctantly accompanying him inside the Honda showroom.

Chapter 29

Tradition

'Dr Madanmohan Mishra, PhD'. Adi stared at the gleaming brass nameplate affixed on the top centre of the plywood panelled front door and realised his life would change forever the second he rang the doorbell.

Mustering whatever semblance of courage he possessed, he raised his hand and pressed the switch next to the door. He almost fled on hearing the chimes echoing but managed to flash his charming smile when a middle-aged lady wearing a traditional sari with a part of it (the pallu) covering her head, answered the door. Unsure if she was the resident maid or Trisha's mother, Adi joined his palms together and greeted her in the traditional Indian greeting in Hindi, "Namaste, I'm Adivteya Ahlavat."

"Beta, please come in, I am Sita, Trisha's mother," the lady responded in flawless English, reminding Adi sheepishly of Trisha sharing during their initial days of dating that her mother had done her MA in Linguistics from Nalanda University in Bihar, and she was a professor in St Xavier's College, Ahmedabad.

"Thank you, Aunty," Adi responded, stepping into Trisha's childhood home, totally taken aback by her mother's modest demeanour.

"Adivteya beta, meet Trisha's father Dr Madanmohan Mishra. He has done PhD in Textile Technology and is a scientist with ATIRA, that is 'The Ahmedabad Textile

Industry's Research Association'", Trisha's mother introduced in chaste English when they entered the tastefully decorated living room.

Adi immediately rushed to touch Trisha's father's feet as per the traditional values ingrained in him.

"May the almighty God give you a long and fruitful life," Trisha's father blessed him before requesting him to take a seat on a chair adjacent to the one he was seated upon.

"Adivteya, we invited you for dinner tonight because Trisha told us she wants to marry you. Son, we respect her decision and have no objections to the man she has decided to choose as a life partner but, being her parents, we wanted to clarify one thing. Trisha told us that you belong to the upper cast Jat community of Uttar Pradesh. As far as I know, this community demands a lot of dowry for their son's wedding. Well, we also belong to the Brahmin community i.e., the upper cast community of Bihar and we too pay dowry to get our daughters married, so we wanted to understand the demands from your family before consenting to this marriage, immaterial of it being one initiated out of mutual love," Trisha's father came straight to the point before Adi could even sip the water Trisha served him.

"Sir, I understand your apprehension, but I don't want any dowry," Adi responded, nervously gulping down the water.

"Do your parents feel the same?" Dr Mishra responded.

"I know my mom wouldn't want dowry, Mishra sir. She is the most educated lady in my family, in my village. She had done her MA in English literature from Kanpur and is the only English teacher in our village. People pay her Rs 5000 per month for private tuitions so that they are well versed in English and can get good jobs in neighbouring cities," Adi tried to confirm.

"I understand son, but did your mother's family pay dowry to get your father to marry her?" Dr Mishra questioned sagaciously.

"Stop right there. I don't want my father to pay even a single paisa to get me married," Trisha objected.

"Good, so stay single because no man will marry you," Trisha's mom retorted, pulling the slipped edge of her 'pallu' firmly back over her head.

"Is that so Adi? Will you not marry me if I refuse to allow my father to pay a dowry for my hand? You claim to love me, so will you allow dowry to raise its ugly head in a 'love marriage?'" Trisha turned defiantly to Adi.

Chapter 30

Skip Tracing

'Damn, I hate Mondays!' Trisha exclaimed inwardly, exiting the mini conference room on her floor, post an exhausting team meeting. It had been the usual bitter volleying of accusations, with sales voicing their frustrations because of the mounting rejections and her credit team retaliating by blaming their dubious cases.

"Hello Trisha, how are you doing?"

"Hey, Ishan, long time no see." Trisha's face lit up on seeing Ishan Gupta, the Collection Manager of *FirstCredit*, the bank she had joined after resigning from *TCI*, waiting for her in her cubicle. She had secretly nicknamed him 'Gentle Giant!' because while he intimidated defaulters with his burly 6 feet 2" muscular physique, and curt attitude, he was a very chivalrous person who respected women.

"I've been terribly busy 'skip tracing', chasing 'non-starters' and defaulters. I'm sorry to be the bearer of bad news but the NPAs have doubled this quarter compared to the same time last year," Ishan informed grimly.

"Skip tracing? How come? Which case?" she responded, sinking wearily onto her swivel chair. She accepted the file he was holding out and started leafing through it.

"Gaurang Shah, a small business owner of 'Gaurang Textile Trading', a firm apparently engaged in textile trading is one of them. The employment FI report of his office in Paldi is positive. He was present at the time of the visit, so were a few employees, busy at their PCs. The executive who conducted the visit had reported examining some orders and invoices.

"The residence visit report was also positive. Same is the case for the income document verifications by the risk team. I checked with some other banks, and he has availed personal loans from almost all of them. So, I went to the Income Tax (IT) office with Som, the owner of the same RCU agency that works for most banks in Ahmedabad, to verify his IT returns. Well, the IT return is fake. The serial number belongs to Nitin Jain, a ninety-year- old man who died last year. Both the residence and employment electricity bills and his bank statement also appear to be doctored.

"This prompted a visit to his place of work on Saturday. Office number 27 apparently hasn't opened since last November, neither were any of the adjoining offices. There was a peon in number 20, but he hasn't heard of a Gaurang Shah or his firm. I haven't yet visited his residence, but I have discretely enquired from his neighbours. No one claims to know a Gaurang Shah."

Trisha felt the room sway as she listened to Ishan. Firing up her PC, she quickly extracted the daily MIS which contained details of all the logins, approvals, rejections, disbursements, and defaults. Filtering the data to only display *Pinnacle's* Personal Loan defaults, her heart lurched on seeing there were at least 10 'non-starters' that is customers who didn't pay their first instalment, and 18 defaulters in the past six months, three of which were doctors with Rs 20 lakh loans.

"What do you propose we should do? Sales is only going to blame us and our agencies. Shall I take up the matter with Sidanshu?" she enquired, still stinging from the meeting that concluded half an hour ago.

"Not now. I'm planning on visiting the residence with Nishant and Surbhi. If we find any lacunae, then we will take up the matter with the respective agencies. It's possible that the FI and RCU executives may be involved," he informed.

"I'll accompany you but Ishan, even if Gaurang turns out to be a case of identity theft, he's one amongst 368 cases logged in by *Pinnacle* in the last six months. I think, *FirstCredit* was the first bank to appoint *Pinnacle* almost two years ago, and there haven't been many issues in his case except in the last few months. Who's the *Pinnacle* executive who logged in this case, has he also logged in any of the 'non-starters'?"

"Raghav 7 of the 10 non-starters."

'Damn!' Trisha groaned inwardly, her fingers turning cold at the information.

"Let's go. If not anything, I'll get *Pinnacle's* executive kicked out," she declared, rising from her chair, and picking up her purse from the bottom drawer of her desk.

Chapter 31

Love or lust?

"Pranam, bade bhaiya."

Adi bent down to touch his older brother's feet upon reaching the spot where Veer was waiting for him in the arrival area of Lucknow airport.

"Jeeta rehe, Adi," Veer responded, blessing him with a long life before hugging him tight.

They walked towards Veer's black Bolero with Veer's hand over Adi's shoulders as Veer updated him about their earnings from last year's harvest. For Income Tax reasons, Adi had insisted the earnings from the plot assigned to his name by his grandfather when he was born, be credited in his mom's account. He was surprised to learn now, that his share of the profits would take the cumulative total in his mom's account to nearly twenty crore rupees in 28 years.

Adi waited till Veer loaded his luggage into his SUV and started it before enquiring, "Do you think I can buy a plot of land of my own with that money?"

"Why? Isn't your inherited property of 20 acres enough?" Veer countered, manoeuvring the SUV out of the airport.

"It is, but I thought maybe it's better to have some land of my own," Adi responded cautiously.

"In that case, Chaudary uncle is going to give you at least Rs 50 lakhs dowry so use that and some of the money accumulated in Ma's account to buy yourself a hefty piece of land. As though, city people like you are going to come to the village to become lowly farmers like us," Veer retorted, laughing heartily at his own joke.

Unable to express the shallowness he had started feeling lately about his life, especially after being squished between Nishant's investigation of *Pinnacle*'s bad cases and Priyansh's pressure to increase his disbursement numbers, Adi turned to gaze at the cotton fields flashing by.

"Is something bothering you?" Veer enquired.

"I can't marry Chaudary uncle's daughter, I'm in love with another girl," Adi blurted.

"Love?" Veer bellowed, letting out another bout of laughter. "Love or lust? Do you even know the difference between the two because I seriously feel you are confused as you haven't gotten laid yet or have you?" Veer paused his mirth to clarify and question.

"You are six years older to me, you tell me the difference," Adi challenged, defiantly, reluctant to share the details of his life.

"I most certainly will. Love is when you are willing to die for a person, when you will not allow anything to happen to him or her. Lust is when you want to satisfy your natural desires and you find a partner who responds to you because she probably has an equal or a higher sexual desire than you. So, what exactly are you going through right now, my baby brother? Is it love or lust?"

"Love and lust," Adi answered confidently, clarifying, "I've been lusting after a lady Trisha, for two years now, but I haven't slept with her yet, even though I've wanted to. I expressed my love for her eight months ago and we want to get married. She responds to me, so I know she wants me, and lust is there from her side too. Unfortunately, I don't know if it will work out or not, as I can't predict the future.

"I requested her father for her hand a few weeks ago. They are brahmins from Bihar and staunch followers of the dowry tradition. Trisha's father is a scientist with an autonomous non-profit association for textile research in Ahmedabad. I guess he earns a decent salary with provident fund and pension. Being aware of his responsibilities as a father as he has two daughters, he has been saving money all his life, to pay dowry when his daughters get married. Trisha's older sister married a dentist five years ago. He was working under another doctor when they got engaged, but her father had to pay a dowry of Rs 30 lakhs to set up his private practice, furnish his newly purchased flat and buy a Mahindra XUV.

"Trisha confided in me that her maternal grandfather had paid the dowry as her father couldn't manage it after wedding expenses that amounted to almost Rs 10 lakhs. Now, if Trisha's dad must pay a dowry for me, well he has to borrow from his Provident Fund and also take a personal loan, I suppose. How much dowry is normally paid for a banker anyway?"

"Rs 20 lakhs minimum, as you have done your MBA, and you are a 'Manager' in a bank. Adi, you idiot, Trisha is probably faking her love for you, so her father doesn't have to pay a dowry for your wedding. Is she good-looking?" Veer answered sceptically.

"Yes, she's gorgeous," Adi responded cautiously, remembering Trisha's objection as to why dowry shouldn't be paid in a love marriage.

"There you go! Any IAS officer or Doctor or Engineer from Bihar will immediately accept her marriage proposal. Forget accepting, their parents will initiate the request for her hand in marriage themselves. Her father will not be able to refuse as a refusal would mean ruining her reputation for any future prospects. So, he will be forced to pay the demanded dowry. By snaring you, maybe he won't have to pay any dowry at all or maybe just Rs 20 lakhs, as those professions would get a minimum of Rs 50 lakhs," Veer stated.

"It's okay, bhaiya I'm willing to take my chances with her love. I haven't discussed this matter with her yet, but she's also a banker earning a good salary. We will take care of the dowry; in case our dad raises the issue. Veer Bhaiya, I'd rather marry a known person, someone who understands me, my job, and my life than someone who has no clue as to what it's like to work for one of the best banks in India and live under target pressure. I can't do this though without your support, so will you help me?"

Chapter 32

The Alleged Perpetrator

Trisha cursed herself for wearing the 2" flesh coloured, *Catwalk* pumps that matched the beige blouse she was wearing over pin-striped, black trousers that day. The pointed ends of the shoes bit into her toes as they climbed the four floors to reach Gaurang Shah's apartment because the 5-storey old building didn't have an elevator.

She hovered at the rear of their group of four as Nishant rang the bell of flat number 402.

"Where is your father?" Nishant questioned a probably six-year-old boy who opened the door.

"Who's there?" a surly voice enquired from within in Gujarati, prompting the boy to open the door wider to reveal their presence.

"How many times should I tell you not to answer the door? Go inside," an old man muttered angrily in his native language, taking hold of the door.

"We want to meet your son," Nishant answered in the same language.

"He's not at home," the old man responded, attempting to close the door.

"Not so fast," Nishant said, placing a foot in the space between the door and the frame while using his body weight to prevent the door from closing. Although Nishant was at least an inch shorter than Ishan, he was bulky enough, if not muscular to wrestle a door with an old man who appeared to be in his late sixties.

"How dare you apply force, I'll phone the police," the old man threatened.

"Go ahead," Nishant responded leaning against the door, forcing the old man backwards.

Ishan's phone rang as the four of them entered the house. Trisha immediately locked eyes with an obese lady seated on a couch to the right of the door. Her arm was around a little girl pressed against her side.

"Good work, bring him upstairs," Ishan spoke into the phone before disconnecting the call and informed his bank mates, "My men intercepted a man who looks exactly like Gaurang, trying to jump the wall in the rear of the building. They are bringing him up right now. I wonder how he knew about our visit?"

Sensing something was amiss, the old man enquired, "What do you want and who are you?"

"What's your son's name?" Ishan questioned.

"Ronak Zala."

"What does he do?" Ishan continued.

"Business."

Two men, Trisha recognized as employees of the off-roll team assisting Ishan in collections, entered the house escorting a man she recognized as Gaurang Shah from his passport-sized photo affixed on the application form in his file.

One of the men shut the front door behind him, while Ishan moved to block the entrance to the passage from the living room and Nishant shifted to the threshold of the balcony.

"Who suggested you should apply for Personal Loans under Gaurang Shah's name in ten different banks in Ahmedabad?" Nishant enquired.

"My name is Ronak, I didn't do any such thing," the alleged perpetrator answered.

"Stop lying. We have your photo in our files."

"Shut up," Nishant snapped at Surbhi's uncalled-for accusation.

Trisha stole a glance at Ishan, and she could have sworn to have seen irritation flash momentarily over his face, before he spoke calmly, "If you haven't, then you won't mind accompanying us to the police station to file a FIR as someone used your photo to apply for Personal Loans from multiple banks under the name of Gaurang Shah."

"It's not my problem that someone used my photo to cheat your banks. You are the ones pestering people to avail personal loans, so someone took advantage of it, not me," Gaurang/Ronak responded defiantly.

"Then what were you doing in office number 27 on the 11th of November 2007 at 11.30 am, pretending to be the owner of Gaurang Textile Trading?" Ishan persisted.

Had the circumstances been different, Trisha would have applauded because the alleged perpetrator looked like a deer caught in the headlights of a speeding vehicle on the highway.

"Get out of my house. You are unnecessarily accusing me of doing something I didn't do," the perpetrator shouted.

"Why are you harassing my son? Can't you see his children are getting upset," the obese lady seated on the couch spoke.

"We are extremely sorry madam, but if your son is innocent, then he won't have any issues in accompanying us to the police station to clear his name, would he?" Ishan responded in chaste Gujarati, flashing his most charming smile.

Chapter 33

Dark Side

Ahmedabad Airport circa 2008 was nondescript, resembling any run-of-the-mill, reasonably clean government building. The Lucknow-Ahmedabad flight touched down at 11 am, two hours late. Adi continued to remain slouched on his seat, waiting for the crowd of impatient passengers who had stood up even before the seatbelt sign had gone off, to subside. He was exhausted; he wanted to go home and sleep, but he knew he couldn't. He had to report for work and somehow get through the day with less than two hours of sleep in 24 hours.

He remembered to switch on his cell phone only upon reaching the baggage claim and wasn't surprised to find 20 missed calls, five of which were from Sidanshu. As if on cue, the phone rang and Adi answered it cheerfully, welcoming the diversion, "Hey, I know you have a car waiting for me and it's not your Mercedes because Tony's not with me."

"It is my Mercedes because I'm waiting in it in the airport parking. We must talk," Sidanshu replied, disconnecting the call.

Adi stared at the blank screen, curbing the urge to phone Sidanshu and demand what was going on. Depositing his now inactive phone back to his T-shirt's pocket, he stared at the immobile conveyor belt, willing it to move. Eerily, it did, startling him, and he stared at the luggage passing over it wondering what was happening to his life.

*

"I was a fool to approach other private and MNC banks of India when I was doing so well with the best multi-national bank in the world, *TM Strides*," Sidanshu exploded the second Adi settled down on the backseat beside him.

"Woah, calm down Sid, what's wrong? Adi enquired, totally flummoxed by Sidanshu's greeting.

"It's that whore you are engaged to who has blacklisted me from her bank. Didn't you tell her I was the one who had bribed the maître d' of the *Fern* so you could get the best corner table and profess your love to her while you had the most magnificent view of Ahmedabad city?"

"I never asked you to do that," Adi answered coldly, a tight vice gripping his heart at Sidanshu's venomous reply. He had only confided his dilemma regarding a romantic proposal to Tony so when did Sid get involved?

"Huh, you think that drunken womanizer Tony is capable of anything?" Sidanshu spat as though he was reading his mind, adding, "Tony told me to handle it, and I did. But now, your bitch Trisha has blacklisted me. I cannot log in PL files at her bank. Fortunately, I have a hold over Surbhi and Nishant, so don't you dare come under your bitch Trisha's influence and try to remove me from *TCI*. I have incriminating evidence against both you, Tony, and Priyansh too, so tread carefully my friend and ditch the bitch you feel is your ideal mate. She is an opportunist."

It took Adi a moment to realise that the car had halted outside *TCI*, and his side of the door was open. He alighted and the car speed away with a squeal the second he retrieved his luggage from the boot.

Pressing the button to release the handle of his trolley bag, he clutched it and dragged it into the building. He was badly disturbed because this was the third time Trisha's character was demeaned in 24 hours. The first was by his brother Veer during their drive home from the airport. The second was by his father who claimed he didn't want a girl with low morals as a daughter-in-law when Veer suggested Adi should marry the woman he wanted, instead of being forced into an arranged marriage, and now Sidanshu.

"Damn Sidanshu. Who the hell does he think he is? Maybe I'm giving him so much importance that he feels he can control my life now, Adi muttered, staggering into *TCI's* opulent lobby, still reeling from the dark side of Sidanshu he had just witnessed.

Chapter 34

Corruption

The elevator pinged upon reaching the 3rd floor, where Jimit Mehta – owner of Mehta and Associates FI agency had his office. What had started as just a flutter of anxiety when they had entered the 'fake identity' culprit's home, snowballed into a full-fledged vice gripping her heart, upon stepping out of the elevator. Trisha took deep breaths, attempting to calm the panic threatening to rise.

Till date her interactions with Jimit had been extremely cordial. In fact, she loved visiting his warmly decorated office which reflected his persona. God knows what's in store for today's meeting, she wondered, following the others. Ishan cursorily knocked on the frosted glass door while turning the handle to open it and entered Jimit's office.

"Hello, Ishan, how are you?" Trisha heard the polite owner greet as she and the others, including the alleged perpetrator Ronak followed suit.

"Let's dispense with the pleasantries, Jimit. Kindly call your executive Samir to your office," Ishan instructed, indicating Trisha and Surbhi should occupy the two chairs in front of Jimit's desk. They complied while Nishant dragged Ronak to a sofa in the room and Ishan paced the ten-foot space between them.

The door opened after a few minutes and Trisha turned to watch a five feet 2-inch man dressed in a white shirt and black pants enter.

The tension on Samir's face was evident to all, as his shifty eyes darted from Ronak to Ishan, Jimit, and back.

Ishan immediately grabbed Samir's collar and demanded, "How much money did you take to give a positive residence visit report of this man?"

"I don't know who he is," Samir protested.

"Oh really? Didn't you meet him when you visited his home six months ago?" Ishan sneered, tightening his grip.

"Six months ago? I have visited hundreds of homes how can I remember all their faces?" Samir responded defiantly.

A resounding slap echoed in the room. Trisha gasped and turned to gaze at Jimit seated calmly in his plush leather executive chair. She hadn't seen Nishant rise from the couch to hit the FI executive and was startled to hear his grating voice, "You reported in the visit report you submitted to *Oakland* Bank two months ago that you met this man in his home."

Diverting her glance back to Samir, she saw Nishant clutching Samir's collar while Ishan had moved to sit beside Ronak.

"Yes, I met him. Didn't you also find him at his home?" Samir answered belligerently.

"You creep. You have clearly stated in your report to another bank yesterday that you confirmed with the neighbours that Gaurang Shah lives in flat number 702 of Regal Heights. This is what you have written in your report to *TCI* six months ago and *Oakland Bank* two months ago. But when we enquired of the neighbours in Regal Heights, no one was aware of a Gaurang Shah living in flat number 702. So, answer the question, how much money did the people from *Pinnacle* pay you to give a false residence visit report to all the banks?" Nishant demanded, raising his fist with an intention to land a sucker punch on Samir's face.

"Rs 25,000. I...er...I needed the money for my father's medical treatment. He has lung cancer and I...I...I was desperate," Samir confessed, stammering.

"Liar. You wouldn't have purchased a new pair of Red Tape leather shoes if you needed money for your father's cancer treatment," Nishant spat, flinging Samir to the floor.

Trisha's eyes reflexively lowered to the shining black shoes on Samir's feet before she turned to Jimit, "You are one of the oldest verification agencies in Ahmedabad and we credit managers base our approvals on your reports. How do you expect us to function if your field executives can be bought so easily?"

"I sincerely apologise for what has happened, Madam and I will take the uttermost care to prevent any such frauds in the future," Jimit attempted to reassure.

"Yeah, sure. A politically correct statement. How will this help the banks recover the lakhs it has lost due to the lacunae in your systems?" Ishan snorted, rising from the couch with Ronak in tow.

Trisha followed suit, shuddering at the corruption she never believed could exist in the agencies the bank depended on.

They took Ronak to *FirstCredit's* office, and after considerable intimidation from both the collection managers, he confessed to having received Rs 50,000 from Raghav, *Pinnacle's* executive, to pose as Gaurang Shah. It became evident to the bankers that the bulk of the defrauded PL was probably split between Raghav and Sidanshu, with the latter getting a larger share.

Chapter 35

The Tide would Turn.

As far as he could remember, Gautam had always been a die-hard optimist. Unfortunately, that feeling had been eluding him for a couple of months now, especially this morning, as he made his way up the two flights of stairs to the crime branch section of Ahmedabad's Police Headquarters at Maninagar.

He entered the huge hall with wooden desks for the two inspectors and steel tables for all the other staff, neatly arranged against the periphery. Technically, Gautam being an IPS officer, assigned to this section under the cadre of Dy. Superintendent of Police (DSP) should have been given a wooden desk, as he outranked the inspectors. He had, unfortunately, been ordered by his boss, the Superintendent of Police, Mr Kamal Arora to sit at the oldest, most rusted metal desk beside the washroom, on his very first day.

'Maybe, I need to prove myself and earn a wooden desk,' Gautam had consoled himself, eager to start work and impress his boss. Things, however, had only gone South with him, no matter how hard he had tried and six months down the line, Gautam found himself being assigned to community policing roles while most of the major crime investigations were given to either the inspectors of Maninagar branch or other major police stations.

Determined to be patient, Gautam pretended he was fine handling cases normally assigned to a constable or a sub-inspector and reported for work, sure that the tide would turn.

He sat at his chair that morning and waited for the clerk manning the squawking police radio to announce cases in their jurisdiction.

"I know Law Gardens is less than 10 kms away from Maninagar police station, but there are no inspectors, sub-inspectors, or head constables available right now. You must understand it's 12.15 pm and all are attending to various cases. They are not answering their phones, either."

Gautam's ears perked on hearing the clerk's response to what appeared to be an emergency, while punching buttons on a console probably trying to phone inspectors and request them to attend to the call.

"I'm trying, but no one's answering their phones," the clerk replied to some more high-pitched squawking emitting from the radio.

Unable to stop himself, Gautam rose from his desk and strode quickly to the clerk, saying, "What's the case? I'll go."

"It's either a murder or suicide in Law Gardens. I'm trying Kamal sir to confirm if you can attend to it as no inspector in the vicinity of 20 kms is available, but sir's phone is switched off."

Gautam's heart sank on hearing the clerk's reply because Kamal had made sure even someone at that grade wouldn't dare to assign such a case to him.

The crackle on the radio continued, prompting the clerk to suddenly request, "Please go to this address Gautam sir, I'll explain to Kamal sir why I had to send you."

Refusing to ponder over the clerk's resigned tone, Gautam grabbed the slip of paper with the address, memorized it and strode out.

Kickstarting his Enfield Bullet, he manoeuvred it towards Law Gardens wondering if things would have been different, had he been posted at Mumbai, his hometown instead of voluntarily accepting the posting in Ahmedabad's crime branch upon completing his IPS training. This was the reason why he couldn't complain about his boss' unfair treatment. To add to his woes, he hated Ahmedabad, especially the unruly traffic and the compulsive 'one-upmanship' he couldn't help sensing each time he interacted with an 'Amdavadi'.

Chapter 36

Housewarming

"How can you drive on these roads? Look at all these unruly drivers! Why is everyone honking so much?"

Adi's heart sank on hearing his father's complaints vocalized in chaste Hindi. 'It's the exact same scene on Lucknow and Kanpur roads,' Adi wanted to retort, but he bit his tongue. His father was just being the grumpy person he turned into when being forced to confront an issue he disapproved of. He would never openly express his displeasure especially when other members of his family felt there wasn't an issue. On the contrary, he would keep finding fault with a stream of unrelated things. Adi was sure his dad deliberately did this to intimidate his family as they often let go of their opinion in the fear of annoying him more.

'God, this is the first time my parents are visiting Ahmedabad, please let it be a pleasant trip,' Adi sent a silent prayer to the Almighty. Taking a deep breath, he drove through a massive gate, manoeuvred the car to the right of a circular fountain built in the centre of the courtyard and eased it into an allotted parking space.

He braked quickly and rushed to open the passenger door, but his father had already alighted and had walked towards the fountain. Adi opened the rear door and helped his mother alight. They joined his father who had tilted his head back in scrutiny of the modern residential complex with a steel and glass façade.

"How tall is this building, and on which floor is your house, son?" his mother voiced the question Adi knew his father wanted to but was refraining from doing so.

"This building has 20 floors, ma, and my flat is on the 9th, er, shall we go up?" Adi responded.

*

"You enter first, dad," Adi gestured respectfully, on unlocking the thick, ebony polished wooden front door.

"Your mother will enter first," his father replied gruffly. Adi could have sworn to have heard a hint of pride in his father's voice He turned to his mother and felt like he was receiving the ultimate reward of his life; his mother was wiping the already gleaming brass plate beside the door proclaiming this flat belonged to Adivteya Ahlavat, with the corner of the loose end of her saree that was wrapped traditionally over her head. Tears were brimming in her eyes as she turned on hearing her husband's voice. She reached out to hug Adi, and kissed his forehead, whispering, "I am so proud of you, son." Clutching Adi's hand she placed her right foot over the threshold and set foot into Adi's newly purchased three-bedroom flat.

*

Adi entered his living room at 5:45 pm dressed in a new off-white kurta and matching churidar purchased by his mother from a famous market in Lucknow. The huge room looked even more spectacular now, decorated with fresh yellow and orange marigolds than it looked with its black leather couch, matching chairs, a recliner and a glass and chrome coffee table. The furniture had been moved to accommodate a portable pit filled with wood for the traditional havan, and a rug for people to sit on.

Extracting his phone from his kurta's pocket, he dialled Hrian. "Thank you for making the arrangements. The priest will arrive on time, right?" he spoke upon hearing Hrian's baritone.

"I am on my way to pick him, boss, don't worry," Hrian reassured, disconnecting the call.

Adi felt a twinge of guilt as he put his phone away. He had literally not paid any attention to Hrian since Sidanshu had consumed his life. He even owed this house to Sidanshu as Sidanshu had used his clout with the builder to get him to reduce the cost by Rs 20 lakhs, so that it fell within the Rs 60 lakh limit at which an employee of Adi's grade could avail a staff housing loan with *TCI*.

Despite all this, Adi had sought the god fearing Hrian's help for the housewarming puja that evening and Hrian had unquestioningly complied. He had even managed to find a pundit from Uttar Pradesh to perform the puja. Adi just hoped his father would be placated with the traditional arrangements and give his approval for the actual reason Adi had gone through all the trouble.

Chapter 37

Déjà Vu

Gautam nudged the partly open wrought iron gates with the front wheel of his bike and rode over the short, paved, driveway flanked by unkept lawns. Parking his bike in front of some flowerpots with dried up stems, he bounded up the flight of three marbled steps. Finding the front door ajar, he pushed it open with his foot and grimaced as the stench of stale alcohol and cigarettes hit him. He entered the house and waited at the threshold for his eyes to adjust to the dimly lit space beyond. Everything appeared to be normal in what looked like a living room, till he turned left and saw a grossly overweight lady sprawled on her back on a leather couch. Her right hand was limply suspended in mid-air while her left hand rested on her curved stomach.

Five quick strides took him to her side, and he pressed two fingers below her left ear. Alarmed on feeling a faint pulse, he whipped out his cell phone and dialled '108', quickly narrating the address. Disconnecting the call, he turned to his right and grimaced on finding a near empty bottle of 'Magic Moments' vodka on the coffee table, along with a piece of half-eaten chicken leg and an open packet of peanuts; most of which was strewed on the table and the carpeted floor. There was also an open packet of Marlboro and an ash tray filled with at least 15 cigarette butts and ash. What alarmed him though was a crumpled strip of medicine, with most of the tablet slots empty.

An eerie feeling of being watched made him survey the room again, and he nearly jumped out of his skin on seeing a plump lady dressed in a sari with the loose end stuffed into her mouth, staring at him. "Who are you?" he enquired softly in the splattering of Gujarati he had picked up.

"He killed her. I know he did. I have often heard them shouting at each other. I phoned him first and told him I know he killed her. Then I phoned the police, so they can arrest him." She let out a barrage of words in the local language in between sobs.

Unsure if he'd understood her right, Gautam enquired, in Hindi, this time, "You phoned him and said he killed her? Who did you phone?"

"Her husband. He's a doctor who is only interested in making money. He doesn't spend any time with her, and he comes home very late, sometimes after midnight, so she started drinking in frustration. That made him very angry, and I have woken up many times at night on hearing their fights. See the half-empty strip of sleeping pills on the table. I'm sure he forced her to swallow them last night on seeing her drunk because he's fed up with her. She was such a beautiful rich lady. Now look at her, all fat and ugly. Go and arrest him, Inspector, he has a clinic in Law Gardens," the lady wailed, walking towards him, and sinking on the carpet beside the coffee table.

"You are their maid?" Gautam questioned tentatively, wanting to confirm that he understood correctly, as she appeared to be well dressed and groomed.

"Yes. I am their full-time maid. My mistress' mother appointed me to work for them when they bought his house," the maid answered, in between tears.

"How long have they been married, and when did she start drinking?"

"For three years, and she started drinking on their second wedding anniversary when he returned home late at 11.30 pm, completely forgetting that her father had thrown a party for them."

"Okay. So, does she drink during the day or only at night? She's not dead, by the way," Gautam questioned, on getting the impression that the maid was not being completely honest.

"She generally starts drinking at 7 pm and goes to sleep at around 2 am, so she wakes up only at around 11 am. She didn't today and I got worried when I tried to wake her, and she didn't respond. Then I saw the bottle of sleeping pills and got scared, so I phoned the police," the maid clarified.

The trilling sound of Gautam's phone filled the ensuing silence. A sense of déjà vu shrouded him when he retrieved his phone from his trouser pocket to see it was Kamal, his boss. He answered it only to hear the curt instructions he was expecting, "Walk away from the scene. No need to file a FIR (First Investigation Report)."

Gautam glanced around the crime scene at Dr Dhiraj Mehta's living room for what maybe the last time and left.

Chapter 38

Insane Connections

"How is she?" Dhiraj paused his pacing of the waiting room to enquire, on spotting his friend Dr Piyush Patel exit the treatment area.

"Let's talk in my office," Piyush suggested, leading the way to a closed thick wooden door a few paces from the treatment room.

Piyush unlocked the door and held it open for his friend.

"She'll survive even though the pills had entered her blood stream because we administered medication to flush out the drugs. She's under dialysis now to cleanse the blood further. Her heartbeats were a bit erratic, but we've medicated her for that too and they have normalized now. She's still unconscious. We'll get a better idea of the extent of the damage on her other body parts only when she's conscious," Piyush updated on closing the door behind him.

"Thank God and thank you my friend," Dhiraj stated, heaving a sigh of relief.

"You owe me, Dhiraj because I really had to pull more than a few strings to prevent this from being investigated as a murder case, as the police were on their way to arrest you either for abetting suicide or murder. Why did your maid make that crazy phone call to the police saying you killed her?" Piyush enquired candidly.

"I don't know, Piyush, maybe to extract more money from me. I'm already paying her a bomb to keep my wife's alcohol addiction from my in-laws, as my mother-in-law appointed her, and I suppose she's using her to keep tabs on me. Thanks for saving my ass, though, Piyush. Her father will destroy me if he gets even a whiff of what happened," Dhiraj responded morosely sinking down on a plush leather chair in Piyush's office and burying his face in his hands

Piyush couldn't help pitying his friend and medical college classmate. Dhiraj's father-in-law was one of the richest stockbrokers in Ahmedabad with insane connections. He had learnt about Dhiraj's wedding only when Dhiraj had visited his house to personally invite him for the same, and had wondered then too, as to why Dhiraj, a simple man with a modest upbringing was entering into this marriage. Things had been good initially, and his stunning wife had been the envy of all the other women in their circle, when she had attended their official and social functions. But that had suddenly stopped, two years into their marriage, and Dhiraj hadn't offered any explanations for the same. It had been almost a year since, and he, Piyush, couldn't believe the svelte, graceful lady, had bloated out of proportion.

"I don't know what hell you have been doing through, Dhiraj, and I'm sorry to say this, but you have to pay a lakh to the police to make this go away, because of your maid's phone call," Piyush stated softly, after a while.

"What? Why? Piyush, I didn't share this with you, but my wife is an alcoholic. She's been one for two years now, drinking half a bottle of vodka each night," Dhiraj confided, incredulously,

"How long was she on the Ativan sleeping pill?"

"I don't know Piyush. I've been slogging my ass out for the past three years to give her the luxurious life she was used to at her father's place," Dhiraj lamented.

"Again, please forgive my candid statement, but the police are not going to see it that way. What they are going to act upon is the fact that a doctor had callously left for work in the morning after overdosing his wife at night," Piyush stated frankly.

"So, am I going to be arrested now?" Dhiraj enquired in a defeated tone.

"Not if you cough up a lakh, cash," Piyush reiterated.

"A lakh! But it's not my fault, she's an alcoholic," Dhiraj countered, stunned.

"Look Dhiraj, your maid dialled the police control room, and the case was assigned to a new Dy SP, an IPS officer. He reached the house before you could phone me and called for a Civil Hospital ambulance. Thank God, she phoned you before informing the police and you contacted me. I have connections with senior-level police officers, and I managed to squash the investigation, but you must pay the money as my contact has to make sure the rookie Dy SP doesn't investigate the case further," Piyush stated.

"This is preposterous! Why would I want to kill my wife when I'm killing myself trying to provide for her? I'm a trained doctor. If I wanted her dead, wouldn't I try some better ingenious method?" Dhiraj questioned, cynically, too hassled to wonder how and why Piyush had such dubious connections.

"Although I'm unaware of the issues you've been experiencing in your marriage, I believe you my friend when you say you didn't try to kill your wife. The police aren't going to have the same trust though, so you must cough up the lakh," Piyush tried to sound practical while voicing the truth.

"Fine, I'll arrange for the money to cover up a crime I didn't commit," Dhiraj muttered, failing to mask the animosity in his tone. He rose from the chair and left.

The gravity of the situation hit him as he walked out of the clinic, towards his car parked on the street as the clinic didn't have a parking lot. Since he had his chequebook with him, he decided to personally go to the nearest *TCI* branch to withdraw the money. He was so preoccupied with his thoughts that he didn't realise a man on an Enfield Bullet was following him.

Chapter 39

Fate

Instinct had made Gautam wait outside Dr Dhiraj Mehta's house after the commanding phone call from his boss. Of course, he had immediately phoned to cancel the local ambulance service first as it would have taken the patient to Ahmedabad's Civil Hospital.

A minute into his cancellation, a private ambulance service had pulled up, and he had followed it to a Sanjeeveni Clinic, which was 10 minutes from the doctor's house. It was located on a busy street, so he had parked his bike across the road from it and had waited. A white Hyundai Accent had arrived five minutes after the ambulance and a seemingly harassed man, he presumed to be Dr Dhiraj, had rushed into the clinic, after hastily parking his car outside it. Unable to contain himself, Gautam had extracted his cell phone and had made a call to his school friend, Raul Da Cunha.

Having been born and raised in Bandra West, Mumbai, Gautam had attended St. Michael's School, a highly acclaimed educational institution on Hill Road, Bandra. Since it's a predominantly Catholic locality, he had many Christian and Anglo-Indian classmates but had formed a strong bond with Raul. It didn't matter that 23-years down the line, Raul had decided to become a professional hacker while Gautam was a government servant, on the side of the law. Considering the compelling circumstances of the current case, Gautam couldn't stop himself from seeking out Raul's talents as he somehow felt this case was different from the many other suicides and murders, he had been called upon to investigate, only to be brushed under the carpet.

Raul had answered on the first ring and Gautam had unabashedly requested him to extract the phone records of both Dr Piyush Patel and Dr Dhiraj Mehta; narrating the numbers that were readily available on the internet. That had been 15 minutes ago. Gautam had been parked outside the clinic for half an hour now, and nothing was happening, invariably churning up memories of his life before Ahmedabad.

Life had always been a cakewalk for him, the offspring of a Police Officer. His dad hailed from a wealthy family of farmers in Rajasthan, where one son usually joined the Indian Armed Forces, so it hadn't been surprising when his father had decided to appear for the UPSC exams, to become a Police Officer. He had just about managed to clear it and had been dismayed when his first posting was in Mumbai. All this had happened before his father had gotten married, so Gautam was unaware of the details as his father never spoke of his job.

As far as Gautam could remember, he had been born and raised in Bandra West, Mumbai, or rather the posh locality of Bandstand. It hadn't struck him when he was young as to how his father could afford a sea-facing flat in one of the costliest areas of Mumbai, with a police officer's salary. 'I'm sure my grandfather would have chipped in for the house as well as our wealthy lifestyle,' Gautam concluded inwardly, sighing upon remembering his carefree youth.

Things had been great until Gautam had expressed interest in following his best friend Pratyush's footsteps and study law. Disappointment had been visible on his father's face on hearing Gautam's decision, but he hadn't voiced a single objection.

One may call it fate or the forces of the universe, but devastation hit their family a week into Gautam's new job in a law firm, post his graduation from one of India's most prestigious law colleges. His father had just been promoted as the Dy Police Commissioner of Mumbai then, but neither could he nor the entire Mumbai Police force find any answers to the tragedy that had struck his family. This had prompted Gautam to give up law and appear for the UPSC exams himself. His father should have been ecstatic, but considering the circumstances, he had stoically given his blessings.

Gautam snapped to attention on seeing Dhiraj leave the clinic. He quickly gunned his bike and waited for the doctor to start his car, the memories of his past retreating into a corner of his mind.

Chapter 40

Shattered Dreams!

"Sir, I'm sorry, we cannot process your request for the withdrawal of Rs 1 lakh because you don't have sufficient balance in your account."

Dhiraj could feel his eyes blinking unnaturally as he stared at the cashier. Since he couldn't afford any support staff, apart from a nurse cum receptionist, he had gone personally to *TCI* with a 'self' cheque to withdraw the money required to keep his wife's suicide attempt under wraps.

"That's not possible, I deposited Rs 45,000 cash yesterday," he objected.

"Sir, I request you to please speak with the officer at counter number 1, he will clarify your confusion. Your account only has a balance of Rs 10,273 so I cannot clear your cheque of Rs 1 lakh. There is a long queue of customers behind you, so please permit me to attend to them," the cashier requested politely, and Dhiraj had no choice but to move to the man handling counter 1.

"Sir, er, Doctor, you did deposit Rs 45,000 cash yesterday but an EMI of Rs 43,484.85 was debited this morning," the man informed.

"You guys have made a mistake. I only have one EMI of that amount and it is debited on the 5th of each month. It's the 20th today. I think your bank had debited this amount twice," Dhiraj protested.

Dhiraj watched the man's fingers fly across his keyboard before replying, "Si…er… sorry, Doctor, two EMIs of the same amount but of different personal loan accounts are being debited from your account every month. The first one started six months ago in June, and the second one a month later."

"Your bank is fleecing me. I don't have two personal loans. I want to speak to your manager," Dhiraj protested raising his voice, oblivious to the fact that counter 1 was right beside the Branch Manager's cabin, and his decibel level had been loud enough to get the Branch Head scampering out to enquire, "Is there a problem?"

The executive behind counter 1 shot to his feet and clarified, "Dr Dhiraj Mehta is an orthopaedic surgeon, sir, and has been an esteemed customer of this bank for the past three years. He presented a 'self' cheque of Rs 1 lakh just now but there is a balance of only Rs 10,273 in his account today as an EMI of Rs 43484.85 was cleared this morning. Dr Mehta is claiming this is a wrong debit as he hasn't availed any loan for it, but sir, this amount is being debited from his account for three months now."

"Dr Mehta, I apologise for the inconvenience. If you may step into my cabin, we can get this matter resolved," the Branch Manager suggested.

Dhiraj did so and watched the Branch Head make a show of ordering coffee for him first and then re-check his account as though his staff were morons. The coffee arrived before the Branch Head could convey the same message to him and hear the same protests.

Realising after a while that he was just banging his head against a wall, Dhiraj stopped talking. He couldn't remember how long he had been sitting across the table from the Branch Head, trying hard to find plausible explanations for the second EMI. The Branch Head probably tried to phone someone for clarifications or maybe he didn't, Dhiraj couldn't remember, because all he could think of was despite working so hard, he had nothing but shattered dreams! His life was on the verge of being ruined forever, and it wasn't even his fault, or maybe it was?

Chapter 41

Work-Life Balance

Adi felt he would have a coronary as his gaze shifted for the umpteenth time between the watch on his wrist and the entrance of his house. It was 6:22 pm. Most of his guests comprising of DSAs, senior DST staff and a few branch executives who were important to him had arrived. Tony and Sidanshu had yet to come.

As per the auspicious time in the Hindu calendar declared by his father 6:30 pm was the time to commence the puja for the housewarming ceremony but Trisha and her family hadn't yet arrived. While he had taken the day off to receive his parents from the airport and help his mother cook dinner for the 20 people he had invited for the event, Trisha had been at work. She had planned to leave early, at say 5 pm, so she could get dressed and reach his house by 6:15 pm. But it was 6:25 pm now and there was no trace of her. Even Hrian and the priest had arrived on time!

Feeling frustrated, Adi headed toward the kitchen where his mother had been slaving since 2 pm, so she could serve his guests authentic food from Bhulandshahr. Hrian had offered to hire a special cook from Uttar Pradesh for the dinner, but Adi's mom had insisted she would cook for everyone. Adi had helped her as much as he could by chopping vegetables and spices like coriander as per her instructions but had been shooed from the kitchen at around 5.30 p.m.

Not finding his mother in the kitchen filled with the aromatic smells of food, Adi returned morosely to the living room and extracted his vibrating cell phone from his kurta's pocket. Disappointed to see the call from the Branch Head of *TCI*'s Law Garden branch, he answered it.

"Adivteya, I have a Dr Dhiraj Mehta in my office. He's claiming that an EMI is being deducted from his current account with us for a loan he hasn't availed. Kindly speak with him," the Branch Head commanded.

"Sir, I'm sorry, but I am on leave right now. Please can I investigate it tomorrow," Adi requested urgently, on seeing Tony and Sidanshu enter his new house. Trisha and her family were the only ones remaining.

"Your department doesn't have even a molecule of professionalism in your body. Dr Dhiraj is a very important customer of this branch. Kindly speak with him just now." The Branch Head apparently didn't care for his response because Adi heard a cultured 'Hello' at the other end of the line.

"Good evening, sir," Adi responded, glancing at his packed living room. Heaving a sigh of relief on seeing Hrian who had met his parents in the afternoon when he had come to decorate the living room, introducing them to Tony, Adi stepped out of his open front door as the doctor narrated his predicament. Trisha walked in just then with her parents. Adi's breath caught in his throat on meeting her exquisitely made-up eyes and his mind tuned off the doctor's monologue while he bent down to touch her parents' feet.

"Why are you on the phone? It's 6.28," Trisha whispered, frowning when Adi straightened up and glanced at her.

"Two minutes," he mouthed, descending a few steps.

"Dr Dhiraj, I'm with Sidanshu, the owner of the agency that handled your first personal loan. Please talk to him, sir, he will positively sort out your confusion unless you have taken your second personal loan from another agent or executive," Adi stated mechanically on realising there was silence on the other end.

"Who is this idiot you have connected me to? I just told him his agent Sidanshu is a fraud and he's telling me Sidanshu will sort out my problems. I'm going to shift all my accounts and deposits from *TCI* to *Oakland Bank*. All you people at *TCI* are greedy for money, so you fleece your customers."

Adi listened in horror to the tirade he had inadvertently precipitated by tuning out of the fag end of the doctor's complaint.

"Doctor, I assure you I will escalate the matter to Mr Uttam Singh, the head of the Personal Loan department right away. He is a friend and a Vice President of this bank," Adi heard the Branch Head try to placate the doctor before the call was disconnected. He stared at the clock he had installed as his screen saver for a few moments before realising it was 6:36 pm.

"Tell me what the call was about before you go in, and I'll take care of it."

Adi startled on hearing Tony's whisper. He quickly sketched the happenings, plastered a smile on his face and stepped back into his living room mentally deriding the hours of HR training *TCI* had subjected their staff through, that stressed on the importance of work-life balance. 'Bankers had no work-life balance, especially the ones in sales,' Adi thought morosely, taking a seat beside his father on the rug, and signalling the priest to begin the housewarming ceremony.

*

Gautam's cell phone chirped to inform him he had an incoming message. He ignored it, his eyes glued to Dr Dhiraj Mehta who was exiting *TCI's* Law Garden branch while talking on his cell phone. The call ended in a few minutes and Dhiraj walked towards his parked car. Gautam's cell phone beeped again as Dhiraj drove his car away from the bank, with Gautam tailing him.

Chapter 42

The Food Chain

Gautam braked and watched Dhiraj enter the looming gates of Zeus Multispecialty Hospital, in Navrangpura. He waited for five minutes before following suit and parked his bike in the space allotted for visitors. Not seeing Dhiraj's car in the lot, he walked towards a sign indicating 'Doctor's parking', and found it parked there. Retracing his steps back to the lobby beside the 'visitor's parking' area, he entered it and headed straight for the board displaying the names of the doctors serving at Zeus. Seeing Dr Dhiraj Mehta's name mentioned as a consulting orthopaedic surgeon, he walked out of the lobby, to the lawns outside the hospital.

Settling down on what appeared to be a reasonably secluded bench, Gautam checked his messages. Both were from Raul, mentioning he had emailed past six months call logs of Piyush and Dhiraj. Gautam glanced at the time displayed on the corner of his cell phone's screen. It was 6.30 pm., almost time to call it a day. He smirked at the irony of his situation. He was an IPS officer, deputed by the Central Government to Ahmedabad to handle 5 police stations in and around Maninagar. His boss, however, was hellbent on ignoring him, hence his phone mostly remained silent in a city where some crime or the other was constantly happening and hadn't assigned ever a single police station to him.

'It's all because of that case involving the death of the local political leader's daughter-in-law,' he reminisced resting his back on the bench, allowing a flashback of the case to play in his mind. He had been only a week into his new job when he had received a phone call in the wee hours of the morning, informing him that the lady had jumped from the terrace of a five-storey apartment building. He had also been curtly told by Kamal that the case had to be handled with care considering her father-in-law's clout. The father-in-law was the state's finance minister and had the power to cut their department's budget; that would have been unacceptable.

Gautam had been horrified on reaching the scene as the body appeared to have been badly beaten up, and the trajectory of the fall indicated it had been thrown from the terrace. Unsure of what to do, he had left the police photographer to do his job and had taken the elevator to the politician's fifth-floor penthouse. The family members and servants all had only one thing to say, 'she was mentally unstable and had often tried to commit suicide. She might have taken this drastic step out of post-partum depression as she had given birth to a second daughter two weeks ago.'

It had been the constant reference to 'a second daughter' that had convinced Gautam her death had been more than a suicide. Being a rookie, he hadn't wanted to take up the cudgels on the lady's behalf and had calmly signed the prepared FIR report stating suicide due to unstable mental conditions as the cause of death.

He had however, refused to accept the bulky white envelope the father-in-law had tried to surreptitious hand over to him on that very morning. The news had reached Kamal's ears as despite having opted for the crime branch, Gautam had found himself being assigned to handle domestic squabbles in the less affluent, community-dominated areas of Ahmedabad. He had also learnt about the 'Food Chain' that day. While many lower-ranked personnel also accepted petty bribes, the top brass were expected to distribute proportions of their bigger kickbacks way down the line to ensure their loyalty. He had learnt this from a clean sub-inspector who was the only one willing to accompany him on domestic crime cases since that incident, as Kamal had taken him too out of actual criminal investigations.

The siren of an approaching ambulance snapped Gautam out of his musings. He decided to head back to his headquarters in Maninagar first, to sign off for the day before going home to check the phone records.

*

Home was a studio apartment on the 6th floor of a high-rise in the Satellite area of Ahmedabad. Rentals were pretty steep in 2007-08 and Gautam had to shell out one-fourth of his salary for the 200 square feet place. It didn't matter as he was a man with modest needs and a purpose in life, which was eventually solving his mysterious family tragedy that had turned him into a Police Officer.

He fired up his desktop computer and headed to his minuscule kitchen to brew a cup of tea while it booted. Tea in hand, he quickly logged onto his broadband Wi-Fi connection and clicked on the email icon. His fondness for gadgets had prompted him to also buy an ink-jet printer for Rs 10,000 when he had purchased his PC, six months ago, but he hadn't yet used the printer. He prayed it would work as he clicked on the email from Raul, downloaded the phone records, and hit print. Sheaves of clearly printed paper spewed from it. He quickly separated Piyush's and Dhiraj's lists, stapled them, and picked up a pencil before scrutinizing Dhiraj's list first as it comprised only of two sheets, while the other had 5 pages printed on both sides.

Outgoing calls were mostly made daily, to his home number, at noon and in the evening. Not finding any major repetitions in the past six months, he quickly glanced at the end of the page, to the calls after Dhiraj had exited Piyush's clinic and then later the bank. There hadn't been any response from the third last call because the column reflecting the duration of the call had zeroes in it. Dhiraj had spoken to the second last number before leaving the bank, for 15 minutes. The last call after leaving the bank had lasted for only 6 minutes. Gautam wrote these three numbers down on a fresh sheet of paper. He then proceeded to recheck the list and found that Dhiraj had received calls from the second last number several times in June and once in July, while there were two calls from the third last one in June.

Setting Dhiraj's list aside, Gautam picked up Piyush's and decided to start from the bottom of the list, i.e. the phone calls made this morning. He noted down the number of an eight-minute call made around the time when the maid had revealed she had phoned Dhiraj Mehta to accuse him of murdering his wife, in a fresh sheet of paper and was surprised to find Dhiraj had dialled the same number on leaving the bank, that is the last number on the list Raul had sent him. He continued to check the rest of the phone numbers on the ten-page long list and found that there had been five outgoing and four incoming calls to and from the same number on different dates. There were no records of outgoing or incoming calls from the second last number on Dhiraj's list, but several calls were received and made to the third last number.

Chapter 43

The Elephant in the Room

"Ahlavat sir, do you rotate crops or stick to only one crop?" Trisha's father, Dr Mishra enquired respectfully, breaking the embarrassing silence in the room.

Although the puja had started late it went off well so, had the dinner. The guests had started trickling out soon after dinner, with Tony and Sidanshu being one of the last to leave. In tune with his usual flair for drama, Sidanshu had presented Adi with a massive brass idol of Lord Shiva in his famous 'Tandav' pose just before leaving. Adi had also been amazed when Sidanshu had greeted Trisha with respect. Of course, that might have been because Trisha had received a phone call from a senior, commanding her to reinstate Sidanshu as a DSA at *FirstCredit*. Trisha too had demonstrated she was a thorough professional and had been cordial with Sidanshu.

Hrian had stayed back with some of his boys to clean up the living room and rearrange the furniture after most of the guests had left. Adi could have sworn to have seen disapproval on Hrian's face for a fraction of a second when he accepted Sidanshu's gift, and it made him feel guilty again. Hrian had always been loyal to Adi, yet Adi had been so focused on Sidanshu, Trisha and all, that he had neglected Hrian.

The women, including Trisha, had started clearing the dinner dishes after Hrian had also left. Adi had wanted to help them but had refrained from doing so as he didn't want to leave his dad alone with his prospective father-in-law. So, he had taken a seat beside his father on his plush new couch and had been wondering how to break the silence in the room, when Dr Mishra took care of it.

Happy to listen to his father's amicable response, Adi tuned out of the conversation to watch Trisha listen attentively to something his mother was saying. Trisha suddenly flashed her '1000 watt' smile at his mom, making Adi feel he was the luckiest man in the world. 'What does she see in me? She looks like a model in that sari,' Adi wondered for the umpteenth time that evening, his eyes roaming over her five feet, six-inch frame covered in a pale, peach-coloured chiffon saree with exquisite silver embroidery on the border. The pleats were pinned immaculately at her left shoulder, revealing the curve of her slim waist exposed by a matching blouse which ended an inch below her chest. Her waist-length, straight, black, silky hair had been gathered into a bunch at the crown of her head, but the rest of it was flowing gloriously, like a silk curtain over her shoulders and back. Silver, high-heeled sandals peaked below the lower pleats of the sari, adding grace to her elegant stature.

Memory of the disastrous start of an auspicious day forced Adi to divert his attention to his and Trisha's fathers still engaged in an amicable discussion regarding the efforts the various political parties in power had made towards the upliftment of the farmers in India. 'Thank God for small mercies,' Adi shot a silent gratitude to the Almighty for giving the two men a common ground. He also voiced a silent gratitude to Dr Mishra for his knowledge regarding the Indian Agricultural system, despite his doctorate in Textile Engineering, his thesis topic being research on manufacturing lightweight, yet extremely durable, waterproof materials, an unrelated field.

Trisha walked in just then carrying a tray, with their respective mothers in tow. Adi's father who had been explaining something about how the browning of the tips of the sugarcane crops is an indication that the crop is ready for harvest stopped talking as Trisha respectfully offered the tray to him first. "Bless you, child," his father mumbled, lifting a glass bowl from the tray. Pin-drop silence prevailed in the room while Trisha served everyone before settling down on a chaise lounge with her bowl.

"I have been eating my wife's kheer for 35 years, and there is no change in the delicious taste. Do you know how to cook, Trisha?"

Adi nearly choked on his kheer, on hearing his father praise his mother's cooking for the first time in his life, only to follow that with the cliched question the groom's side asks the girl during the 'seeing the girl' ritual.

"Well, I cannot make such tasty kheer, but I can cook normal food.' 'Point 1, Trisha,' Adi cheered inwardly at her modest reply.

"Good, so when do the two of you want to get married?"

Adi squirmed now, as the question was directed at him. He had been expecting his father to give a big discourse about the trouble they went through to arrange Veer's marriage with the right girl, so the fact that his father directly addressed 'The Elephant in the room' unnerved him, and he didn't know what to say.

"Er, we thought we'd leave it to you to set the date," Adi replied, hoping he sounded genuine as neither he nor Trisha had discussed when they wanted to get married. Hell, they hadn't thought beyond this meeting.

"Hmm. Under normal circumstances, I would have invited you to come to our village first to see our house, land and so on. However, we had to turn down a proposal from one of the richest men in our village, who was willing to pay Rs 30 lakhs for Adi's hand in marriage to his daughter. Under these circumstances, it would not be right to have you visit our house before finalizing anything. Also, since this is a love marriage, I don't want any dowry, Dr Mishra," Adi's father stunned the room, especially Adi with his declaration.

"I can understand why you don't want us to visit your village, sir. Er, regarding dowry, I'm just a modest scientist, but keeping up with the tradition, I would like to make an offering of Rs 20 lakhs before Adi enters the auspicious area where the actual wedding ceremony will be performed. This is our tradition, sir," Dr Mishra responded.

"That is acceptable to me. Why don't you complete the formalities for the 'shagun'?"

Trisha's mother let out an audible gasp on hearing the request. She pressed the loose end of her sari against her lips, as tears trickled down her cheeks. Everyone else in the room, except Adi's parents were dumbfounded, especially Adi. He hadn't expected them to have come prepared for the tradition of sealing the 'wedding deal' with the 'shagun' (good omen) ceremony.

No one spoke as Adi's mother slipped into the guest bedroom of the new house and returned with a big tray covered with a silk, embroidered cloth.

On seeing her, Trisha's mother rose from her chair, snatched the bowl from Trisha's hands, placed it on the coffee table, and quickly covered Trisha's head with the loose end of her sari, while whispering, "Bow your head, my child."

Adi stared in wonder as Trisha complied. Like a scene from a 'Bollywood Family Drama' movie, Adi watched his mother seat herself beside Trisha, uncover the tray she was holding, extract an intricately carved bangle, lift Trisha's right hand, and slide the bangle over her hand. She repeated the same with the left hand, before placing a heavily embroidered sari or some other traditional outfit in Trisha's hands. She finally opened the red and yellow printed box on the tray, broke a piece of 'peda', a traditional milk confection, and fed it to Trisha.

Trisha's mother reciprocated by feeding the rest of the 'peda' to Adi, after which she extracted three gifts wrapped in silver and gold striped paper and distributed them to Adi and his parents.

'That's it! We're engaged! This is what happens when one worries unnecessarily over things!' Adi could only slump back and declare inwardly, drained from the weeks of worry over his parents accepting Trisha as their future daughter-in-law and the chaotic beginning of this evening's events.

Chapter 44

A Gut Feeling

Gautam stared at the two sheets of paper neatly laid out on his desk. Something about the last common number bothered him. Extracting his phone, he quickly scrolled down the contacts list and paused at a number. He nearly fell off his chair on seeing the phone number in his contact list exactly matched the last common number.

Convinced there was something fishy going on, Gautam dialled Raul.

"Hey, man! Thanks for promptly sending me those call logs," Gautam spoke, on hearing his voice.

"No sweat, man. It was a piece of cake. So, what can I do for you now?"

"I've texted some phone numbers to you. Can you tell me the names they belong to, and their profession, if possible?" Gautam requested, rattling off the two unidentified numbers from Dr Dhiraj's list.

"Sure," Raul replied.

Gautam listened to the clacking of Raul's fingers flying over his keyboard before he informed, "The first one belongs to a Sidanshu Gaur, the owner of Pinnacle Financials, a loan facilitator with several banks, including *TCI*. The second is registered to someone named Priya. Do you need anything else?" Raul informed after a while.

"Hack into Dr Dhiraj Mehta's email account and forward any emails pertaining to correspondence with the banks Sidanshu is attached with. I'll text you the names. Something's not right here," Gautam requested on realising the phone call Dhiraj had made from the bank that had gone unanswered had been to Sidanshu, while the second 15-minute call had been to Priya, and the last one after leaving the bank was of course to SP Kamal Arora.

"Done. Just a friendly caution, though. I know you have studied law, but you are just a rookie IPS officer. None of the dirt I unearth can be used as evidence if there really is something wrong," Raul stated.

"Yes, man. I understand. Hell, even my father will be forced to resign if anyone comes to know I opted for the easiest way to investigate a case, which is taking the services of a hacker. But Raul, a suicide or maybe murder is being covered up by educated people in power, so why should I feel guilty for employing illicit means to get to the bottom of it?" Gautam countered.

Ending the call, he opened the first drawer of his desk and extracted a Nikon digital camera. It had been an indulgent purchase a month ago in an attempt to overcome his frustration at being ignored by his boss and subordinates. He quickly switched it on to check if it was charged. Satisfied to see it was as he hadn't used it since he bought it, he quickly abandoned his desk to change into a pair of blue jeans and a nondescript black T-shirt.

Picking up wrap-around clear glasses from his desk along with a cap, he quickly laced sneakers onto his feet, grabbed the keys of his bike and house and bolted out. He impatiently zipped his bike through several by-lanes to avoid the traffic on the main road, hoping he wasn't late. It took him exactly 10 minutes to reach Maninagar Police Station and he heaved a sigh of relief to find his boss' Innova parked in the station's compound, indicating that SP Kamal Arora was still in the station, otherwise, the car would have been parked outside his residence.

Gautam halted his bike across the road from the Police Station, quickly donned the cap and glasses and waited, wishing for the first time that he didn't have an Enfield Bullet because the distinctive sound of the exhaust made it the wrong vehicle to use while following someone.

Half an hour passed, and several junior officers left the station, causing Gautam to wonder if his hunch was right. Another half hour later, he started questioning his intentions of waiting outside the Police Station as even if his boss was the person Dr Piyush had phoned immediately after Dr Dhiraj's call, and the person Dr Dhiraj had phoned after he left the bank, why would SP Kamal Arora meet with Drs Piyush and/or Dhiraj that evening, and why would he take his official car to do so?

Gautam's logical side told him he was on a wild goose chase, but a gut feeling prompted him to hang out a while longer, as payments for coverups were generally made before the FIR report was filed. Since he, Gautam, was officially at the scene, he would have to sign the FIR, so maybe Kamal would accept the money?

Deciding to continue with his gut, he kept his eyes glued to the entrance of the Police Headquarters, wondering why his boss hadn't left yet as it was nearing 9 p.m. He gripped his bike's handle a few minutes later, on seeing the familiar 6 feet 4" stout figure, with a long face and silky, straight salt and pepper hair, exit the Police Station. The guards outside stood to attention and saluted him as he descended the stairs. His driver emerged from nowhere, unlocked the car and held the door of the back seat open.

Kamal stuffed his tall, bulky frame in the car and the driver dutifully shut the door. Gautam waited for the car to cover a few feet before starting his bike. He maintained a two-car distance as the Innova wound its way from Maninagar. His heart started thumping faster when the car turned left, then right again after a few minutes indicating it was on its way to Law Garden. The driver braked on the left, just after the roundabout at the corner of Law Garden and Kamal got out. Gautam rode past and parked his bike a few feet away. He quickly crossed the road and ran to the entrance of Ahmedabad's famous garden, hoping he wouldn't miss Kamal.

He did for a while, as he frantically ran down the path to the left, then abandoned it to return to the entrance and take the one to the right. His instincts proved him right once again, as Kamal's tall frame loomed over the other walkers and joggers. Taking deep breaths to calm his mounting excitement, he followed his boss. Kamal suddenly turned to the left and started walking on the grass. Gautam stayed on the path beside it, grateful for the several hedges and trees that bordered it.

Kamal stopped beside a bench under a tree, so Gautam also halted to take refuge behind a hedge opposite the tree. Gautam's heart nearly stopped beating on seeing Dr Dhiraj emerge from behind the tree. Extracting his camera with trembling fingers from his jeans pocket, Gautam aimed it at the duo and willed his arm to stop shaking as he clicked away. Fortunately, winter hadn't yet set in and the light from a nearby lamppost was sufficient for him to get photos of SP Kamal Arora accepting a package from Dr Dhiraj Mehta.

Chapter 45

From Cloud 9 to Cloud 0

Adi leaned back on a chair in the conference room of *Kremlin Enterprises Pvt Ltd* and watched the employees of the company file into the opulent conference room to submit their applications for Personal Loans. It had taken him months of presentations and convincing to finally crack a deal with one of India's upcoming pharmaceutical companies a week before their IPO (Initial Public Offering).

The company had also declared Employee Stock Options (ESOPS) for their senior level employees, enabling them to purchase shares of their company at Rs 50 per share while the IPO was valued at Rs 100 in the open market. Adi had managed to work out a special Personal Loan scheme so they could avail loans at 11.50% rate of interest (1% lower than *TCI's* competitors) for their ESPOS. He had been confident many would opt for loans as the stock price was predicted to double a few days after the IPO.

He was right because the executives of his direct sales team (DST) were busy helping around 35 odd employees of the company to fill out the loan application forms. Satisfied with the progress of the deal, Adi strode out of the company's Corporate Office and headed for his car parked in the area reserved for the top brass. His phone rang just as he unlocked his Honda. He answered it on seeing it was Tony, and conveyed, "Boss, a minimum of Rs 100 lakhs will be logged in today, as most of the employees are opting for loans of Rs 2 to 5 lakhs."

"That's great, Ahlavat, when will you return to the bank?" Tony questioned.

Tony never enquires. In the eight years that Adi had worked with Tony, he had learnt two things, everyone was Tony's friend, but nobody was his best friend & Tony never enquired about his subordinates' whereabouts. His leadership style commanded performance and loyalty which he almost always received, so his question alarmed Adi into answering while enquiring tentatively, "in 20 minutes. Is something wrong?"

"I want you in the office ASAP, Ahlavat," Tony replied, disconnecting the line.

'Tony never enquires.' The thought continued to play in Adi's mind while he mechanically manoeuvred his car through Ahmedabad's unruly traffic.

*

Adi walked into the sales section on the fourth floor and felt his blood turn cold on hearing his sales coordinator inform, "Tony's boss is waiting for you in the first meeting room."

He turned to the right where the meeting rooms were located. His heart plummeted to his knees on seeing Priyansh and another man closeted in the room with Tony. Their laptops were open, and they appeared to be in a serious discussion. Adi knocked before entering.

"Come in and take a seat," Tony commanded.

"An official complaint has been launched against you, Adivteya, for logging in fraudulent, fake identity cases. Sahil Malhotra from human resources, HR, will be investigating the issue along with me," Priyansh declared, introducing the third person.

"This is preposterous. I haven't engaged in any fraud," Adi protested.

"A joint report signed by both Surbhi and Nishant seems to state otherwise," Tony countered, pushing a paper towards Adi.

Adi felt his earlier euphoria plummet from cloud 9 to cloud 0, on reading the report declaring loans to the tune of Rs 5 crores which were logged in by his team were defaulters for several reasons. The top four on the list were doctors who claimed they hadn't availed the Personal Loans of Rs 20 lakhs each, for which the bank was asking them to pay EMIs. A Mr Gaurang Shah with a PL of Rs 5 lakhs was fifth on the list and had been classified as a case of an identity theft. So were the other five below him. No comments were mentioned against the rest of the names on the list. While only two cases belonged to Hrian's DSA and five to his DST team, all the other identity thefts, defaulters, and the doctors' cases had been logged in by Sidanshu's DSA *Pinnacle Finances.*

"Look, I seriously have no clue about these cases. At least give me time to confer with my sales managers and investigate them," Adi requested.

"I'm sorry Adi, but your sales manager who was assigned to *Pinnacle* has been asked to resign and you are being investigated now. There is a large, unexplained credit of Rs 15 lakhs in your salary account with *TCI.* Apart from that, you are overleveraged because you have availed a car loan of Rs 12 lakhs, a home loan of Rs 80 lakhs for a house which costs Rs 60 lakhs and there is no record of any prepayment amount of Rs 20 lakhs for the home loan from your account. Further, you have submitted a Personal Loan application for Rs 10 lakhs.

"Surbhi, the area credit manager has gone on record to declare that your DSA *Pinnacle Financials* has a reputation for bribing bank officials to disburse dubious loans. Most of *Pinnacle's* loans were declined by her, yet you have fought for them and have gotten them approved by higher authorities by submitting false facts, so maybe you are taking kickbacks from them? The builder from whom you have purchased your new house doesn't have any record of a down payment made by you. Nor is the same reflecting in your bank accounts. So, Mr Adevitya, kindly explain all this."

Adi stared at Sahil as he droned on about his overleverage loans and financial condition. After a few minutes, Adi shifted his glance to Priyansh who met his eyes for a fraction of a second before diverting his gaze. Tony's light brown eyes were expressionless when Adi searched them for answers.

Chapter 46

The Horrors he had Been Living With

Gautam took a long swig from the Pepsi bottle he had purchased on his way to work that morning and immediately regretted it. His desk was right beside the washroom, and a constable had opened the door on his way in, letting out a waft of stale urine. The stench triggered nausea from the hangover Gautam was nursing, and although the hall he occupied with the other police personnel was practically empty, he didn't want to pound at the washroom door nor puke in the washbasin outside it.

Taking deep breaths to quench the nausea, he glanced at the clock on the corner of his screen and realised it was noon. Deciding to head home, as he had nothing to do, he shut down his computer, holstered his gun and walked out, not bothering to inform his boss that he was leaving for the day as he wouldn't be missed.

He kickstarted his Bullet and allowed the signature sound of the bike's exhaust to elevate his mood. It took him half an hour to reach home in Ahmedabad's sweltering October heat which worsened his hangover. Unlocking the front door, he turned on his air-conditioner first before his computer. Extracting a chilled beer from his refrigerator he took a long swig before shedding his sweat-soiled clothes.

Placing the beer on a table beside his bed, he headed for his tiny bathroom for a quick shower. Emerging in a towel, he hastily slipped on grey Nike shorts and a loose black singlet. Retrieving his beer from the table, he gulped thirstily as he walked towards his PC. Excited to see six forwarded messages from Raul, he clicked on the first one and saw it was a simple sanction letter from *TCI*, dated the 23rd of June 2007 stating that Dr Dhiraj Mehta had been sanctioned a Personal Loan of Rs 20 Lakhs, at an interest rate of 11% for the purchase of a Medical Equipment. The other three were marketing emails from *TCI*. Feeling defeated, he drained the rest of his beer and headed for his refrigerator to pick up another can. That's when it struck him that he didn't have any proof that Kamal had accepted cash from Dhiraj.

Feeling like an idiot for forgetting his law training, he returned to his PC and clicked on Raul's fifth forwarded email from an undisclosed address only to find two video attachments. Assuming it was just some marketing junk, he clicked on the first attachment only to stare disbelievingly at the screen. Dr Dhiraj Mehta was slumped on an executive chair. A slim lady clad in tight jeans and a dark blue printed top was kneeling between his legs with her long, curly locks of hair covering her face The bobbing of her head and a clear image of Dhiraj's contoured face left little to the imagination.

The video ended in two minutes, so Gautam quickly clicked on the second video only to find himself staring at Dhiraj's hairy right thigh, flaying blue shirt and the right profile of his face with his eyes shut as he pumped widely into the same girl prone on his desk, her bare left leg bent at the knee with her foot resting on his desk. Again, her face wasn't visible as it was hidden by her thick hair. Her shirt was opened though, and her black bra was bunched above her chest, with Dhiraj's right palm kneading her left breast, so none of it was visible.

He shut the video; cold sweat dripped down his neck and forehead. Firmly curbing the urge to smash the screen of the desktop computer, he took a couple of deep breaths before draining the rest of his beer. Realising he needed a stronger drink, he crumpled the empty beer can in his hand, flung it into a dustbin, and extracted a bottle of *Royal Challenge* whisky from the bottom shelf of his desk.

He chugged at the bottle for nearly 10 seconds before surfacing for air. The neat 40% alcohol in the bottle hit him within seconds and he started babbling, "I had a steady girlfriend since eighth grade and a life plan ready even before I could pass twelfth grade: join a private law firm with my friend after graduation and marry my high school sweetheart.

"My sister's disappearance during my final year changed everything. She was just a year older than me and in love with a software engineer, who worked with a renowned MNC company. He was her senior, while she was a trainee. Both parents approved the match and had hosted a lavish engagement for them. But she just vanished a week after the engagement. My father was the Deputy Police Commissioner of the Mumbai police then, and no efforts had been spared in trying to find her.

"He had even gone to the extent of hiring a private investigator to stalk her fiancée for a year, in vain. We had tried hard to accept the situation when her fiancée finally married another colleague, five years after her disappearance.

"I had managed to graduate from law school with my childhood friend Pratyush, but I suddenly wanted to be the actual 'foot on the street', instead of fighting in a courtroom for justice. So, I had decided to crack the IPS exams, much to my girlfriend's chagrin. Leveraging on the double whammy of betrayal by my girlfriend, who was quick to enter an arranged marriage with the heir of a popular chain of departmental stores, and the bafflement of my sister's disappearance, I aced the IPS exams and sailed through the rigorous training.

"I continued to party with my friends and use my wit to keep women at bay, but I soon realised this alcohol-driven existence wouldn't help me find my sister. I also realised that I wouldn't learn anything if I served in Mumbai, so I grabbed the Ahmedabad posting, the nearest big city, with the hope that I would get exposed to the underbelly of crime.

"Yes, my aim is to raid every brothel in the country, or scope every street I cruise, trying to contain crime while searching for my sister, foolishly in Ahmedabad now, but eventually in Mumbai. Who knows which state of India she's in or if she is abroad or even alive?" Gautam sobbed at the question. The sight of an older man having his way with a young girl ignited the horrors he had been living with for a while now, obliviating the fact that maybe the girl in the video had deliberately initiated the intimacy for devious reasons.

Chapter 47

Benched

The sun was somewhere in the sky, probably getting ready to make its descent or was the earth rotating away from it so the other half of the world could wake up? Adi shook his head at the bizarre, irrelevant thoughts flowing through his numb mind. It was 4 pm; he was sitting on a white wicker swing in the serene place he had created for himself on the balcony of his newly purchased house instead of being at the bank or on a call with a team member. The plants he had purchased to adorn his balcony all looked healthy, thanks to his new maid who dutifully watered them. They didn't have the answers Adi sought though, as he lowered his gaze from the sky to them.

The leaves rustled in response to a strong, warm breeze; so, did the sheaf of papers in his hand, forcing him to acknowledge their presence. He raised them to eye level and tried to comprehend the details printed out in an organized, tabular form. His mind refused to cooperate. Instead, it kept playing back the parting conversation between him and the team of three investigating his alleged misdeeds.

"Sahil, I may have fought for my cases and gotten them approved by seniors, but I have never deviated from the policies laid out by *TCI*. I've never submitted fake evidence to get my cases approved. Please let me go through the files, and meet the defaulters, so I can give you a proper explanation," he had requested the HR Manager.

"Adivteya, three of them are untraceable, five are identity thefts with no money of their own and then there are doctors claiming they haven't availed the loans. You have a month to get to the bottom of this. Nishant, your collection manager is also willing to accompany you when you visit them, in the hope that some money can be recovered," Sahil had responded.

"I'll do that. I'll also make sure my sales numbers don't suffer because of this," Adi had assured, relieved they weren't going to ask him to resign.

"Yeah, that's another thing, Ahlavat. You cannot login any more files until we get to the bottom of this mess. Bharat is taking charge of your territory, North Gujarat, and your team will be reporting to him. I will personally convey this to your team. You cannot interact with them anymore. In fact, you must hand over your company-provided cell phone and sim card right away," Tony had candidly conveyed.

"No. Please. I've just closed the deal with *Kremlin Enterprises* and will be logging in around Rs 100 lakhs today," Adi had pleaded, stunned that he had been benched.

"Tony, you get them logged in your name. Adivteya, you better move your ass if you want to clear your name."

Feeling encouraged by Priyansh's decision, Adi had decided to visit the defaulters on his own, because he and Nishant had developed a mutual hatred for each other long ago. He had started with some oil and grain traders who had shops in the Kalupur area of Ahmedabad. The shops were opened, but all three shop owners had only one thing to say: "We only requested loans of Rs 1 to 2 lakhs and signed blank application forms and agreements. Your bank has deposited Rs 5 lakhs in our bank accounts, only to withdraw the extra Rs 3 to 4 lakhs for their personal use, but we are being charged EMI on the entire Rs 5 lakhs, so we stopped paying it. Further, the rate of interest mentioned in our sanction letter is 21%. This is too high. We were promised a rate of interest of 12%. Your collection manager came here, demanding we at least return the Rs 2 lakhs we wanted to borrow, but how can we? We used the money to buy new stock, but the recent floods destroyed everything in our shops."

All these loans had been logged in by Raghav, a sales executive of *Pinnacle*, so Adi had immediately phoned Sidanshu, but his phone had been switched off. A futile visit to his office and residence had been Adi's breaking point. Feeling tired and hungry, he had headed home, taken a long shower, and had settled down on the balcony, wondering what to do.

The chiming of his doorbell startled him. He decided to ignore it, sure that it would be a nosy neighbour wondering why he was home so early. The ringing didn't stop, so he forced himself out of the swing and opened the front door to find a nearly six-foot tall man dressed casually in blue jeans and a blue and black plaid shirt enquire, "Mr Adivteya Ahlavat?"

"Who wants to know?" Adi enquired cautiously.

"I'm Dy SP Mittal from Ahmedabad's crime branch. I need to talk with you about certain loans your bank has sanctioned to some customers, especially doctors," the man stated, placing a foot on the threshold, lest Adi should slam the door in his face.

On the contrary, a white-faced Adi opened the door just enough for Gautam to enter, and then quickly shut it behind him.

"Crime branch? But the bosses told me I have a month to get to the bottom of this. Please, I hail from a respectable family in UP. My mom wouldn't be able to bear it if you arrest me like this," Adi started blabbering.

Gautam regarded the trembling man who appeared to be of the same age as him and toned down his 'tough guy' demeanour a notch to clarify, "Relax, I'm not here to arrest you. I've been investigating certain people who have availed loans from your bank, and I wanted to talk to you about them." Gautam deliberately left out the fact that he was unofficially investigating only Drs Dhiraj and Piyush.

He had been following Adi for a week now and had decided it was time to have a face-to-face conversation with the sales manager of the bank that had disbursed Dhiraj's PL, especially after seeing the way Adi had been running from pillar to post all afternoon.

Chapter 48

Blackmail?

"Please come in Inspector, I'll tell you all I know, in fact, maybe you can help me save my job. Er, may I get you some tea or coffee?"

'I'm not an Inspector,' Gautam wanted to correct but refrained on seeing the glimmer of hope on Adi's face.

"Tea would be good. I'll prepare it, while you talk, just point me in the direction of your kitchen." Gautam suggested.

"I'm in deep trouble, Inspector. Sales executives of my DSA, *Pinnacle* have been...." Gautam's ears perked up on hearing *Pinnacle* and Sidanshu, but he silently went about the motions of brewing tea the way he liked it while absorbing each word Adi narrated.

"Do you think Sidanshu has disappeared as I couldn't find him at his residence and his office? Oh, by the way, these are the list of defaulters I must investigate and try to recover money from in a month," Adi concluded his side of the saga, thrusting the stack of papers still clutched in his hand towards Gautam. That's when he realised the tea had probably been ready for a while now, as Gautam was holding two mugs in his hands.

"Inspector, I'm so sorry, let me take mine," Adi quickly reached out for a mug and pressed the papers in Gautam's free hand. "Can I get you something to eat? I'm starving, shall I order a pizza?" Adi inquired graciously while they made their way back to the living room.

Gautam almost felt sympathetic on seeing some of the tension lift off Adi's face as they settled down on opposite sides of the coffee table, but he quickly checked himself; it was too early to trust Adi completely.

"Yeah, pizza would be good," Gautam responded, scrutinizing the list while sipping his tepid tea.

"I ordered a large vegetarian pizza from *Pizza Hut* with all the toppings because I'm a vegetarian. I hope it's okay, with you. I can order a non-veg one for you, otherwise," Adi informed after a while, draining his tea in one gulp.

"Veg's fine. Tell me about yourself." Gautam regretted the general question because it took Adi about the same time as the pizza delivery to give him a verbal description of his hometown in UP and his stint in Mumbai. The doorbell chimed just as Adi had started talking about *TCI*. Grateful for the interruption, Gautam started asking specific questions after Adi paid for the pizza, regarding the functioning of the personal loans department.

That didn't help though, and Gautam had to tactfully change the topic when Adi lingered for too long on irrelevant information like Trisha's support and Surbhi's attitude. Adi's tendency for detailing helped, however, while he described Sidanshu's office and opulent penthouse.

"Inspector, I've told you whatever I know. You must help me clear my name. Even Priyansh and Tony have attended Sidanshu's parties, why should only I be accused of taking kickbacks from him? So how should we start?"

Gautam couldn't figure out if he should feel sympathetic or laugh at the audacity of Adi's last statement; he had come looking for answers, but Adi had turned him into a saviour.

"Okay. First, please call me Gautam, and I think we should start by visiting Dr Dhiraj Mehta," Gautam suggested.

"Dr Dhiraj Mehta? Why? He's not on the list?" Adi objected.

"Do you have a laptop or a PC? I want you to see something."

"I have a PC in my bedroom, please come this way, Gautam," Adi replied, rising from the couch to lead the way.

*

"God, this is pornography, why am I watching this?" Adi grimaced as the scenes unfolded. He suddenly recollected the Branch Head's phone call on the evening of his housewarming ceremony, and enquired suspiciously, "From where did you get these videos and what do they have to do with me being benched?"

"It doesn't matter how I got these videos. What matters is are you responsible for your high net-worth clients being blackmailed this way?" Gautam countered.

"Blackmail? I...responsible...What makes you feel they are being blackmailed?"

"It's just a hunch. You have at least five doctors on your list claiming they haven't availed loans for which they have to pay EMIs, so they are defaulting. What about the other doctors who have availed loans from TCI? Maybe similar incriminating videos have gone to them, forcing them to pay EMIs on loans they haven't availed? This Sidanshu could be running a racket here," Gautam declared.

The ringing of the doorbell interrupted the sudden silence that had settled upon them.

"Who on earth could it be now?" Adi muttered, striding out of the room.

Gautam logged out of his email and followed suit.

"Oh my God! Trish. What time is it? Come in. I...was going to phone you from my other number, but it's been an unbelievable day," Adi spluttered.

Gautam tried not to stare as a beautiful woman walked in. Her smart black trousers, tucked in pale blue formal top, 4" black pumps and neatly tied hair gave the impression she was just starting her day, barring the faint shadows beneath her doe-shaped eyes which were locked questioningly with his.

"Er, this is Gautam, my friend. Actually, he's not, but please don't freak out. Gautam is a Police Inspector," Adi introduced.

"Good evening, inspector," she greeted calmly, holding out her hand

"Good evening, ma'am," Gautam returned a firm handshake and greeting before turning to Adi to state, "It's 9.30 pm, I'll better get going. Let's meet tomorrow and take it forward from there."

"No, please stay. I want to hear what both of you have to say," Trisha suggested, taking a seat on a winged chair beside the couch.

"Let me order some food first. Trish, you must be starving. Have you eaten anything?" Adi enquired.

"No."

"Adi, you start talking while I order the food," Gautam suggested and Adi agreed, so he moved to the balcony.

Chapter 49

Bunty aur Babli

Gautam felt as though the forces of nature were handing the investigation to him on a platter when Trisha asked him to stay. She was as beautiful as Adi had described her that was why Gautam had planned on meeting her soon as he was highly suspicious of beautiful women. 'Baggage I probably need to deal with later,' he made a mental note to himself as he walked towards the balcony with his ear firmly on the conversation between 'Bunty aur Babli' the childish name he conjured up for the duo from the Bollywood version of Bonnie and Clyde, an American criminal couple infamous for their bank robberies. This of course appeared to be a 'white collar' crime.

Being a bachelor Gautam had the phone numbers of all the 'home delivery' restaurants, so it took him less than five minutes to order Chinese food. Adi, in the meantime, was dramatically replaying the tale from this morning. Gautam pretended to talk on his phone as he listened, waiting for whispers or pauses. He even stole frequent glances in their direction, but nothing appeared to be out of the ordinary. Adi paced as he talked, and Trisha watched him as she listened.

'Maybe I'm just being paranoid,' Gautam mentally concluded, returning to the living room when Adi reached the part of him ringing the doorbell.

Frown lines creased the smooth area between Trisha's brows on hearing Adi say, "Damn, I thought Gautam had come to arrest me! "

Gautam shifted his scrutiny from Trisha's face to Adi's to gauge his expression as the statement appeared to be what a straightforward person would have made. Unfortunately, Gautam didn't have enough experience to conclude if a nervous laugh and an unsuccessful attempt at masking the worried look on his face was an act of a perpetrator.

"So, why did you come to meet Adi, Inspector?" Trisha questioned.

She didn't divert her gaze for even a second as she listened attentively to Gautam's part. The food arrived just as Gautam concluded, so they moved to the sturdy wooden dining table with six matching chairs, to the right of the living room.

"Were you born and raised in Ahmedabad, Inspector?" Trisha questioned as they dug into the food.

"No, Mumbai."

"Then why are you working in Ahmedabad?"

"I was offered Ahmedabad upon completing my training."

"You seem to be of our age. Doesn't it take time to become an Inspector?"

Gautam met her eyes from across the table, unsure of how he should answer her question, at the same time struggling to mask his admiration at her astuteness.

"Yes, it does," Gautam replied, knowing where she was going.

"Oh, okay. So, do you head the Law Garden Police Station? Don't Inspectors have a bunch of Sub Inspectors, constables etc. who conduct preliminary investigations?"

"Ma'am, I don't head the Law Garden Police Station, because I'm not an Inspector, I'm…"

"You're not an inspector! Then who are you and why did you lie to me?" Adi exploded.

"I didn't lie. I introduced myself as a Dy SP."

"May we see some identification?" Trisha requested.

Gautam reached into the pocket of his jeans, extracted his badge, and handed it over to her.

"Wow, you're an IPS officer! Shouldn't the inspector of Law Garden's police station be investigating this case? Hey, if everyone has finished eating, how about we clear the table?" she suggested, handing the badge back as she rose from her seat. She picked up their empty plates and headed for the kitchen.

Gautam grabbed a few empty cartons and followed her, marvelling at her shrewdness once again. Two thoughts simultaneously crossed his mind, 'How on earth did an unperceptive person with average looks land a lady like Trisha?'; 'Could Trisha be the mastermind of this scam, and Adi her puppet?'

"Inspe...er DSP, is this case so serious that it warrants an investigation from an officer of your rank?" she suddenly stopped and turned to question.

"Ma'am, I was the only available officer when the 100-emergency call was made to the police control room regarding Dr Dhiraj's wife's suicide. One thing led to another and now I'm investigating a probable blackmail," Gautam replied, calmly meeting her eyes, "Another thing, please, let's dispense with the titles. Call me Gautam."

"Oh, okay," she turned on her heel and entered the kitchen.

It took them five minutes to clear the table, post which they gathered again in the living room. Trisha broke the silence by suggesting, "Adi, if you don't want to work with Nishant, I think you should take Ishan's help. People in the Loan Recovery department are better equipped to handle such situations. Ishan is the collection manager at *FirstCredit*, the bank I work with Gautam, and he has a much better disposition than Nishant."

"I don't want to work with any collection guy at the moment," Adi objected

"You must, Adi, because Ishan and Nishant questioned Sidanshu's executive Raghav about the Gaurang Shah skip case and he led them to some offices in a building in Shahpura where there is a fake identity racket going on…"

"A what?"

"Why didn't you tell me this before?"

Gautam and Adi interrupted her with their respective reactions.

"To answer your question first Adi, all this happened just before our engagement. You were so busy with your new house and getting everything right for your parents' visit, I thought I'd tell you later. Regarding the issue of counterfeit documents, we need to have an ironclad strategy to trap them, lest they get suspicious, shut shop, and vanish. Now that you are here, Gautam, maybe you can officially investigate the place and put an end to it? Let me give you a background about it first…"

Chapter 50

Guilty until Proven Innocent

Adi stared unbelievingly at the blank screen of his cell phone. Dr Dhiraj Mehta, the very same doctor who had barged into *TCI* demanding an explanation for a Personal Loan he hadn't requested for, had politely declared a few seconds ago that his confusion had been sorted out and had hung up on him.

"What do we do now? Dr Mehta is refusing to meet us," Adi turned to Gautam who had heard the conversation as Adi had activated the speaker.

"Go get dressed in 5 minutes," Gautam instructed.

"But why? Where are we going? Okay, I'll go change." Adi agreed on seeing the sour expression on Gautam's face.

*

"Good morning gentlemen. Who's the patient?" Dr Dhiraj Mehta greeted amicably.

"I am," Gautam declared, moving towards a stool beside Dhiraj's executive chair before Dhiraj could suggest it.

"Okay, what seems to be the problem, Mr…?"

"Gautam. I have this nagging pain on my left shoulder which is hampering my work and my sleep."

"Okay, please remove your shirt so I can have a look."

"Er, doctor, before that, may I show you some x-rays I took last week. To be honest, I had consulted Dr Harshad Patel, and he wants to operate on my shoulder. I'm consulting you for a second opinion."

"Oh, okay, show me the x-rays."

Adi watched in amazement as Gautam extracted a 12" x 10" envelope from his satchel, removed a sheaf of photographs from it, and handed it to Dhiraj.

"What on earth? This is preposterous," Dhiraj exploded, flinging the photos on his desk.

"Who are you?" he questioned after a few seconds, rising from his chair, trembling.

"I'm DSP Gautam Mittal, from Maninagar Police Headquarters," Gautam informed, flashing his badge.

"Has your boss Kamal sent you to find out if I am going to talk about what happened? I won't, I swear I won't. Tell him that," Dhiraj pleaded, sinking back in his chair.

"SP Kamal Arora didn't send me. I request you to trust me and tell me everything. You have my word your reputation will not be tarnished."

"Are you also a Police Officer?" Dhiraj shifted his eyes to Adi.

"Er, I'm Adivteya Ahlavat." Adi replied, nervously.

"Huh," Dhiraj snorted, "Sure, I was a fool to have fallen in that 'Honey Trap', but I'm not talking in front of the person who supported Sidanshu in his felony."

Gautam placed a firm hand on Adi's arm to stop him from protesting and conveyed, "Doctor, Adivteya is also under investigation. According to me, he's guilty until proven innocent. He'll wait outside if you don't want to talk in front of him, especially if you want to share something that will incriminate him."

Dumbfounded by Gautam's declaration of him being 'guilty until proven innocent', Adi regretted his straightforwardness. 'Considering the circumstances, what else could I have done?' he mentally cajoled himself, feeling a tad relieved on seeing Dhiraj press a button on his desk phone and speak when his receptionist answered, "How many patients are waiting?"

"None, doctor," the receptionist's voice floated over the speaker.

"Okay. You may leave now. Please lock the office behind you."

Dhiraj pressed the button again to end the call and addressed Gautam, "How do I know that either of you will not tape this conversation and start blackmailing me for it?"

Chapter 51

A Pattern

Trisha checked her watch for the umpteenth time on Tuesday morning, but it was only 11.15; barely 5 minutes had passed since she had last checked. The restlessness had settled in around midnight. She too had wanted to take leave and assist Gautam and Adi in their investigation, but Adi had objected vehemently, stating, "It's bad enough that I'm on the verge of losing my job. No need for you to put yours too in jeopardy."

Gautam had offered to escort her home last night since it was late. She had declined and had spent the night tossing and turning. She was doing something similar now, picking up a file, glancing unseeingly through it, and either setting it aside or approving it if all the verification reports were in place. Realising she wasn't going to accomplish anything if she didn't do what she wanted to in the first place, she pulled up the records of the defaulting doctors at her bank *FirstCredit* and was stunned to see a pattern. Realising she had to discuss this matter with Ishan, she rose from her desk and walked over to his workstation at the far end of the room.

"Hey, how is it going?" she enquired, pulling up a chair, wondering how to approach the matter.

"I'm under a lot of pressure to recover money in these high-value cases, but I just can't seem to get hold of the doctors. They are not answering my calls, their receptionists don't allow me to meet them, and their wives or maids at home simply say they are at work."

Trisha got the opening she was looking for and said, "Ishan, I was just going through their files and in most of them, the first loan was disbursed in the name of a medical equipment supplier. The second loans were mostly disbursed a month later, directly to the doctors' accounts, and the reason for availing the second loan varied from hospital/clinic renovation to education and so on. Can you pull out their bank records to check if the entire disbursed amount was withdrawn in one shot? I could have done it myself, but I thought you would have their bank statement handy."

"Yes, I do. Okay, here's the first one," he agreed amicably, pulling up a bank statement.

They spent the next hour pouring over the statements and a printout Ishan had taken with the loan details. Trisha kept noting down details in her notebook as they proceeded.

"Damn, my hunch turned out to be right. Ishan, go to the Excel file with the loan details. Okay, now look at the cheque number in the bank statement and compare it with the cheque numbers on the post-dated cheques submitted to the bank. In each case, one of the Post-Dated Cheques has been used to withdraw the entire loan amount from the doctors' accounts, post the disbursement.

"People always issue cheques in the numerical order they appear in the chequebook. So, if 5 PDCs must be submitted to the bank as security, obviously they would issue them in the consecutive order. Fine, we could give them the benefit of the doubt if they used the next number to withdraw the entire disbursed amount, but in several cases, the first or subsequent cheques have been used. This can only mean that the perpetrator collected one extra cheque apart from the mandatory five PDCs to be submitted to the bank and used it to withdraw the entire loan amount." Trisha pointed out excitedly.

"Oh God! You're brilliant, Trish! What made you think of this?"

"I kept having this nagging doubt as to why a doctor with a good reputation would default. I know, we are legally not allowed to use strong-arm techniques to get them to pay, but we can file a court case and make it public," Trisha lied, not ready to share what Gautam had disclosed about Dr Dhiraj Mehta last night.

"These are all Sidanshu's cases. I can't believe he'd be so foolish. This is too easy, Trish."

'Damn! He's baiting me. Why did I come to him? I should have waited.' Doubts churned in Trisha's mind as she met Ishan's calm gaze. She hadn't seen the 'sex tape', but she was sure it was enough to keep the doctors silent.

"Hey, how about we check the bank statements of the other high-profile defaulters, maybe the same thing is happening with them," she suggested, lowering her eyes.

Ishan agreed and Trisha felt oddly comforted by his silent strength. She loved Adi immensely, especially for his straightforwardness, but at times like this she could really use some support from a calm, matured person like Ishan.

"Here's another one," Ishan declared, bringing her back to the present.

'Wow, that makes it three businessmen. How are we going to get to the bottom of this and clear Adi's name?' She couldn't help wondering as she updated the manual record of the pattern they had uncovered.

Chapter 52

A Murky Aspect

The clicking of the levers in the front door lock echoed in the medium-sized clinic while the receptionist turned her key eight times to lock it properly. Dhiraj's eyes were on the two men seated across him. Although he had been sceptical initially, an odd feeling of relief settled upon him. He was glad he could finally discuss the quagmire he had gotten himself into with somebody.

"Priya, that's how she introduced herself when she phoned me for the first time, three months ago, to inform me about the special scheme *TCI* had come up with for doctors who wanted to buy medical equipment. I badly needed that X-ray machine, but I didn't want to avail another loan as I was already paying EMIs for my house and car. She wouldn't give up and kept insisting I should meet her boss, Sidanshu.

"I agreed and he managed to convince me to take the first Rs 20 lakh loan. A month later, she phoned me again, requesting for an appointment as I had to sign some more papers. I told her to meet me at Zeus Hospital, but she insisted on coming to my clinic after 7 pm."

He paused his narration, his thoughts drifting to that fateful night when Priya had entered his office.

"It had been a particularly busy evening, and she waited for my last patient to leave before walking into my room. I had sent my receptionist home, thinking it would take me only five minutes to sign whatever Priya wanted. I was meeting her for the first time. Nothing was stunning about her, but now that I think about it, she has seemingly endless long, shapely legs. They were clad in denim that evening. Her feet were encased in pencil healed stilettoes. That had mesmerized me the second she had stepped into my room and had shut the door behind her. I probably gave her the vibe that I found her alluring by the way my eyes had travelled over her tight shirt emphasising her slim waist, and ample chest.

"She is sexy, damn it. The entire package; shoulder length, curly, black hair framing her round face with full lips, dark skin giving her an exotic look, and husky voice."

Gautam felt his jaw drop at the incredulity of Dhiraj's description. It was as though Dhiraj was talking about an amazing date and not the lady who had conned him.

"I had requested her to take a seat, but she had remained standing at my table. She opened the folder she had been holding and had extracted a form. I was seated at my desk while signing at the places she was indicating, but she moved to my side, her fingers brushing against mine as I signed."

Dhiraj stopped speaking again and shifted his dreamy gaze from the spot above Gautam's head to meet his eyes. He continued to look straight into Gautam's eyes as he declared, "I am not a womanizer, Inspector. Unfortunately, I hadn't been 'intimate' with my wife or any woman since my wife became an alcoholic. Priya's enticing personality and heady lemon-scented perfume weakened me. She had placed her soft palm over my hand when I had signed the last of the Post-Dated Cheques, a total of 6 in number, and had thanked me for my valuable time; her red-tipped fingers caressing the back of my hand.

"I reacted like a typical man and caressed her back, wondering how I could get so lucky when she pushed me back against my chair, straddled me and started kissing me. She made me lose control. That's why I didn't notice the camera she had probably placed on the right-hand corner of my desk, as I had proceeded to satisfy my carnal needs. I'm sure that was where she had placed the camera for the first video and probably turned it for the second. What a fool I was not to have noticed her doing it."

Gautam rose from his seat to the spot Dhiraj indicated, concluding after a while, "Hmm... I agree with you about the camera positioning. We seem to be dealing with one smart girl here."

"When did she start blackmailing?" Adi enquired.

"The evening my wife's attempted suicide."

"You think she knew about it?" Gautam baited, curious to listen to Dhiraj's side, because the hacking had indicated Piyush, the doctor who had attended to Dhiraj's wife, had phoned Sidanshu on multiple occasions before the day of the suicide but not on that day, at least not till the time Raul had obtained Piyush's call logs.

"I didn't explicitly mention it, but I did phone her after leaving *TCI*, demanding an explanation of why another Personal Loan was disbursed in my name. She said she has no clue, and that maybe the bank did it by mistake, on seeing another application form with my signature on it. Apparently, she had taken my signature on one more application form at the behest of the bank because there was a mistake in the first one. I was at my wits end because I couldn't go back and demand an explanation from the Branch Head, as he had already spoken to you, the PL sales manager of *TCI*, Adi…, er, I don't know how to pronounce your name, on a call with me, so I tried Sidanshu's number. He didn't answer the call," Dhiraj replied.

"Please call me Adi. That means she sent you the email immediately after answering your call!"

Gautam couldn't help diverting his gaze to Adi on hearing him exclaim, as he was sure he detected a trace of relief in Adi's voice.

"Yes, at least that's what the time stamp on the email indicates. I unfortunately, saw the email only when I reached Zeus Hospital where I'm a consulting surgeon," Dhiraj confirmed.

"I can't believe her audacity!" Adi exclaimed once again.

"Maybe someone else sent it because some weird email address appears in the sender details," Dhiraj informed, turning suddenly to Gautam to enquire, "maybe you can throw some light into this matter. How did you get the incriminating photos you showed me?"

"I suppose you received the email from newage@manda.co.in, right? Well, so have many more doctors who have lodged an official complaint with us, and our cybercrime cell has been monitoring emails from this account. It's futile to reply to this email though, as you won't get a response," Gautam lied.

"My God! So, have these other doctors paid the money and to whom? By the way Dr Dhiraj, how much money was demanded? Did you pay it and to whom?"

Gautam winced mentally on hearing Adi's question and the puzzled look on Dhiraj's face as he enquired, "What exactly are the two of you investigating?"

"As per my boss, Mr Kamal Arora's instructions, I'm investigating blackmail, while Adi here is trying to figure out the lacunae in the bank, resulting in honest professionals like you defaulting in their loan repayments," Gautam lied once again, praying Dhiraj would buy the implied message that Kamal accepting money from him was part of a ploy to catch the actual perpetrators.

"The email didn't demand any money but had a curt message instructing me to continue to pay the EMIs for a loan I didn't avail from *TCI*," Dhiraj answered, tentatively, his eyes fixed on Gautam.

Gautam mentally heaved a sigh of relief at Dhiraj's reply, as Kamal's involvement was literally a murky aspect to the sordid saga that was unravelling.

Chapter 53

And the Plot Thickens ......

An onlooker would have probably described the scene as two pals enjoying chilled beer after as hard day's work, in a perfectly serene setting. It was 7 pm. The lingering hues of dusk, coupled with the city lights reflected an orangish purple sky. A cool breeze rustled the leaves and flowers of the potted plants. All this was lost on Adi slumped over a wicker chair and Gautam seated on the swing; both nursing beers; lost in their own mind space.

Adi suddenly started laughing, startling Gautam.

"What's so funny, man?" Gautam enquired frowning.

"This. I mean, I was a teetotaller, now I'm drinking bootlegged beer with a police officer," he managed to convey in between bouts of laughter. He suddenly sobered up and said, "G, that night, at Sidanshu's house, when I drank alcohol for the first time, I woke up at noon to find the other side of the bed rumpled, as though someone had been sleeping beside me. What if it was one of those stunning women at his party and Sidanshu recorded it? Is he going to blackmail me now?"

"Chill man. We'll deal with it when we must. I'm going to get dinner started," Gautam comforted rising from the swing.

He didn't feel so comforted though as he walked towards the kitchen. In fact, he also felt as lost and confused as Adi post their meeting with Dhiraj. That was probably the reason why he behaved in an unprofessional manner by stopping at his residence first to grab some beers and then returning to Adi's house. Of course, he also had an ulterior motive. He wanted to continue to observe Adi, especially after Adi downed a few beers and would, maybe say something to incriminate himself.

Gautam also couldn't understand if the bankers should be blamed for pushing sales numbers or the defaulters, or people like Priya and Sidanshu, for their blatant disregard of putting some hardworking person's savings in jeopardy. History had evidence of banks going under due to NPAs (Non-Performing Assets).

"Hey, I'll take care of the parathas while you cook the rice and dal. The utensils are in the bottom drawer and the groceries are on the side table," Adi suggested, following him into the kitchen.

"Sure," Gautam agreed, reaching out for an unopened packet of lentils. He loved to cook, especially when he was disturbed. Cooking relaxed him. It helped him gather his thoughts. As if on cue, events of the past few days started unravelling in his mind as he washed the lentils. It was only when he turned off the flame under the pot of steamed rice, that he realised he was alone in the kitchen. Also, the incessantly chatty Adi hadn't spoken a word while he had prepared the parathas. Grabbing a beer from the refrigerator, he left the kitchen.

The doorbell rang and Adi sprang from the couch Gautam found him seated on, in the living room. "Hey, beautiful. We've got a surprise for you," Adi conveyed on opening the door.

Gautam paused mid-stride on hearing the bell and was alarmed to see the broad smile on Adi's face vanish as he backed away from the door.

"Er, Adi, this is Ishan, *FirstCredit's* Collection Manager. Ishan, this is my fiancée Adivteya Ahlavat. Please call him Adi.

His name is quite a mouthful," Trisha introduced, walking into the room with a well-built, tall, clean-shaven man in tow.

"Hey, Adi. I hope you don't mind me arriving uninvited at your doorstep," Ishan greeted amicably holding out his hand.

"No, not at all, welcome Ishan," Adi managed to plaster a smile on his face as he grudgingly returned Ishan's handshake, before introducing, "Ishan, this is DSP Gautam."

It was Gautam's turn to feel wary at the intrusion Trisha had sprung on them, but he was better than Adi at hiding his resentment.

"Please take a seat, Ishan, make yourself at home. You guys are drinking beer? How did you manage it, Adi? Do you have more, can Ishan and I have some?" Trisha requested.

Gautam almost guffawed at Adi's shocked expression. Realising the time was not right to analyse Adi's ideals about alcohol, women and alcohol, or his fiancée and alcohol, Gautam responded, "I brought the beer. There are enough cans stocked in the refrigerator, please help yourselves."

"So, what's your surprise, Adi?" Trisha enquired, on returning to the living room with two cans in hand.

"G and I cooked dinner for you," Adi replied a sour expression flitting over his face on seeing her offer a can to Ishan.

"Aw, that's so sweet," Trisha responded, taking a seat beside Adi on the couch. "Let me tell Hrian not to bring dinner. Hope you've cooked enough for all of us," she declared, pressing some keys on her cell phone.

"Why is Hrian coming to my house now?" Adi shouted, losing it. He grabbed Trisha's cell phone before she could connect the call. She grabbed it back and disconnected the line. 'And the plot thickens,' Gautam couldn't help thinking, leaning back against the chair he was seated on and listened to Trisha calmly state, "Adi, I know you're tensed and worried about your future, but you've got to trust me. I spent three hours investigating similar defaulting cases at *FirstCredit* with Ishan and we've come up with a plan. Then we went to meet Hrian as our ploy can succeed only if Hrian helps. Please hear us out, Adi, it's a terrific idea."

The doorbell chimed again before Adi could respond.

Chapter 54

The Mastermind

"Trisha, why don't you answer the door while Adi and I get some more beer?" Gautam suggested.

"Sure," Trisha agreed.

"Pull yourself together you idiot and listen to what she has to say," Gautam whispered when they were out of the ear shot.

"But how could she have confided in Ishan and Hrian without discussing things with me first?" Adi protested.

"Please don't take it the wrong way when I say this Adi, but Trisha is a smart lady. She isn't going to wait for you to tell her what to do. I think you owe it to her for standing beside you when you are on the verge of losing your job for allegedly conniving with Sidanshu, a conman and trying to clear your name. So please be a gracious host and hear her out," Gautam advised.

"Okay," Adi reluctantly agreed, opening the fridge to extract some cans. 'Let me also see if Madam Trisha is a loyal fiancée or the mastermind behind this whole racket,' Gautam thought, re-entering the living room with Adi.

*

Gautam stuck to beer, Adi switched to water, but the other three indulged in the Vodka Hrian had brought along with food. Adi fortunately was back to his normal chatty self and the conversation during dinner centred around the loans department. Trisha had insisted in between that Gautam talk about himself. He had been painfully brief about it, vaguely mentioning his upbringing in Mumbai and had steered the conversation back to their profession.

Everyone helped to clear the table once they were done eating and took their bottles and glasses back to the living room.

Trisha started talking first, and Ishan pitched in while they revealed their findings of the pattern Sidanshu seemed to be following to con doctors and high net worth businessmen. Adi then disclosed everything Dr Dhiraj Mehta shared. Gautam continued to be the spectator, surreptitiously looking out for signs in Trisha and Adi for being hand in glove in the whole scam, especially when Ishan expressed his shock regarding the honey trap as Trisha had obviously not disclosed that part to him.

"Okay, so if Sidanshu is using this modus operandi to defraud doctors and businessmen, as confirmed by Dr Dhiraj, then Ishan and I have come up with a plan. We realised we needed help to execute it, so I suggested we confide in Hrian. I'm sorry, Adi and Gautam, that we went ahead without consulting you, but we discussed it with Hrian, as he is the only DSA we can trust and he has agreed to it," Trisha conveyed.

"I trust you sweetheart, so what's your plan?" Adi enquired.

"A sting operation. Hrian knows a Dr Shailesh Shah. He's a cardiologist with a modest clinic in Ambawadi. If you guys agree to it, then Hrian will make sure Raghav, Sidanshu's executive is made aware of the fact that Dr Shailesh wants a personal loan to purchase a Colour Doppler Ultrasound. He really needs the equipment, and he will go through the formalities of availing a loan to purchase it. Then we'll wait for Sidanshu to spring the 'honey trap'. Only, this time, we'll have cameras and microphones ready to record the whole scene and we'll follow the lady to see where she lives and works," Trisha revealed.

Silence descended upon the living room and all eyes turned to Adi after Trisha conclude the plan. Adi's eyes, however, were on Gautam, waiting for his take on the plan. Gautam hoped he was successful in maintaining a deadpan expression as his eyes lingered over each person in the room, before finally looking Trisha straight in the eye and responding, "it's a brilliant idea, but I think Sidanshu waits for at least a month before sending in his accomplice to set the stage for fraud and blackmail.

Chapter 55

Aukaat

It was almost 2 am when Hrian unlocked the door to his bachelor pad, a modest 1 BHK flat in a nondescript building. The neighbourhood was predominantly middle class, at least 10 kilometres away from the affluent areas of Ahmedabad. He walked in the dark towards his bedroom, switched on a night lamp, extracted a pair of clean track pants and a T-shirt from his wardrobe, and laid them on his bed. Shedding his sweaty clothes, he carried them to his bathroom, dumped them in the laundry hamper, took a long shower, and re-entered his bedroom to wear the clean clothes.

Flopping down on his bed, he extracted an unopened bottle of Johnny Walker Black Label from his nightstand, switched on the 21" wall-mounted flat screen TV and started watching a re-run of his favourite show, *Kaun Banega Crorepati* playing on *Sony*. It didn't take long for his mind to drift from the charismatic host Amitabh Bachchan to the happenings in Adi's house less than an hour ago. Opening the bottle in his hand, he took a long swig of the blended whisky, unmindful of the fact that he had already consumed two beers and four pegs of vodka that night.

The neat alcohol hit him instantly, but it wasn't enough to obliviate his contempt for bankers, if not for ever, then at least for that night. Unlike Adi who was probably just a year or two older than Hrian, betrayal and despair had struck Hrian four years ago, numbing him to any feelings of compassion or empathy or rather, he had numbed himself with alcohol when he had been faced with a choice to give up or survive.

Life had been so good nine years ago. He and Sonia, the love of his life, were 18, fresh out of college, with dreams of working and earning enough of money to support each other. She had landed a job first with *TCI* as Tony's predecessor, Vinay Deshmukh's sales coordinator. It was her responsibility to keep track of the performance of the sales managers reporting to Vinay, collate their data and manage Vinay's emails.

Hrian should have noticed and paid more heed to her obsession with Vinay when a month into her job, all she could talk about was how smart Vinay was, or the way he got his team to perform or his flawless English, general knowledge, MBA degree and so on.

However, he had been so blindly in love then that he had dismissed her adoration as hero worship. Then Vinay had offered him a job as a sales executive with his DST and Hrian had been so absorbed in performing and earning incentives that he barely had time to meet Sonia. She in the meantime, had joined an English-speaking class and had enrolled herself in a distance learning MBA marketing program. He had felt proud and had encouraged her.

Almost 18 months after he had started working with Vinay's DST, Hrian had gone one evening to *TCI* to log in some files only to learn Sonia had resigned. He had rushed to her house and had found her crying in her bedroom.

"I'm sorry Hrian, but I've been having an affair with Vinay for the past six months. I broke it off last night when I came to know he's married. I can't work with him anymore, so I resigned. I don't want to live in Ahmedabad after this humiliation, so I'm moving to my uncle's house in Vadodara. Vinay has spoken with his friend, an Area Sales Manager with

HDFC Bank and he has assured me of a sales manager's job in Personal Loans," she had conveyed through her tears.

"No, there's no need to relocate just because that creep had fun with you. Let's get married, forget about what happened. I'll also resign and join another bank," Hrian had pleaded vainly.

"I don't love you Hrian. If I had, I wouldn't have had an affair with Vinay. I'm getting an on-rolls job with HDFC Bank, Hrian, the second-best bank in India. I'll also be completing my MBA in a few months. I'm confident that with my MBA and hard work, I'll rise very soon to the same level Vinay is in now," she had declared.

Hrian had been besides himself. He had rushed out of her house and had driven like a mad man to *TCI*. It had been almost 8 pm when he had entered the loan department. Most of the outsourced back-office staff had left for the day. Vinay had been cloistered in one of the meeting rooms with his team. Hrian had walked up to it, yanked the door open, and had brushed aside the sales managers. He had grabbed Vinay's collar and had punched his face.

"Don't. Just leave the room," Vinay had instructed his sales managers when they had tried to pull Hrian off.

"Mujhe marne ka tera koi aukaat nahi hai saale. Ttaali do haath se bajti hai. She knew I was married. She has met my wife long before we slept together. It was she who made the first move, so why should I have turned down someone as sexy as her. There is no use of being a hero, trying to defend her honour," Vinay had stated calmly, the statement in Hindi conveying that Hrian had no rights to hit him, and it takes two to tango.

Hrian had released Vinay's collar and had gotten drunk on reaching his own house. He had turned up for work the next day and had worked so hard that Vinay had no choice, but to promote him as a Team Leader at the start of the new financial year. No amount of hard work could help Hrian sleep at night though, and he had to resort to alcohol to forget the fact that he had been a fool to have loved so much. Although it hadn't entirely been Vinay's fault, Hrian had also started hating bankers especially for the way they treated their subordinates as lackeys, expecting them to always do their bidding.

While he continued to perform at work, his alcoholism had worsened. Aware of the fact that he didn't have the educational qualifications like his sales managers or Vinay, he had childishly resorted to drinking more expensive brands like Johnny Walker Black Label and bulk of his salary and incentives were being eaten up by his addiction and ego. He had moved out of his parents' house when his mother had started nagging him about his addiction.

Today, seven years later, he was still an addict but thanks to Adi, he was making so much money that an indulgence of Rs 1 lakh per month meant nothing to him. In fact, he was so rich that he had bought land in one of the affluent localities of Ahmedabad and was in the process of constructing a palatial house for himself.

He hadn t disclosed this fact to anyone in *TCI* though and was happy about it now that a flamboyant person like Sidanshu was under their radar.

He had known all about fake identities and fraudulent cases, and had deliberately not cautioned Adi about it, due to his hatred for bankers, although Adi had always treated him with respect and was responsible for his progress. He hadn't known about the doctors and businessmen being blackmailed though, and while taking his last swig of the neat whisky in his hands, he vowed, he would ensure Adi's name was cleared.

Chapter 56

Just another Day at Work

Gautam guided his Bullet into an empty spot between two gearless scooters and turned off the ignition. After spending two days in close contact with Adi and his banker life, Gautam felt philosophical about his job as he entered the Ahmedabad City Police Headquarters in Maninagar. He didn't have to achieve targets or worry about retaining his high-paying job because he wasn't overleveraged, that is neck-deep in debt to maintain a certain lifestyle. His mundane, low-paying job was fine, and it gave him time to understand the functioning of the police department.

Granted, being a rookie, excited about investigating his first unofficial case, he may have adopted an unprofessional and unethical approach by being in close proximity with Adi and Trisha, but what the hell, he had been on official leave and done it in his own time.

"Good morning, sir," a sub-inspector greeted as he absentmindedly walked towards the desk allotted to him, right next to the washroom. Several more greetings followed suit, thoroughly puzzling him this time as he was generally ignored after he turned down his first bribe. He reached his desk, and a cold vice gripped his heart on seeing a constable polishing the badly scarred sunmica surface of his metal desk; again, a practice discontinued when he had become a pariah at the station. Gautam mechanically returned the constable's salute and sat down on his rickety wooden chair.

'Uh-oh, Kamal has found out about my clandestine investigation. That's why he has instructed his staff to be good to me. What am I going to do now? What if he asks me about it? Orders me to drop it?' Crazy thoughts churned in his mind. Feeling or maybe imagining that the eyes of the other officers and constables on him, he snatched the first case paper from a pile of around 10, neatly stacked at the right-hand corner of his desk, yet another novelty, as no one left any files on his desk. On the contrary, he had to often spend hours searching for case papers he wanted to scrutinize.

The pain in his chest intensified upon opening the first file and scanning through contents. It was the case of a 26-year-old male who was found dead in a ditch two days ago. The cause of death was stated as 'heroin overdose'. The file would have eventually been dumped in the pile of unsolved cases, had it not been for the boy's father who was a reporter with a prominent Gujarati newspaper '*Gujarat Mirror*'.

Gautam remembered reading about the incident in the papers as the father had raised hell, claiming that his son was murdered by his in-laws because he had eloped with the daughter of a famous criminal lawyer. The body had been found two days ago in Narol, only 5 kms from Maninagar Police Station, so sub-inspector Madhav Shinde had been assigned to conduct the preliminary investigation.

Beads of perspiration dotted Gautam's forehead and his hands felt clammy upon reading a memo from Kamal attached to the FIR, stating that the investigation has been officially transferred from Madhav to Gautam as it demanded the attention of a higher ranked official.

Being an IPS officer, Gautam, technically should have been assigned at least 5 police stations in Ahmedabad, but Kamal hadn't done so. On the contrary, since his open refusal to be corrupt he had only been sent on investigations that required the presence of a Constable, with rare exceptions of being ordered to accompany Madhav on burglary cases. Madhav's sickeningly obsequious nature led Gautam to presume he was Kamal's sycophant; the best person Kamal could use to learn about what made him, Gautam tick.

After what may have been their fifth investigation of a home break-in together, Madhav had confided in an almost convincingly sincere manner, "Sir, my father was a head constable in Vejalpur Police Station. He never accepted a single paisa as bribe, despite my younger brother being born a special child. We used to live in a one-room kitchen in Juhapura with whatever income my dad earned. Mum used to contribute to it by stitching clothes for the poor people around us, but she hardly earned anything.

"My dad was killed in a shootout with some drug dealers when I was only 16 years old. That prompted me to study for the state police exam and clear it. I was appointed as a constable in Vejalpur Police Station, and I worked very hard sir, but unlike my dad, I started accepting bribes because I knew my mum wouldn't be around for ever to take care of my sibling. I also learnt a very important truth once I started working; it's better to be diplomatic, even to the extent of being subservient to succeed in certain professions if one wants to rise.

"I know you won't believe it when I say that I wish I could take a stance of being incorruptible like you or my dad, sir, but l was able to buy a proper house for my mother, two years after joining the police force. She has her own bedroom with an attached bathroom and 24x7 running water. The day I was promoted as a sub-inspector, and assigned to Maninagar, I hired a full-time maid to assist mum, and take care of my brother, so that she could finally get a few hours to do something for herself, rather than only cater to my brother all the time.

"What I shared right now may seem like a justification for wrongdoings sir, in fact, I don't even know why I felt compelled to tell you all this, but somehow, I felt I should. I felt the need to justify my actions in front of a fearless senior. I don't know anything about your life, sir, but I admire you for having the courage to openly oppose corruption."

Madhav's last statement had wiped out the minuscule shred of sympathy Gautam had almost felt for him, and he had continued to be cautious in what he said or did around him, until one night, two months later. They were both manning a roadblock with a sub-inspector from Fathepura Police Station, and three other constables, on the lookout for illegal sand transporters in Pethapur, Gandhinagar. Apparently, illegal sand mining was going on in a nearby riverbank at midnight and the perpetrators were using a road in Fatepura to transport the sand.

They had managed to nab three trucks at around 2.30 am and Gautam had offered to drop Madhav home, on his Bullet, as the jeep Madhav had been travelling in had to follow the truck back to Fatepura Police Station. Madhav had agreed, and Gautam had found Madhav's mother waiting for them at the gate of his house. She had insisted Gautam come in and eat a hot meal. Gautam had accepted and had been saddened to see an obviously physically and mentally challenged man of around 22, totter into the small dining room after a while.

Madhav had immediately abandoned his food to rush to his brother's side. The lopsided smile of happiness on the hapless man's face on seeing his brother had melted Gautam's heart. While he had continued to remain guarded around Madhav, he had firmly put a pin on his doubts regarding Madhav's loyalty to the police force and had moved on.

Holding on to that same belief that morning, Gautam calmly closed the file, placed it to his left and reached out for the next in the pile to his right. This one was of an unidentified dead body found drowned in Kankaria Lake, again with an official memo from Kamal stapled on the FIR, stating that Gautam could assign it to any officer he wanted and had to only take regular updates on the progress of the investigation.

Raising his head, he managed to curb the manic laughter threatening to burst on realising he was the cynosure of every officer and constable in the room, he randomly called out to a sub-inspector and handed him the second file. This charade continued for the remaining eight files on his desk, all with the same stapled official memos.

Rising from his seat upon assigning the last file, he announced, "I want an update at 6 pm from all of you. Now kindly start your investigation. Madhav, please come with me."

"Yes sir." A collective consent echoed in the room, accompanied by some salutes. Nonchalantly picking up the controversial case file assigned to him from the left side of his desk, he sauntered out of the station like it was just another day at work, with sub-inspector Madhav Shinde in tow.

Chapter 57

Contempt for Bankers

The fish tank had a height of at least 2 feet and the width spanned the entire left wall of the waiting area in Dr Shailesh's clinic. Determined to end his obsessive need to keep checking his watch and willing the time to move faster so they could finally meet Dr Shailesh, Adi started focusing on the spectacular landscaping inside the tank, including the myriad of fish.

Well, it failed to hold his attention for more than 2 minutes and his eyes wandered over the rest of the modestly decorated waiting room with black plastic bucket chairs lined in rows, opposite the fish tank. A plump, middle-aged lady manned the reception. Her eyes followed him as he jumped up restlessly from his chair and started examining Dr Shailesh's certificates hung on the wall beside her table.

A bell resounded in the room announcing the exit of the patients who were in the consulting room. Adi looked hopefully at the receptionist, and she nodded, indicating he, Hrian and Ishan could enter.

Hrian entered first and introduced the other two. Dr Sailesh politely shook their hands and requested them to have a seat. Adi regretted the fact that he was in the middle because Dr Sailesh's penetrating gaze was upon him. He tried hard not to squirm, wondering if he should break the silence.

"Er Doctor, about that case I discussed with you yesterday, er," Hrian started to speak but Dr Sailesh interrupted him,

"Yes, I remember. I insisted on personally meeting you Mr Adivteya Ahlavat because I wanted to meet the banker who allowed people in my profession to be blackmailed by that scum."

"I'm sorry doctor, but we honestly have iron-clad systems in place to safeguard our customers against fraudsters," Adi protested.

"Yeah, I'm sure you do, but they wouldn't work if people on the inside were involved, would they? That's precisely what I told your collection manager, Mr Ishan. A doctor's wife had to commit suicide and the police had to find evidence of blackmail to make you guys realise you are just leaches, greedy for money. See what your counterparts have done in the US! They are reeling under the biggest financial scam of the century because of callous bankers like you. The 'sub-prime' crisis. I'm sure it's going to impact India very soon and all of you will lose your jobs. I have nothing but contempt for bankers," Dr Shailesh snorted.

Adi did squirm now, at the truth behind Dr Shailesh's deride of his profession. It was not only the bankers but insurance companies and the Wall Street that had precipitated the current financial meltdown in the US. Lehman Brothers, a global financial services company had declared bankruptcy last night. The Federal Home Loan Mortgage Corporation, and The Federal National Mortgage Association, both United States government-sponsored enterprises, commonly known as Freddie Mac, and Fannie Mae respectively, had gone under due to foreclosures by banks as the homeowners were unable to pay their second and third mortgages. Property prices had crashed to an all-time low in the US and the impact was already being felt in Europe.

"Dr Shailesh, I understand your disregard, your contempt for bankers mainly because of what Hrian disclosed is happening to your peers and the current US crisis. Yes, I do admit the salespeople are under pressure to perform, but in the case of the doctors being blackmailed, well, we never anticipated deviousness of this level. We came to meet you today because Hrian assured us of your help to get to the bottom of this mess," Ishan responded with uttermost politeness.

"Hmm, I will help you only for Hrian's sake as we hail from the same village. Before I do so though, I need it in writing that *TCI* will only process the Rs 20 lakh loan for the purchase of a colour Doppler machine, no matter what ploy the alleged perpetrators adopt. I will furnish the invoice for it, and you will pay the vendor. Further, if that lady Priya approaches me to sign some additional documents and Post-Dated Cheques and tries to seduce me, I will permit it only to a certain point, with enough evidence to incriminate her. I will not go beyond that. I want you guys to barge in and erase the recording in her camera. I will have my own hidden camera to prove that I am not a sex-starved prey.

"If you don't barge in at my signal, I will end it, snatch her camera, and call the police. So, let me reiterate my stand, I will not undress her, I will not kiss her. She can initiate the kissing if she wants, I'll play along, but I will stop at the point when she reaches for my pants," Dr Shailesh clarified vehemently, his eyes boring into Adi's again.

Adi could only adjust the collar of his Allen Solly shirt and wish Gautam was with him. They had been apart only for 10 hours, but he was already missing his presence.

Chapter 58

The Crime Scene

Gautam flashed his badge at the constable on duty in the side lane that led to the ditch Rahul, the alleged unwanted son-in-law of the criminal lawyer had been found overdosed in, and commanded, "Take a break, but come back in 10 minutes."

The constable immediately scurried away. Gautam waited till he was sure the constable was out of the earshot to sternly spew a barrage of questions at Madhav, "Tell me everything, starting from when you were assigned to this case, what you were doing then, who ordered you to attend to it, what you saw at the crime scene and everything that happened after that."

"Sir, I was in the jeep the day before yesterday, accompanying Inspector Popat at 10 am to investigate a jewellery shop robbery in Thaltej when I received a call from Kamal Sir, instructing me to investigate a dead body in Narol. Well, Inspector Popat told the driver of the jeep to take a U-turn and he dropped me at the spot."

"Did Inspector Popat drop you exactly beside the dead body? Did he alight from the vehicle to poke around?" Gautam interrupted, as he knew Popat was Kamal's most trusted Inspector.

"Yes sir, he did. It was he who picked up the syringe found in Rahul's right hand and placed it in an evidence bag. Then he ordered us to search the perimeter for any other evidence," Madhav answered hesitantly.

"So, did you find any?"

"Er, I think I did sir. I think, no I'm sure there were another set of tire marks, there on the dirt road, but most of them were messed up when the jeep took a turn to reverse out after a while," Madhav answered, hesitantly.

Gautam immediately diverted his eyes to the spot Madhav indicated and a set of tyre marks partly obliterated by the jeep's tracks were visible.

"Did you point this out to Inspector Popat?" Gautam inquired his eyes boring into Madhav's.

"No, sir, I didn't."

Gautam turned his gaze back to the tyre marks and started following them. Unable to believe his luck, he found the partly wiped-out tyre marks suddenly swerve to the left and a clear print was visible. Extracting the digital camera he had started carrying with him in his jeans pocket, since Kamal's Law Garden's rendezvous, he clicked pictures of the tracks.

Okay, what happened next?"

"Well, the constable who was with us extracted a wallet from the victim's pant pocket which had a driver's licence identifying him as Rahul Joshi, son of Bipin Joshi. Inspector Popat immediately handed over the wallet to me and instructed me and the constable to re-enter the jeep, saying he would drop me off at the address mentioned in the driver's licence which was in Basant Nagar, only a few kilometres away. I had no choice but to agree and I found myself standing alone outside the deceased's house. His mother answered my knock, and I introduced myself before I showed her the driver's license. She confirmed it was her son's but, sir, despite my 10 years in the police force, I couldn't reply directly to her question as to why I had her son's driver's license with me, so I took the coward's route and asked for his father.

"She replied he was at work and gave me his number. Well, Rahul's father turned out to be Mr Bipin Joshi, Sr. Reporter at Gujarat Mirror, who asked me to meet him at his office. It was painful to tell him that his son was found Oded in a dirt track, off the Narol main road. Well, the rest of it is history, sir, with Mr Bipin making the headlines of Gujarat Mirror, stating that his son was murdered by his nefarious father-in-law because he dared to marry above him."

Ignoring the cold vice gripping his heart at Madhav's statement, Gautam messaged the pictures of the tyre tracks to Raul, requesting him to try to identify the make and possibly the vehicle it belonged to as most of the tyre manufacturers had distinct thread marks.

Chapter 59

Dilemmas

Adi watched the children frolicking on the ground in front of the Sabarmati Riverfront. It was the venue for the annual international kite festival. The city of Ahmedabad has been hosting the International Kite Festival as part of the official celebration of Uttarayan since 1989, bringing in master kite makers and flyers from all over the world to demonstrate their unique creations and wow the crowds with highly unusual kites.

The festival of Uttarayan is a uniquely Gujarati phenomenon when the skies over most cities of the state fill with kites from before dawn until well after dark. The festival marks the days in the Hindu calendar when winter begins turning into summer, known as Makar Sankranti or Uttarayan. On what is usually a bright warm sunny day with brisk breezes to lift the kites aloft, across the state, almost all normal activity is shut down and everyone takes to the rooftops and roadways to fly kites and compete with their neighbours.

Right now, though, the ground was open to the public, and children were having a field day, playing cricket or 'tag' or just kicking a football around.

'My God! I'll be a father one day. Should I even become one? Will I be able to handle the responsibility, considering the mess I've made of my life?' Adi couldn't help panicking as he listened to the carefree laughter of playing children.

"You want to turn back the clock and become a kid again?"

He startled on hearing Trisha's cheerful voice. A sudden reality had hit him the second Hrian had dropped him home, post their meeting with Dr Shailesh, and he had frantically phoned Trisha, on a Thursday afternoon, insisting she should meet him immediately. Well, Trisha had been immersed in work and had requested they meet at 6 pm. Disappointed, he had phoned Gautam, but his phone had been busy. Unsure of what to do, he had gone home and had taken a few neat swings from the near empty Vodka bottle, leftover from last night. That had helped him sink into oblivion.

Fortunately, he had woken up at around 5.20 pm, had showered, changed into clean clothes, and had rushed to the waterfront where he was supposed to meet her.

"No, my love. Just enjoying their innocence," he replied, swallowing a lump in his throat, firstly for drinking in the afternoon, and secondly for being so foolish.

"So, what happened, did the meeting with Dr Shailesh go well?" Trisha enquired, snuggling up to him on the bench.

"Not really, Trish, please don't be mad when I say this, but I completely forgot about Priyansh's instructions that I couldn't log in any files till I recover some money from my defaulting cases when I agreed to meet with Dr Shailesh. But I'll find a way out, Trish. Dr Shailesh has agreed to proceed with the plan," he blurted, clasping her hands in his.

She snatched her hands away and walked up to the railing to gaze at the flowing river.

Adi watched her, unsure of what to do. In the two years that they had been romantically involved, she had been forthright whenever he had done something that had displeased her, which had been rare. Now, he had deliberately withheld Priyansh's order from her out of vanity. He hadn't wanted to disclose that his boss had lost faith in him. But the worst was, she had come up with this plan for a 'sting operation', only to save him, and now they couldn't execute it because of his ego.

"Phone Priyansh and request him to permit *Pinnacle* to log in files till we get to the bottom of this. Tell him both credit and collections will keep a close eye on *Pinnacle's* files," Trisha commanded after a while.

"But why will Surabhi and Nishant agree to cooperate when we haven't kept them in the loop," Adi protested, a tad comforted by the fact that she hadn't walked away, leaving him in the lurch.

"Priyansh will work it out with Surbhi. Ishan has already informed Nishant about our plan. They are friends, Adi, and Ishan owes Nishant for teaching him the ropes of collections. Phone Priyansh," she instructed steely.

Adi extracted his cell phone and tapped a few keys till he reached Priyansh's number. He connected the call and held the phone with trembling fingers.

"Yes."

The phone almost slipped from Adi's sweaty palms on hearing Priyansh's curt response.

"Sir, I need to talk to you, is this a good time?" Adi enquired, his heart thumping wildly.

"I'll have my secretary book you on tomorrow morning's 10 am flight to Mumbai. We'll talk during lunch," Priyansh declared, disconnecting the call.

Adi stared dumbly at the blank phone in his hand for a few seconds, before turning to Trisha to narrate Priyansh's response.

"Damn it! You should have specified you wanted to talk on the phone," Trisha responded angrily.

"He didn't give me a chance, Trish. Why does he want to meet me personally? Is he going to fire me?"

"I don't know Adi. Look, I must head back to the bank to attend a con call. Bye, take care," she stated, leaving without so much as a hug.

'God, she must be fed up with me. How did I land up in this mess?' Adi wondered, staring at the flowing river for answers to his dilemmas.

Chapter 60

A Time Bomb

'One, two, three,' Gautam nervously counted the rings, unsure whether he wanted to make the call.

"Gautam, I am angry with you. This is the first time you have phoned since you began your stint at Ahmedabad," Mani, short for Manikantan reprimanded jokingly, on connecting the call.

"I'm sorry, Mani uncle, I was a bit tied up with work here," Gautam lied, though feeling strangely comforted by the familiar voice.

"I understand beta. How have you been?"

"I'm fine uncle, how about you?"

"No complaints. So, what's up?"

Gautam bit his lip and paused. Manikantan Nair had been an officer with the Mumbai Police when Gautam's father, Amrish Mittal, was appointed DSP upon completing his IPS training. Two years later, Amrish, Mani, and a few other police officers had stormed into a building in Versova on receiving information from the Intelligence Bureau (IB), Delhi, that a terrorist unit had set up shop on the fourth floor and was planning the bombing of Chhatrapati Shivaji Terminus, formerly Victoria Terminus Station, today a UNESCO World Heritage Site in Mumbai.

The IB had been right, and a shootout had ensued. The Mumbai Police didn't have Kevlar Vests then, so the police team had barged in with only fibreglass shields. A few seconds into the attack, Amrish's shield had been kicked away, with a gun aimed at his heart. Seeing this, Mani had promptly dived, pushing Amrish aside, taking the bullet in his left femur.

Unfortunately, the disintegrating bullet had considerably damaged Mani's thigh bone. A plate had to be screwed in, ending Mani's active service in the Mumbai Police. Amrish, couldn't bear Mani leaving the service and had insisted on Mani being retained as his assistant. Soon, Mani had become indispensable to Amrish as he rose in the ranks; their bonding extending to their families, with Manikantan becoming 'Mani uncle' to Gautam.

"Er... Mani uncle, I phoned because I'm in a bit of a pickle. You see, I'm informally investigating a corruption case here, and I don't know if the suspects have got wind of it?" Gautam finally confessed.

"What do you mean by informally?" Mani questioned in his typical South Indian accent; a trait untainted by his three decades in Mumbai.

"Come on Mani uncle, you know how it is," Gautam responded.

"No, I don't son, please explain."

'Damn it,' Gautam cursed inwardly, wondering if he should disclose his predicament. Realising he may be sitting on a ticking time bomb, he started talking, revealing details of the 'Honey Trap' and their plan to record her.

"Uncle, I know I took advantage of my hacker friend, but look at the muck it has unravelled!" he exclaimed excitedly, only to conclude in a more subdued tone, "Unfortunately, I think my boss, Kamal, is suspicious, that's why, probably, he's assigned the Rahul murder case to me. God, how am I going to handle such a high-profile case? It's only a matter of time now before the reporters reveal I'm the son of Mumbai's Dy. Police Commissioner. They'll surely publish Divya's story. Uncle, I've screwed up big time."

"Son, Kamal didn't assign this case to you because he thought you have dirt on him," Mani spoke after a pause.

"Then, why?"

"Rumours of his corruption had reached the office of Gujarat's Director General of Police (DGP), around the time you were finishing your IPS training. The DGP was on the lookout for a rookie to be appointed under Kamal, as he felt that was the best way to smoke him out. Fresh recruits are generally full of passion and righteousness Given your pedigree, you were his best bet, so he had discussed the matter with your dad. While Amrish sir wasn't too happy with you being used as a pawn, he agreed when you declared you wanted to start your career as a Dy SP in any place other than Mumbai. So, Ahmedabad, Lucknow and Kolkata were presented as options. Believe me, this decision was taken at the highest level because SP Kamal Arora has political connections.

"Before you could even consider, Lucknow and Kolkata were filled up, leaving only Ahmedabad. We have been monitoring you since day one, son... I, your dad, and Gujarat's DGP. It was a deliberate leak from the DGP's office to one of Kamal's minions that the seniors were aware you were not being assigned cases that fit your rank. We never bargained for you to oversee such a sensitive case though."

Gautam reeled under the shock of Mani's revelations. He was sitting on a time bomb. Now, it was a matter of his dad's reputation; he had to handle both cases sagaciously, somehow covering up the fact that he used a hacker to access the videos, and there was only one way to do it.

"Mani uncle, thank you for confiding. I'll phone you if I'm stuck," Gautam stated.

"You take care, son, and remember, I'm always around for you," Mani assured, disconnecting the call.

Chapter 61

If a Criminal Lawyer wants to Commit Murder, He will Cover His Tracks.

In all his 28 years, Gautam had never felt claustrophobic, yet right now, he wanted to run out of the 5 x 10 feet cubicle he had been asked to wait in, screaming.

Almost 20 minutes had passed since he had disconnected Mani uncle's call and had approached one of the many security guards manning the entrance to *Gujarat Mirror's* building. Madhav had left immediately after briefing him, so he was alone, which was in a way good. Visitors wanting to meet personnel inside the newspaper's office had to be screened before they were allowed entry, so Gautam had flashed his badge and had requested for a meeting with Bipin Joshi, the aggrieved journo father demanding justice for his son.

The guard had immediately dialled a number, listened for a while and had personally escorted Gautam to the cubicle, stating that Mr Joshi was out and he would return as soon as possible So, Gautam had waited, trying to assimilate Mani uncle's disclosure and decide if he should be flattered or flabbergasted by what he had learnt. Unable to deal with his present, his mind started reminiscing about how life had been a breeze with good friends, and doting parents. That had been until his sister had disappeared.

His father had started returning home late, and his mother generally spent her days crying or in temples. So, post completing his LLB, Gautam had started spending more time in Mani uncle's office, whenever he was free of his duties at the private practice he had joined, trying to understand how the police force worked.

That was probably what motivated him to join the police force and Mani uncle had been the first person he had shared his decision to appear for the IPS exams, a month after his sister's disappearance. He had tried to dissuade Gautam, but had encouraged him when he understood his frustration, so had pushed Gautam into disclosing his decision to his father. Fortunately, Amrish had been indulgent. That had helped him deal with his mother's vehement objections.

Now, here he was, called upon to officially handle his first difficult case, and he was nervous.

As per the newspaper's policy, visitors had to hand over their cell phones before entering the premises; he had dutifully done so and hence had been unaware that Adi was trying to reach him. While waiting and trying to think about anything other than what he would say to the grieving father, he had remembered that Adi was supposed to have met Dr Shailesh by now and had hoped the meeting had been fruitful.

A man suddenly entered the tiny cubicle and was staring at him from the door he had closed behind him. Gautam stood up and extended his hand while speaking, "Er, I'm DSP Gautam Mittal from Maninagar Police Station."

"Oh, so my son's case has been assigned to a greenhorn IPS because the experienced Inspectors cannot handle it," the man snorted, occupying the second chair in the room.

The deriding tone triggered Gautam's sense of righteousness, spurring a retort, "Fresh eyes often result in a renewed perspective."

"Okay, let me answer the obvious questions. Why do I feel my son was murdered? Because his father-in-law never wanted a garage owner to marry his daughter. A month into their registered marriage, the police barged into Rahul's garage on a Sunday evening along with cameramen and reporters from local news channels. They found a packet of 'ecstasy', a drug, stashed in Rahul's cabin, behind the trophies he had won for local cricket tournaments. My son doesn't do drugs. Hell, he hasn't touched a cigarette in his life. Anyway, the matter was plastered all over the local news and his regular customers took their cars elsewhere.

"Next question, why did my son want to become a garage owner? Because he loved cars and had a flair for repairing them. Now the cliched question, what proof do I have that Mr Atul Gandhi, a successful, Ahmedabad High Court criminal lawyer would murder my son? Well, the answer is that I don't have any proof because if a criminal lawyer wants to commit murder, he will cover his tracks," Bipin declared.

"Thank you, Mr Bipin, for your insightful information. One question from my side, if Mr Atul is the murderer because he didn't want your son to marry his daughter, then why did he wait for six months after their court marriage to murder Rahul, when being a lawyer, he would have anticipated that they would have registered for a court marriage because he would have objected to the alliance right from the start?"

Chapter 62

What might have Transpired?

It was the September of 2008, and the world was still reeling from the subprime crisis that had struck the US in the previous financial year. Adi entered the then nondescript Ahmedabad airport and walked sluggishly towards the Kingfisher Airline counter. It had been the talk of the town when India's liquor baron Vijay Mallya had launched an airline in 2003, under the same brand name that had made his beer famous. Right from the start, the airline's motto had been exclusivity and luxury at a price marginally above that of other Indian air carriers.

Had Adi been travelling to Mumbai under normal circumstances, he would have sauntered down the red-carpeted check-in area of Kingfisher which set it apart from the other airlines, but he felt the opposite of elation or success that morning as he stood in line for his boarding pass.

The feeling of helplessness continued during the flight too, and the exquisite high-end food tasted like cardboard. He was relieved when the plane finally landed in Mumbai and he was en route to *TCI*'s Corporate Office in Maker Towers, Cuffe Parade.

*

The meeting with Priyansh ended in 15 minutes. Adi tried to appear cool while exiting Priyansh's cabin. He paused for a few minutes to chat with some known people and managed to curb his straightforwardness when questions got awkward. One-upmanship was rampant in the loans department, and so was gossip. The fact that he had been suspended and under investigation for fraud had been conveyed to all the personnel of the PL vertical, hence, the pointed questions regarding his Mumbai visit. Fortunately, years under Tony's tutelage had enabled him to deflect the loaded queries and he managed to exit the Corporate Office, leaving people guessing as to what might have transpired.

He was trembling though, on making it outside, and whipped out his phone to dial the one person he knew had the suaveness to guide him.

Chapter 63

Gimmick

'Be strong," Gautam mentally cautioned himself as he sat on a plush sofa in Mr Atul Gandhi's living room. It was 10 pm. He had been trying in vain to meet either Mr Atul Gandhi or his daughter for two days. Mr Gandhi had finally granted him a meeting, insisting Gautam should come to his house if he also wanted to meet his daughter, at 10 pm, as that was the only time Mr Gandhi was free.

In the meantime, Gautam's fears had come true; he had made the headlines of all the local newspapers in Ahmedabad and eight of the prominent ones were neatly arranged on the glass-topped table in Mr Atul Gandhi's living room right now.

'It probably hadn't taken Bipin, an investigative journalist more than 15 minutes to trace my family's history,' Gautam thought, totally dejected on seeing a photograph of his elder sister plastered alongside his on the front page of the *Gujarat Mirror* newspaper with Bipin Joshi's name in the tag line. The photo had been taken on her 18th birthday and had been used by the police when she had disappeared, to try to trace her.

Madhav had translated the scathing news item, an attack on the corrupt Ahmedabad Police, stating that transferring the case to Gautam was nothing but a gimmick to cover up their weaknesses. They were all 'bought' by Mr Atul Gandhi, maybe so was Gautam.

'Gimmick,' Gautam had snorted inwardly at the irony of the situation because no one at Maninagar Police station knew his history till this morning, or at least that's what he assumed because Kamal hadn't summoned him, nor had he answered Gautam's phone call that morning when Gautam had deliberately phoned him on the pretext of updating him about his meeting with Bipin. What he was waiting to see was how Kamal would treat him, now that the cat was out of the bag. Kamal not answering his call only increased Gautam's paranoia regarding Kamal's intentions of assigning this high-profile case to him.

Well, all the other staff had fawned over him this morning. Even his desk had been moved from beside the washroom to an airier location, next to a window.

A movement in the corner of his eye diverted his attention from his sister's smiling photo. Gautam turned his head and stood on seeing a tall man with silver grey hair that only added to his charisma, enter the opulent living room with a young girl and an older lady in tow.

"DSP Mittal, how gracious of you to agree to meet me at my home. I apologise for the inconvenience. The issue is that my daughter, Kamini, has been so distraught since her husband's murder, that she hasn't stepped out of the house," Mr Atul Gandhi greeted in a booming voice that matched his personality and profession.

"I can understand sir," Gautam responded, diverting his eyes from the formidable man to the pale, young girl seated on a couch in front of the one he had occupied.

"Oh, this is my wife," Atul introduced, on seeing Gautam's gaze rest on the older lady seated beside his daughter; her heavily made-up face adding to her stoic demeanour.

"So, I guess we must repeat all the answers we gave to your predecessor, right? You know I too agree with Mr Bipin that assigning you to this case is nothing but a gimmick on the part of the Ahmedabad Police. I can't understand how the DGP agreed to it. I must ask him this Sunday when we meet for golf," Atul spoke.

Gautam started at him, shocked by the casual reference to Atul knowing the very same man who had wanted him to spy on his boss. 'No wonder he's such a successful lawyer. He almost threw me off guard with his name-throwing.' Gautam brushed aside the distracting thought and addressed the widow, "I know this is a hard time for you, but did your husband start taking drugs in college or after you got married?"

His question caught her unawares. She gasped and looked at her father, giving Gautam the feeling that she had been coached to expect certain questions and the one he just asked was probably not on the list. 'Maybe it's a good thing I decided to study law and practice it for a bit before becoming a Police Officer,' Gautam couldn't help wondering inwardly as a part of his lawyer training had been to lead with the most unexpected question.

"Er, I... he di... er... I don't know," she stammered, shakily.

"There might have been some evidence like mood swings, sniffling, traces of white power on his nose or beard. What about smoking, how long has he been a smoker?" Gautam persisted.

Gautam noticed the mother close a palm over her daughter's trembling fingers and squeeze it.

"He never smoked in front of me," Kamini whispered, a sob escaping her lips.

"Look, son, we never knew he was a drug addict until his garage was raided. The thing is, like any other father of a daughter, I felt he wasn't good enough for her, so I objected initially, assuming it was just a crush, and it would fade when my daughter realised, she couldn't enjoy the comforts I have provided for her, in his house. It didn't, they got married. I tried to reconcile but my daughter was so blind in her love for him that she didn't allow me to visit her even once at her in-laws' house. It was only after he died that she returned home to grieve because her in-laws kept accusing me of getting him killed. Why would I do that to my only child?" Atul intervened; his distraught tone unnervingly convincing.

"So, there was never any issue of him not having enough money, because heroin is an expensive addiction or increased sleeping, or decreased attention to personal hygiene," Gautam rattled off some of the signs of heroin addiction he could remember.

"No, I was so busy adjusting to my new life, that I didn't notice any," she answered flatly, tears rolling down her pale cheeks.

"What about his friends? Did he spend a lot of time with them? Return home late at night? What about your friends? Did you have common friends because you both did study in the same college, right?"

"No, he always came home straight from the garage and took me out for a drive. We then ate dinner, watched TV in our room and slept. All his friends became my friends when Rahul and I fell in love in college. They are all hard-working people with jobs and families."

"Okay, but surely you have different childhood friends. Were they also friends with Rahul?"

"With due respect, DSP Mittal, Rahul's best friends already confirmed he wasn't an addict so has Kamini. I fail to understand how Kamini's childhood friends will be of any help. They are from a different stratum of society. I hope they'll take Kamini into their fold again, as she needs to put this unfortunate incident behind and move on."

While his eyes were on Atul during his courtroom-like objection to Gautam's questioning, Gautam had managed to sneak a glance at Kamini and could have sworn to have seen a flicker of hatred in her eyes when her father mentioned her childhood friends.

Chapter 64

Quid Pro Quo

The cab dropped him off in Lower Parel at the famous High Street Phoenix, formerly known as Phoenix Mall, one of the largest shopping malls in India. Adi strode inside and scoped the swanky outlets of the globally famous brands on the ground floor for *Jimmy Choo*, the brand he knew Leila favoured. He found it opposite the entrance, and sauntered casually towards it, curious to know what it was so famous for. 'Who wears such shoes?' Adi wondered staring at a silver crystal studded sandal with a 4" heel on display, costing Rs. 1.53 lakhs.

"Hey, country boy."

He turned on hearing Leila's familiar voice, hugged her and shifted slightly to glance at her feet encased in delicate black sandals "You would," he muttered, as she was wearing the same shoe that was on display beside the silver one.

"I would what?" Leila questioned, puzzled.

"Wear shoes like that," he clarified, pointing to her shoe on display.

"Yeah. I do have a pair. It costed me a month's salary. So, do you want to window shop, or shall we sit somewhere, so you can tell me about the issue you wanted to discuss with me?"

"Yeah, let's find a place to sit and talk," Adi agreed, sobering back to reality. The glam fest followed them though as they stepped on an escalator, and Adi shamelessly gawked the myriad brands and stylish public floating through the mall.

He followed Leila into the TGIF (Thank God it's Friday) restaurant and sat down across her in a corner booth. An energetic waiter was at their table in a jiffy with two menus.

"I'll have a Budweiser and a Tennessee Burger," Leila declared without glancing at the menu.

"Make mine a Kingfisher Light and whatever veg burger you have," Adi followed suit.

"Wow, beer huh! I can't believe you started drinking after going to Ahmedabad," Leila responded when the waiter was out of the earshot.

"Yeah, I kinda got roped into drinking."

"By whom, Tony?"

"No, it's a long story."

"Well, this restaurant is open till 1 am, so we've got five hours, would that be enough?" Leila quipped. Her impish grin faded on seeing the grave look on Adi's face.

The waiter arrived with their beers. Adi took a long drink before launching onto the Sidanshu saga. The food arrived just as he reached his first, wild, alcohol-infused party.

"Hmm, so the mighty Sidanshu managed to finally corrupt you, huh," Leila commented sardonically after the waiter served them.

"Come on Leila, I didn't get corrupted," he started to protest, only to have her cut him off, "but you clearly are in trouble."

"Yeah, I am," he sighed, revealing the rest of the mess.

"Wow, even I didn't see that coming. No one could have, so why are you in trouble?"

"Because they feel I was taking a cut from Sidanshu for pushing bad cases. The issue is I took a lot of loans for my house, car, and personal expenses, so HR sees me as a vulnerable person, living beyond my means, hence an easy prey for people like Sidanshu to use for fraud," Adi confessed, filling her in on the meeting with HR, Tony and Sidanshu 28 days ago and how he hadn't made any leeway regarding clearing his name or recovering the money.

"How come you are in Mumbai today?" she finally poised the question Adi had been dreading all evening.

"Priyansh called me for a meeting," he replied, looking at her squarely in the eye

"Why?" she enquired, her eyes narrowing suspiciously.

"Quid pro quo. You to drop the attempted rape charges against him and he will use whatever I've unearthed against Sidanshu to convince HR I had no knowledge of what Sidanshu was up to."

Chapter 65

Just Lucky

"May I come in, Sir?" Gautam questioned, opening the frosted glass door to Kamal's cabin.

"Yes, Gautam, please have a seat," Kamal instructed, raising to shake his hand.

Gautam managed to maintain an impassive look on his face while returning the gesture, a first, in the seven months he had been reporting to Kamal.

"So, do you have anything new to add to Madhav's investigation of Rahul's case?" Kamal got straight to the point.

"No sir. We don't have a single witness willing to testify that Rahul was a drug addict or that he displayed any signs of heroin addiction. Sir, it is very hard to hide heroin addiction...," Gautam tried to plead his case only to be cut short, "I didn't summon you for a lecture on heroin addiction. You are a ranked officer. Your duty is to assign cases to your subordinates and oversee them, not investigate on your own. Do you have the status of the other cases you have assigned?"

"Yes, sir," Gautam confirmed, rattling the progress from memory, and thanking his stars he had the presence of mind to take regular updates, despite the complicated case he was personally handling, not to mention the unofficial one.

"Good. Now, I want you to instruct Madhav to record a formal statement from the two employees of Rahul who said he used to scream at them for the slightest mistake," Kamal instructed, meeting Gautam's eyes.

"But, sir, they were only two, amongst five who said he was an ideal employer," Gautam deliberately protested.

"That's because the other three were bribed by Rahul's father."

It took a superhuman effort to quench the scoff that almost escaped Gautam's lips on hearing Kamal's bizarre conclusion. A chilling thought struck him, 'This man is definitely in cahoots with Atul. They are so confident of their power that they don't care for my pedigree or the fact that my father can invoke an investigation from the Home Ministry. No, I'm not going to go running to Daddy. I'm going to find a way around this.'

"Sir, with due respect to your experience, please give me some time to gather concrete evidence that Rahul was a heroin addict and he overdosed," Gautam requested humbly.

"Sure, you have two weeks to close this as an overdose," Kamal declared, dismissing him.

Ignoring the urge to retrieve his phone and make the call to the one person who could expedite the connection between Kamal and Atul, Gautam calmly sat down at his desk and proceeded to call each of his subordinates for an update on the cases they were investigating.

He left the police station after two hours and took a longer route to the *Gujarat Mirror* office, deliberately making several random stops to check if he was being followed. He parked his bike a kilometre away from the newspaper's building and walked towards it, constantly checking for shadows, and made the phone call only when he was in the building's parking.

"Yes, DSP Gautam, what can I do for you?" Bipin answered on the first ring.

"Sir, I'm in your parking. I need to discuss something very important with you," Gautam replied.

"Okay, let me instruct the security guard to make a special pass for you. We'll talk in my office," Bipin stated disconnecting the call.

*

Pain for an aggrieved father gripped Gautam's heart on entering Bipin's spacious cabin, awash with natural light. Drawing strength from the man behind the desk who looked haggard yet determined, Gautam greeted him and sat on a plastic chair placed at his desk.

"Sir, I got a very brief opportunity to speak with your daughter-in-law last night in her father's house, in the presence of both her parents. She was very distraught, and petrified, yet she confirmed your son was an ideal husband and never showed any signs of heroin addiction. I also spoke with his college friends and his employees. Barring two new employees, not a single friend or employee confirmed having spotted any signs of heroin addiction. What I can't understand is if Atul murdered Rahul, then why with a heroin overdose when at least some evidence of Rahul being an addict is required?

"Then comes the matter of Kamini's personal friends, you know the ones she hung out with before falling in love with Rahul. Atul didn't allow Kamini to give me any details about them. Atul just dismissed it as unnecessary. Do you know anything about her friends? Did any visit her at your home?"

"Yes, a girl Davina did. She often arrived in her red Mercedes to take Kamini out to lunch. Kamini went on a few occasions, but my wife overheard her objecting once, saying she could no longer afford buffet lunches at the Grand Bhagvati. Davina didn't accept it and insisted she would pay, so my wife called Kamini to the kitchen under the pretext of discussing something with her, gave her Rs 500, and asked her if it was enough. Kamini broke down and refused, saying she didn't want to eat lunch with her friends, and that she was happy eating with her mother-in-law, but my wife urged her to take the money and go.

"Well, Kamini started taking tuitions after that, to pay for her jaunts with her other friends, because they apparently ate the buffet lunch every month, I think on the last day," Bipin disclosed.

"Hmm, can you describe Davina?"

"Er, she's very thin, has blonde hair with brown streaks and wears very short dresses."

"Okay. One more thing, since you are an investigative journalist, I'm sure you are aware of the drug dealers who operate in Ahmedabad and have questioned them on several occasions. Now remembering the fact that we are dealing with one of the leading criminal lawyers of Ahmedabad, what if those two new employees who spoke against your son were planted by him just to make them the 'usual suspects', you know the ones who would be investigated, while the actual fatal drug was procured by a seemingly loyal employee who went rogue? Can you investigate Rahul's older employees as well as the friends he used to meet regularly? I also want you to probe into your daughter-in-law's acquaintances and buddies," Gautam requested.

"I most certainly can," Bipin confirmed.

"Just one more thing, sir. What would an investigative journalist do if he suspects a senior police officer of taking bribes to ensure FIRs are not filed for suicides, murders, and other fraud?" Gautam voiced the question which was the actual purpose of his visit today.

Bipin raised his head to meet Gautam's eyes. He held them for a while before replying, "Just as the police force has informers, so do we journalists. Give me names if you can, and if you can't, I know who to investigate, so, correct me if I'm wrong."

"Please proceed with a discrete investigation, sir," Gautam replied, rising from his seat.

"Er, I need you to also investigate one more thing for a friend. There is this building Lalitha Towers near Gita Mandir bus stand where some people may be running a fake identity scam. Can you explore that too and update me before publishing it? If my informant is right, I'd like to make a few arrests first with you, the only journalist on the scene when I do," Gautam requested from the doorway, hoping it would appear as an afterthought.

Bipin was too smart for him though, and his eyes narrowed as he remarked shrewdly, "I will explore your tip. Looks like you have stumbled upon a lot of underhand businesses in Ahmedabad in less than a year than most police personnel who have spent a lifetime in this city. Is it that you're just lucky or have a nose for sniffing out such things?"

"Just lucky," Gautam quipped, leaving the room.

Chapter 66

A Convenient Label

The most distinctive feature amongst all her other physical attributes were Leila's almond-shaped eyes, emphasised by her high cheekbones and heart-shaped face. They were almost always skilfully made-up to highlight her light brown irises. She could seduce, cajole, or melt anyone with her beautiful eyes

Right now, in the trendy interiors of the TGIF restaurant, they were blazing scorn as she listened to Adi unravel Priyansh's cowardly scheme. Adi concluded his monologue and waited, his eyes never leaving her face. She too held his gaze, for a while, then drained her beer, stood up and snapped, "Do as he says, I don't care. I'm going for a smoke."

Adi followed suit, flinging a few five- hundred- rupee notes on the table. "Damn it, Leila, just because I told you what he said, that doesn't mean I'm going to paint you as a slut," he objected angrily when they reached the main road outside the swanky shopping centre.

"A slut! What a convenient label to soothe a man's ego in the wake of a rejection. How did he know about us anyway? Did you suggest this outrageous ploy just to save your job?"

"Look I know you are hurt and probably feeling disgusted right now, so you want to download it to me. Do it, I can take it, but I swear, I never told Priyansh about our brief fling. Is that what you think of me?"

"You're a man, Adi. You don't have to put up with the demeaning we women have to, just to work and make something of ourselves in a man's world. If we look good, men hit on us. If we don't meet the conventional standards of attractiveness, we are ignored or dismissed. Men don't see us for our abilities, our capabilities.

"Yeah, I check all the boxes of a 'good-looking' woman's list; I'm slim, fair, and I wear trendy clothes, shoes, and accessories. I also smoke, drink, and enjoy sex like a man. What does that make me in the male-dominated world of sales? An easy lay, someone who should be available to a man who has the 'hots' for her, even if she doesn't want him or doesn't desire him?

"That's what's been happening with Priyansh. He's my boss, he recruited me. I don't want to sleep with him. I want him to acknowledge that I am good at sales just like any other sales manager in his team. But no! He must make a pass at me!"

She paused and lit another cigarette. "It happened in the very first week I joined. It was around noon, and I was supposed to meet the HR Head of *PR Traders* to work out a special rate of interest for Personal Loans for their 100-odd employees. One of my Sales Managers was with me. We had decided to have a quick smoke before a nearly two-hour taxi ride from Cuffe Parade to Andheri East. Priyansh walked out of the building just as we lit up and extracted a cigarette. Naturally, my sales manager flicked his lighter to light Priyansh's cigarette, but boss man brushed it aside, plucked my cigarette from my mouth, and took a puff from it before using it to light his own cigarette.

"His eyes never left my face the entire time. My skin crawled; I felt like flinging my cigarette to the ground and lighting another. I should have done that because Adi, he licked his lips when I took a puff from what was left of my 'tainted' cigarette. God, I just stubbed out my cigarette.

"My SM had watched the whole thing. Thankfully he didn't utter a word and continued to treat me with respect. I did my best to avoid Priyansh after that incident, but he would keep coming to my workstation and would stand very close to me or call me to his and insist I check something on his screen without turning it towards me, so I used to be forced to lean over his shoulder.

"Anyway, the worst was that Germany trip six months ago. Adi, I shouldn't have been on that trip, I was two crores short of the qualifying target," she confided, pausing to light another cigarette.

"Oh, my god! You mean he manipulated things so you could go?" Adi gasped.

"Yeah."

"So, what happened there if I may ask? No, you don't have to answer if it's too painful."

"Didn't you notice, because Tony surely did?" Leila surprised him with a counter-question.

"Leila, I apologise. I was too excited to notice anything," Adi confessed sheepishly.

"Since ours was a corporate booking, the bank probably checked us in before we boarded, so I was allotted seat 1A and Priyansh 1B on the two-seater aisle. He didn't even wait for the plane to take off before leaning against me on the pretext of peering into my in-flight entertainment console. Drinks were eventually served, and he kept insisting I drink scotch instead of wine. A couple of pegs under his belt, he tried to grab my hand. I wrestled it out of his grip and stood up. Tony, who was exiting the washroom diagonally opposite our seat saw it. He looked at me and thankfully understood my pained look, so he suavely asked me to occupy his seat 27F, claiming he wanted to discuss something with Priyansh.

"I grabbed my hand baggage and ran to Tony's seat. He returned after a while to request a Delhi SM who was sitting beside him to occupy my seat and he settled down beside me. Priyansh had passed out from way too many pegs, and Tony asked me how long Priyansh had been harassing me. I told him everything and he assured me he would look out for me during the trip.

"Anyway, Priyansh came to our seat just after we landed in Munich and sneered, 'It's fine if you're currently shagging Tony, I'll wait my turn.'

"Things didn't end there. On our very first night in Germany, during the party the hotel had arranged for us, Priyansh followed me into the ladies' loo, forced me into a cubicle, locked the door and started pawing me. Fortunately, I was wearing my 4" Louboutin that night, so I managed to slip one out and jab the heal into his temple. That took him by surprise, and he let go of me. I ran out of the loo and searched for Tony, only to find him dancing with some lady, so I approached you, dancing with some guys and joined you, requesting you to keep Priyansh away from me," Leila narrated.

"Yeah, I remember that part. Also, how he tried to grab you on the dance floor and Tony came between you," Adi confirmed.

"Tony did his best to make sure I was never alone during the rest of the trip," she clarified.

"Gosh, Leila, I am so sorry it didn't register in my dumb brain that if you, a lady who can generally take care of herself is asking for help, then it must be something serious."

"That's okay, country boy. So, what are you going to do about Priyansh's escape scheme of you telling HR that I am a tease who played with you too?"

Adi felt his heart constrict in his chest on seeing her feeble smile and hearing her teasing tone. "You are simply amazing Leila to have complained to HR, despite knowing that people like Priyansh have enough clout to ruin you. I know you won't stop at that. I know you will create a stink if either Priyansh or HR takes any action against you.

"Unfortunately, while I would love to get Priyansh also implicated in my current predicament, I know I cannot do that. However, I will certainly never demean you. Regarding Priyansh's current backup, Bharat, I'm sure he's calling my bluff as he knows we are rivals. Even if Priyansh's serious, if I tell Tony about Priyansh's offer, he will fire Bharat before allowing him to taint you," Adi replied.

"Don't be too sure Adi, Priyansh has too many sales guys who will be more than willing to support him for their career advancement. But I don't care. You know my pedigree, right? I'll quit, join my dad's company, and then hire the best lawyers in India to ruin Priyansh. My family will support me in my endeavour. Unfortunately, you or any other Sales Manager who dares to stand up against me will be dragged into this," Leila pointed out.

Chapter 67

Nonchalant Revelation

Nostalgia for his carefree life as a newly appointed lawyer in Mumbai hit Gautam, the second he entered the restaurant in *The Grand Bhagvati* Hotel that was supposed to serve the most lavish buffet the city had to offer. He unwittingly compared the room to the one in *The Taj Mahal Hotel*, just opposite the Gateway of India, which had an airier interior and looked out to the majestic Arabian Sea. He and his friends, especially Pratyush, had often dined at the Taj, especially during FIFA or cricket World Cup matches, because the Taj had a massive television screen which telecasted the live matches.

Remembering the purpose of his current visit to the hotel in Ahmedabad, Gautam took a seat at a corner table from which he could observe both the entrance to the restaurant as well as all the guests seated in the big room. A waiter approached him to enquire, "Shall I bring you some soup and starters, sir?"

"Yes, which soup are you serving?"

"Chicken Man chow and veg clear soup, sir."

"I'll have the chicken."

"Shall I make all your starters non-veg too, sir?"

"Get me a mix."

"Very good, sir," the waiter replied, walking away.

Relieved he could continue sitting for a while, Gautam checked the time on his cell phone. It was only 1.15 pm, on the 31st of August 2008, exactly 25 days after Rahul had been murdered. Nothing had turned up in the investigations of Rahul's employees, including the ones who had spoken against him so, Gautam's only hope was Kamini's friends, and that too was just a hunch.

He had tried to phone Kamini on several occasions, but her mum had always answered the call and had curtly informed him that her husband had insisted Kamini didn't have to talk with Gautam. He had tried very hard, to find out about Kamini's friends from Rahul's friends, but as Atul had pointed out, they belonged to different societal strata and hence, didn't mingle. So, eating the buffet lunch at the Grand Bhagvati on the last day of the month had been his last resort, with the hope of running into Davina, if she continued with their ritual.

Well, here he was, surveying the 50-odd people stuffing themselves with food in the most expensive restaurant in Ahmedabad. There was only one group of youngsters, but none of the girls matched Davina's description, although two of them were reed thin. Wondering if he was on a wild goose chase as Davina could have easily changed her hair, Gautam diverted his eyes to the entrance while the waiter placed a bowl of soup and an assortment of starters in front of him.

Absentmindedly chewing on a breadstick, Gautam extracted his phone and opened the email from Raul stating that the tyre threads found on the crime scene were of a 120/80 R17 61P size, generally used in a sports motorbike, especially a Suzuki Hayabusa.

It was almost 2 pm when he finally ate the last of the starters. The waiter who had served him earlier approached his table and suggested politely, "Why don't you check out our buffet sir?"

"Er, are you serving any fish?"

"Yes sir. There's Goan Fish Curry, fish fry and chilli fish."

"Please can you get me a plate of plain rice, fish curry and some green salad?" Gautam requested, wondering if he should eat fish in a land-locked city.

"Most certainly sir."

The waiter left his table just as a group of twenty-somethings entered the restaurant. Trailing them, engrossed in her cell phone was a tall blonde girl with brown streaks, wearing a beige micro-mini dress. Gautam's heartbeats accelerated as the group was ushered to the corner diagonally opposite his, where a waiter was joining two tables for them.

Diverting his gaze from the girl he was sure was Davina, Gautam glanced at the rest. There were two more girls who appeared to be thinner than Davina, and four boys, all donning leather jackets over chest-printed black T-shirts and blue jeans.

The moment Gautam had been waiting for had finally arrived, but he was clueless as to how he would approach Davina. Thanking the waiter for bringing his desired food to his table, Gautam placed a spoonful of the rice and curry in his mouth, only to regret his choice; the curry almost tasted bitter due to over spicing. Realising he had to make a ploy of eating, he reached out for a cucumber, as he watched Davina rise from her seat beside to inspect the buffet.

Half an hour passed with the boys in Davina's group heartily indulging in the non-veg fair and the girls picking at their food. Davina's phone suddenly rang, and she walked out of the restaurant to answer it. Gautam too, stood from his table, placed 8 Rs 100 notes below a dish to cover the buffet cost which was Rs 750 plus a tip and followed her out.

Heaving a sigh of relief on finding her seated on a couch in the lobby, he hovered nearby till she ended her call, and sat down beside her before she could get up.

"Miss Davina, I'm DSP Gautam Mittal from the Ahmedabad Police Force. Please may I take a few minutes of your time?"

"Wow, I didn't know Indian detectives could be as sexy as the ones in Hollywood movies. Sure, inspector, you may take as much time of mine as you want, but not now. I should have probably approached you first as I think I know who could have killed Rahul. So does poor Kamini, but I'm sure her dad isn't allowing her to talk to you. I've been her bestie since kindergarten, but I too am not allowed to go anywhere near her now when she needs me the most.

"9099213094. Phone me this evening, after 6 and I'll give you my home address. We'll talk there, as my folks won't be at home. Dad will be at work, and Mum will be at the parlour, getting spruced up for a dinner party she's throwing for Dad's business associates at our farmhouse.

"Oh, our housekeeper will be home, but I'll tell her you are one of my friends' older brothers, who has come home to talk to me about him, so please don't introduce yourself as a policeman to her. One more thing, please call me Diva like all my friends do. Miss Davina sounds so old," Davina conveyed all of it in one breath before abandoning the couch to walk back towards the restaurant.

Stunned by her nonchalant revelation, Gautam glanced down at his cell phone in his hand, grateful to have reflexively punched in the numbers Davina had rattled out. Shaking his head at the bizarreness of the conversation he just had with the lady he had been waiting to interact with, he walked out of the hotel and entered the parking where he had deposited his Enfield Bullet.

Something made him scan the rest of the bikes parked in the lot and his heart beats accelerated again on spotting a Hayabusa. Trusting his gut once again, he continued to wait at the parking. Two of the boys of Davina's group walked towards the Hayabusa after 45 minutes and Gautam was able to click a clear photo of the boy mounting the bike before racing it out of the parking.

Chapter 68

Practical Logic

Tony Braganza personified the phrase 'good upbringing'. He often fondly remembered his mum telling him he was quite a mischievous child, always playing pranks on others. Also, he was highly competitive, a strange trait, because both parents were the 'happy-go-lucky' kind. Having been born and raised in Bangalore, at a time when BMX bikes were a big thing in metro cities, his father had gifted him the cool bike for his 10th birthday.

It had only been a matter of time when he had discovered BMX racing and had started participating in local races. Being taller and sturdier than most of the kids of his age, he had clinched almost all the local races and had entered a district-level one upon turning 15. His father had accompanied him.

It had been a tough race for Tony and there was only one rider in front of him as they neared the end. Determined to win, Tony had peddled hard and had tried to make it look like an accident when he had nudged his cycle against the leading rider, resulting in him losing his balance. Tony had been the first to reach the finish line but had been disqualified for foul play.

His dad had rushed to the finish line and had suggested, "Hey, kiddo, how about we go to Whimpy's for burgers."

"What? Aren't you ashamed of me?" Tony had enquired in a wobbly tone, as he fought to control the tears of humiliation.

"I will be if you don't apologise to that guy before we leave," his dad had responded.

Tony had swallowed his shame and had done it.

Later in the restaurant, his dad had given him a very valuable piece of advice, "Son, don't ever try to achieve anything in life by intentionally harming anyone. It's not worth it."

Tony couldn't help recalling that advice and the entire episode that night, as he started at Adi who had just concluded his verbatim account of his meetings with Priyansh and Leila.

Unmindful of the fact that his flight from Mumbai had landed at Ahmedabad airport at 11.30 pm, Adi had rushed to Tony's house as he had been at his wit's end regarding his next course of action. Tony, fortunately, had answered the door and had patiently listened to everything Adi had to tell him, including details of Leila's family.

Firmly curbing his seething anger at Priyansh's insinuations that he would 'throw Adi under the bus', as well as the callousness of Priyansh's ploy, Tony stated calmly, "Screw Priyansh. you tell Hrian to proceed with the plan. I will phone Sidanshu tomorrow and give him some 'cock and bull' story about how the bank was just experimenting with a crazy idea of not logging in any files sourced by DSAs."

"Thanks, boss, I knew I could count on you," Adi responded, fighting back tears of relief, only to remember, "but we have a problem. Dr Shailesh wants it in writing that ...."

"You idiot! I heard you the first time. How could you have committed to something so stupid? Ask Hrian to set up a meeting with me and this doc ASAP, I'll explain things to him. Also, I want to meet this detective you are so gaga about. I mean what are we going to do with a recording other than use it as proof to blacklist Sidanshu? Adi, you disclosed all of this to Priyansh. What's the guarantee he won't convince the seniors both you and I knew about this 'Honey Trap', and we covered it up because Sidanshu was paying us to do so?" Tony interrupted with his usual practical logic that made his subordinates worship him.

Chapter 69

The Two Alpha Males

"The number you have dialled is currently busy...."

Adi disconnected the call before the recorded message could be completed and flung his cell phone on his bed in frustration.

Two days had passed since his desperate nocturnal visit to Tony's house. While Hrian had arranged for a visit with Tony and Dr Shailesh the very next day, and Tony had convinced Dr Shailesh to proceed with the plan, Adi had been unable to reach Gautam, despite dialling his number at least 10 times daily. The pressure was killing him especially because Priyansh was also constantly phoning him, probably to find out what he planned to do about Leila, but he hadn't been answering Priyansh's calls.

Realising he had to take matters in hand, Adi started updating his resume, intending to upload it on some of India's best job portals. He was about to enter the achievements' part when his cell phone chimed. On seeing Gautam's name flash on the screen, he grabbed his phone and connected the call, admonishing, "I know you are Mumbai's Joint Police Commissioner's son, currently handling a high-profile case in Ahmedabad, and you have made it to the front page of all the newspapers in Mumbai and Ahmedabad, but that's not an excuse to ignore my calls."

"Adi, I'm sorry, it wasn't intentional. Look, I have found a way to clear your name at least partially, but I need your help for that," Gautam tried to clarify.

"G, before you ask me to do anything, you must meet Tony. Things have worsened since we last spoke at my house, and now Tony seems to be the only person who can help me get out of the grave I've dug for myself," Adi pleaded, feeling like an incompetent fool.

"Set up a meeting tonight at your place, I'll bring the beer. Tony does drink beer, doesn't he?" Gautam enquired.

"Ya, I suppose he does, or he can bring his alcohol, I don't care. I'll set it up," Adi confirmed, dejectedly.

"Oh, please invite that DSA guy who offered to ask his doctor friend to support us in trapping that blackmailing girl. I need his help," Gautam casually mentioned, before hanging up.

Adi could only stare unbelievingly at his blank cell phone for a few seconds before dialling Tony's number to convey the message, followed by Hrian. He then texted Trisha to request her not to come over after work that night and honestly stated the reason. She had been so understanding when he had revealed all the details of his meetings in Mumbai and his subsequent visit to Tony's house straight from the airport. She had even gone to the extent of surprising him by suggesting that maybe they should just leave the banking industry behind and become farmers in UP. He had been tempted to do so but had earmarked her suggestion as Plan B, in case he couldn't find a better one with Gautam and Tony's help.

*

As expected, Hrian arrived first with a bottle of Black Label whiskey, twenty-four cans of Budweiser, and an assortment of snacks. Tony was next with yet another bottle of Black Label. Gautam rang the bell an hour later and handed

Adi a backpack filled with 24 cans of Corona beer as he walked straight from the door to the balcony while talking on the phone. Unsure of what to do, Adi laid out the alcohol, glasses, and ice alongside his contribution of soda, and an assortment of non-veg and veg starters on his coffee table. He had also ordered a lot of dinner which was in cartons in the kitchen, ready to be warmed in case anyone wanted to eat.

"Do you drink beer, Hrian, 'cus you're so thin," Tony remarked, opening a whiskey bottle, and pouring four fingers into one of the glasses. He added some ice to it, raised his glass at them and took a sip.

"I do, sir. I guess, I'm lucky not to put on weight," Hrian replied modestly.

Gautam returned to the living room, and walked straight up to Tony, extending his arm, "Hey, Tony, great to meet you."

"The pleasure is all mine. Adi told me you're an IPS officer," Tony responded, rising from his chair to shake Gautam's hand.

"Yeah. It's a tough role to live up to. Hey, why aren't you guys drinking?" Gautam replied to Tony before addressing the others.

"Er, we were waiting for you," Adi stated, picking up a Corona.

"Sorry, man. Hrian, what will it be?" Gautam answered, turning his attention to Hrian.

"I'll also start with a beer," Hrian replied.

"Great, so Adi, I have confirmation that a fake identity racket is going on in an office in Lalitha Towers in Narangpura. We need to bust this racket and provide proof to the bank so that the blame for most of Adi's fake identity cases will go to the third-party verification agencies for not having done the due diligence they are being paid for. Unfortunately, my source told me the people engaged in this fraud will entertain only cases recommended by trusted sources. That's where you come in, Hrian.

"You are a well-known DSA in Ahmedabad. Do you think any sales executive of yours will be able to help? One of my sub-inspectors is willing to be a decoy, but I need your guy to approach them to avoid suspicion," Gautam got straight to the point. It was Bipin who had confirmed the fake document business. An easy task for him. All he had to do was contact an informant, a former gold smuggler, who had been a mule himself, using fake passports made at the same office.

"Sure, sir, I'll give you my most trusted executive. He knows some of the guys who are involved in all this," Hrian confirmed.

"That's great Gautam, but how will this or even the video evidence of the 'honey trap' clear Adi's name? I don't suppose he has told you about his trip to Mumbai on Monday. Things have certainly become murkier for him," Tony voiced his doubts.

"Adi, sorry once again man, I haven't been able to answer your calls. Tell me about the new development," Gautam urged.

Adi glanced away from the two alpha males in the room, Tony, and Gautam, each trying in their own way to get him out of this quagmire that seemed to be sucking him deeper and deeper into it. He diverted his gaze to Hrian, who had turned into a loyal associate and felt ashamed about what he was going to reveal.

Gautam's eyes kept darting between Adi, Hrian and Tony as Adi narrated his sordid tale. He could have sworn to have seen contempt briefly flicker in Hrian's eyes, but he let it slide as a thought suddenly struck him. He waited for Adi to finish talking before speaking, "In the wake of what Adi just disclosed and with due respect to your concern about how evidence of the honey trap will clear Adi's name, if we logically examine the string of events, starting right from the parties Sidanshu threw for you guys and Priyansh, Sidanshu may have incriminating evidence implicating all three of you, not just Adi.

"Just in case Priyansh is in cahoots with Sidanshu, then one way in which we can try to clear Adi's name is to request Dr Dhiraj to approach other doctors in the list and get them to confide if they were also trapped by Priya. Tony, I think you will be the right person to approach Dr Dhiraj with this request as you are Adi's boss and I have already lied to Dr Dhiraj that an FIR has been issued against Sidanshu. You can say you are conducting an independent investigation to check if Adi is involved. Since Dr Dhiraj is a bit disgruntled with Adi, maybe he will cooperate with you?"

Adi didn't know whether to feel worried or hopeful at Gautam's suggestion. He glanced at Tony who hadn't bothered to hide his scepticism as he continued to stare at Gautam. "Yeah, you're right DSP Gautam, we're all in deep trouble. I'll do it, let's see where it goes," Tony finally spoke.

"One more thing, try to get Dr Dhiraj Mehta to find out the influential people Dr Piyush Patel socialises with or is in touch with, especially if Mr Atul Gandhi is one of them," Gautam requested.

"Why? What does that have to do with our case?" Tony's eyes narrowed.

"Please do it as a personal favour for me," Gautam replied, smiling.

Chapter 70

It takes a Crook...

Bipin unscrewed the cap of the Digene syrup bottle and took a quick gulp, followed by three gulps of water. He waited for a few minutes and then reached out for the half-eaten vada pav on the left side of his desk. Vada pav was his comfort food, something he turned to whenever he was stressed, which was quite a lot lately since he was investigating his own son's death. Biting off a piece, he chewed absentmindedly while his eyes flickered over the five neat bunches of papers on his desk. Each had a photograph of the employees who had worked for Rahul, including the three who had given him pristine character certificates.

Five of Bipin's most trusted reporters had been assigned to investigate them a month ago, and they had compiled their findings into neat, systematic reports. All of them lived in lower middle-class areas and had only one bank account with the State Bank of India, India's largest public sector bank. Rahul had opened these accounts to deposit their salaries, and the Branch Manager of the Paldi branch had been very cooperative when Bipin had requested for their past six months' bank statements to check for any unusual transactions. Nothing turned up in them, obviously because an astute person like Atul would have given them cash.

Each of the reporters had questioned their neighbours too, to dig up some dirt. They had also assigned interns to follow the five, after getting the interns to sign official 'non-disclosure agreements', so they wouldn't, even out of fear, talk about what they were doing with anyone. The cumulative hard work had paid off and they were able to narrow down their suspicions to two employees, one with a weakness for *Teen Patti* a gambling card game and the other who had mounting medical bills because his father suffered from renal failure. The gambler should have been the obvious choice, but Bipin felt it was too easy. So, he sat there, munching on the remains of his vada pav and tried to think like a criminal lawyer who wanted to stage the perfect murder.

Five minutes later, Bipin washed down the last of the unhealthy, fast-food snack with a round of Digene and water, plucked the photographs from the sheaves of paper, and exited his office, locking the door behind him. He climbed into his weather-beaten red colour Maruti-800, adjusted the seat to accommodate his wide girth and started the car. It was time for him to personally do some legwork and what better place to start than Ahmedabad's underbellies? Like policemen and lawyers, investigative journalists also cultivated informants. None of them could be trusted though as they would switch their loyalties to whoever paid them the most money.

It took Bipin fifteen minutes to reach Bhadra, an area in the walled city of Ahmedabad which still had the remains of the old Bhadra fort. Fortunately, he found an empty parking spot beside the famous Bhadrakali Temple and started walking towards the old fort. He turned right into a narrow lane just before the fort and kept walking down a street flanked by almost identical, old, wooden houses till he reached a fractionally better-looking one. Cursing his weight which made the climb up the narrow wooden stairs laborious, Bipin made it up to the first floor. The entrance door was wide open, and Bipin immediately spotted Sombhai, the man he came to meet, seated casually on a couch, in conversation with some men occupying chairs in front of him.

"Bipinbhai, I knew you would come to meet me. I am so sorry to hear about your son. Tell me, how can I help you,"

Sombhai spoke in chaste Gujarati, as he stood up and reached out to embrace Bipin.

"Thank you," Bipin responded, clearing his throat to control the sudden surge of emotion.

The other men, who had also jumped to their feet helped Sombhai lead Bipin to the couch. Someone pressed a glass of cold water in his hand. Bipin drained the glass and then reached into his cloth satchel. Extracting three bundles of photographs, Bipin addressed Sombhai, "These 5 used to work for Rahul, these 3 are Rahul's friends, and the other 4 photos are my daughter-in-law's childhood friends who didn't go to the same college as her, so they were not so friendly with Rahul. My son wasn't a drug addict. Someone overdosed him. Can you find out if any of these 12 people purchased heroin from a drug dealer?"

It was Davina who had given the 4 photos of Kamini's rich friends to Gautam. They were all children of Ahmedabad's most affluent citizens. Gautam was particularly suspicious of Karan Malhotra, a lawyer, and the son of Atul Gandhi's partner, Mr Ramesh Malhotra, a well-known corporate lawyer in Ahmedabad, who handled high-level mergers, acquisitions, and other legal matters for Corporate Houses in Gujarat. According to Davina, Karan was obsessively in love with Kamini, and had gotten totally drunk the day she had married Rahul.

"Most certainly, sir. Please have some tea or something cold to drink. It's been a long time since you have graced my humble home," Sombhai requested.

"I'll drink tea with you after we've caught my son's killer," Bipin confirmed, rising from the couch. He couldn't help chuckling at the irony of the situation while descending the steep steps. Sombhai was one of the senior members of a gang that supplied drugs in Gujarat and his humble home which looked like any lower middle-class house was a Den', the focal point of most of the drug dealing in Ahmedabad. Illegal gambling took place on one half of the second floor, while the other half was used as a brothel. Many local politicians, reporters and police personnel were aware of the activities. The police had also often tried to raid his 'Den' at night, but due to the proximity of the houses on this lane, there were corridors connecting one house to another, so escape was easy, and they hadn't been able to find any evidence of illegal activities.

So, they did the next best thing. They cultivated Sombhai. The politicians used him to mobilize votes, while the reporters and police turned a blind eye in exchange for information. As the saying goes, at times, it does take a crook to catch one.

Chapter 71

Needle in a Haystack

"I need your help, Bipin," Gautam spoke the second the call connected, and he heard Bipin's curt greeting.

"Okay, you want to meet somewhere outside or come to my office?" Bipin responded.

"Your office."

"Fine, I'll intimate the security guard."

Twenty minutes later, Gautam was seated across Bipin, staring back at the senior journalist, wondering how to poise his question. Deciding to take the bull by his horns, he started apologetically, "I know it's wrong on my part to ask this of you under the current circumstances, but would *Gujarat Mirror* by any chance have records of suicides/deaths in the past year that were not investigated by the police?"

"Why?"

"It could be that the police were bribed into not investigating the case."

"According to a report published in a leading national newspaper on the 31st of March 2009, there were around 50 suicides from Jan to March 2009 alone, while in 2008, there were 39 suicides in the same period. This was as per the data provided by the city police commissioner's office to that newspaper," Bipin's eyes narrowed while rattling out the statistics.

"Meaning the figure of the un-reported suicides could be much more. What about unsolved murder cases? Would you have any such records?"

"Why?"

"I have a hunch on something, and I assure you of exclusivity if it works out."

"In that case, let me disclose something unofficially. Like any other news agency, we have a team whose job is to monitor 100/108 calls and dispatch our reporters to the scene. Apart from that, we have cultivated insiders in every municipality ward where death certificates are filed. We do investigate unnatural deaths, make a detailed report, and publish them immaterial of whether the police have filed FIRs or not. I'll arrange for you to go through our archives if you want but trust me it's akin to searching for a needle in a haystack. The victim's relatives won't talk especially if they've paid money to bury the case," Bipin reasoned.

"Would you also have records regarding the clinic or doctor these bodies were taken to for a death certificate?" Gautam enquired, unfazed by Bipin's discouragement.

"Yeah, we do. I'll take you to our archive room, but make sure you keep your word on the exclusivity part," Bipin declared.

"Done," Gautam conceded, rising from his chair.

He followed Bipin through the massive hall outside his cabin, filled with employees glued either to their desktop computers or files. Bipin paused beside two elevators and pressed a button. They entered the one that opened on their floor and descended five floors to what looked like a basement. Gautam held the doors open and waited for Bipin to step out first into a long dimly lit corridor. He strode alongside Bipin to an open door with a security guard outside.

They entered a room with a desk on the left, manned by a middle-aged lady reading what looked like a religious book. Gautam glanced around the massive room which appeared to cover the entire basement of the building, because only the part being dusted by a peon was lit up, the rest of it was in shadows.

Bipin quickly introduced Gautam to the lady as an intern doing some research for him and instructed the peon to light up the right-hand side of the room. He then led Gautam to it and waved his hand at two five and a half feet tall steel racks neatly labelled month-wise as suicides/murders 2008, "Knock yourself out, son. I'll try to arrange for a table and chair for you to sit down while going through the files. Although we maintain such records they are rarely accessed. If they are needed, they are taken out of this room to be examined. We unfortunately cannot do that now."

"Not an issue Bipin, I'll manage," Gautam reassured, picking up a stack of 20 files from a rack labelled April 2008, the month he had joined Ahmedabad circle and had investigated his first murder turned suicide case. He squatted on the floor with it, extracted a pad and pen from his satchel, and proceeded to examine the files.

Chapter 72

Beating the System

Sub Inspector Madhav Shinde loved his job, despite the politics and corruption, and although it had been against the principles inculcated by his parents, he had accepted the bribe money percolated down to his level and had done as he had been told. His diplomacy had paid off three years ago, earning him a promotion as a sub-inspector. Nothing had changed though apart from his grade. The strings were still pulled by the seniors. That was until Gautam had joined and had openly defied the precedent set by his superior.

Madhav had been happy for the first time in his career as a police officer and was glad to assist Gautam. Then the bomb of Gautam's pedigree had dropped. While Kamal had assured his minions that Gautam didn't have proof to implicate anyone, Madhav hadn't been so sure.

There was something about Gautam that reminded him of his father's gospel, 'Never be afraid to walk on the path of truth.' That's why Madhav was super excited when Gautam asked him to go undercover to expose a 'fake document' racket. Madhav didn't have much knowledge or interaction with banks and bankers, and as he sat in Hrian's huge cabin that afternoon, waiting for the alleged tout to appear, he couldn't help wondering how a loan agent like Hrian could have such a big office with so much staff.

Hrian escorted a man who appeared to be in his 30s into his cabin just then. Madhav noted his jeans, a T-shirt with Calvin Klein written across his chest, and what appeared to be expensive, black sneakers. His curiosity was picued because he had been instructed to wear scruffy clothes and try to appear desolate.

"This is Madhav Shinde, a jobless migrant from a remote village in Satara. He used to work as a farmhand in his village but decided to move to Ahmedabad to start his own popcorn-making business. For that, he needs a Rs 2 lakh personal loan to buy an industrial grade popcorn maker, lease out a shed, buy packing material and so on, but he doesn't have any documentation," Hrian conveyed, the second the tout occupied a chair beside Madhav.

"That's not an issue. How old are you, Madhav?" the tout enquired.

"I'm 27."

"Great. We'll portray you as an accountant working with a Private Limited company, earning a salary of Rs 50,000 per month. Where do you live in Ahmedabad?" the tout responded.

"In a dormitory," Madhav answered as he had been coached, although he lived in a small, independent house with his mum and brother.

"That won't work. No bank will sanction a loan to you. I'll find a rented residence for you and fabricate a rent agreement. I'm going to click a photo of you now, so please sit straight," the tout requested, extracting a digital camera from his pocket.

*

Adi's heartbeats accelerated on hearing his cell phone ping. Scrolling down with trembling fingers, he read a text message from Hrian, 'Our part is done. He'll be leaving the building any minute now.' Adi gunned Hrian's motorcycle, borrowed for the occasion of tailing the tout, as it was more convenient than his car. Taking deep breaths to calm his frayed nerves, Adi watched the man who had entered the building with Hrian 15 minutes ago, exit it, and walk towards a black Skoda Rapid parked outside. Since Adi was waiting across the road, he allowed the car to pass him before taking a U-turn. 'Wow, this man could easily pass off as a wealthy businessman and not a crook apt at beating the system,' Adi wondered, following the tout.

As per the plan devised that night with Gautam and Tony, Hrian had to videotape the entire interaction between the tout and Madhav, while Adi was assigned to follow him because Gautam wanted to double-check if the documents were being forged in Lalitha Towers or elsewhere.

Chapter 73

Digging his Own Grave.

"Good morning, DSP Mittal. It appears that you have put in an all-nighter. Would you like to go home and shower before our meeting, or shall we proceed right away?"

Gautam sprung to attention on hearing his boss, SP Kamal Arora's unusually warm greeting. 'Meeting? What meeting?' The question churned in his mind as he saluted his superior while trying to recollect if he had received any message or email regarding a meeting.

Sure, he had put in an all-nighter because he wanted to meticulously organize all the evidence he had gathered till now, but there hadn't been any email or message about a meeting.

"Do you need more time to answer my question, DSP Mittal?"

The hint of sarcasm in Kamal's tone prompted Gautam to respond, "Er, sorry sir, let's have the meeting right away."

"Hmm, thank you," Kamal replied, turning towards his cabin with Gautam in tow.

Kamal sat on his desk, fired his laptop, connected the USB cable that would enable him to present reports from his laptop on the flat TV beside his desk, and turned on the TV.

The contents displayed on the 52" screen hit Gautam like a sucker punch. It was a mirror of the virtual notice board he had created on his laptop that was lying at that very moment on his desk and had the entry he had updated 5 minutes ago before Kamal had requested for the meeting. It had been set up some months ago so that the Director General of Gujarat Police could monitor his progress in the 4 major investigations he was handling.

Speechless, he turned to meet Kamal's eyes boring into him. Ominous silence shrouded the room as the men assessed each other. Gautam blinked first and lowered his eyes, only to raise them in surprise at Kamal's declaration, "This is first-rate sleuthing. I never knew *Gujarat Mirror* kept such detailed records of attempted suicides or murders that may have been brushed under the carpet. So, did you cross-reference all 45 cases that had passed through Dr Piyush Patel and the other 5 doctors with FIRs on your own or did Madhav help you?"

Gautam wondered if he was digging his own grave with his answer, "I did it on my own."

"Hmm, so you'll need a warrant right to subpoena the doctors' phone records."

His fingers turned cold at Kamal's calm conclusion, yet he decided to play along and answered, "Yes."

"Okay, you take printouts of the reporters' records and the death certificates, and you file an FIR against Dr Piyush and the other doctors. We'll use it to request Judge Smita Mehra, a magistrate of the first class for a warrant to subpoena the doctors' phone records. Now tell me about this Sidanshu Gaur. How did you stumble on this con man?"

Realising he had nothing to lose, Gautam confessed to having tailed Dr Dhiraj after his wife attempted suicide, but left out the hacker part and fibbed that Dr Dhiraj had confessed to being blackmailed, which led him to Adi, the honey trap, and the fake document racket, finally concluding, "Sir, I have reasons to believe that Dr Piyush Patel is in cahoots with

Sidanshu, and has furnished information about doctors who need loans to purchase medical equipment."

"Great, so we already have Dr Dhiraj's FIR on record to request the judge for a search warrant of Sidanshu's premises and an arrest warrant if incriminating evidence is found. Ask Madhav to file an FIR to obtain a search warrant for the office in Lalitha Towers," Kamal instructed, leaving Gautam wondering if all this was happening or if he was dreaming.

"Hmm, now I would say you are playing with fire Gautam by requesting for the fourth warrant to seize Karan Malhotra's sports bike to match the tyre prints with the ones found on the murder scene based on the journo's FIR. Do you know how many such sports bikes there are in Ahmedabad?"

"There are 5 Hayabusas, sir, but only one of the owners is a heroin addict with a connection to the victim."

"Fine, let's place a request for that warrant also. We'll deal with the aftermath, if any. You may leave now and let me know when you are ready with all the paperwork. I'll accompany you to meet Judge Smita Mehra," Kamal declared, dismissing him, only to state, making it appear like an afterthought,

"Just to set the record straight, it was the DGP who phoned me this morning and shared the virtual notice board. He requested me for my full co-operation to ensure the smooth execution of these raids."

Gautam left the room, mentally raising a hat to the DG for shrewdly neutralizing Kamal.

Chapter 74

All in a Day's Work

It was nothing like the stakeouts one sees in movies, or maybe a bit because there was a car parked a few feet from Dr Shailesh's clinic, with dark windows, Tony's Hyundai Elantra, with only Tony and Adi sitting in it. Gautam was perched on a bike, taking updates from his subordinates as they waited for Priya to arrive. They had been stationed outside Dr Shailesh's clinic since 6.45 pm.

Gautam had been apprehensive about using civilians, but he had no choice. His trusted sub-inspector Madhav was on another important mission. Like a jigsaw puzzle, a lot of pieces were falling in place. Tony's charm had worked on Dr Dhiraj and Dr Dhiraj had managed to convince at least five other doctors who were defaulting because of Priya's trap to allow Madhav to record their statements. Bipin had managed to trace and convince some of the aggrieved businessmen to at least permit the police to place their predicaments on record, with the guarantee their names wouldn't be revealed, nor would the videos be released to the press, should the case go to court. Gautam had also reassured them of anonymity, but everything henceforth depended on how the next hour would pan out.

Gautam's breath suddenly caught in his throat on seeing a tall, lithe girl wearing a flowing black dress and oversized dark glasses push open the front door of Dr Shailesh's clinic. Sure, it was Priya. Gautam quickly disconnected the call he was on and dialled Tony.

"Ya, we too saw her. I've turned on the clock facility in my camera, so the photos Adi clicked of her will show the time she entered the clinic as 7.04 pm.," Tony responded before Gautam could say anything, so Gautam hung up, and dialled Dr Shailesh.

As per their plan, Dr Shailesh had to activate a camera hidden in a wall-mounted bookshelf upon receiving Gautam's call, so it would start recording even before Priya entered his consulting room. Dr Shailesh answered the call and stated, "I'm about to finish with a patient. I will get back to you ASAP."

Gautam's heart started pounding as he slipped the phone into the breast pocket of his shirt. He had shed his uniform for plain clothes that evening for obvious reasons. Well, everything was in place, now all they had to do was wait, which was the most painful part.

Unprofessional thoughts started churning in his mind. 'What could be compelling Priya to cheat people this way? Is Sidanshu coercing her into it?' Seeing the young girl brought back memories of his sister and he couldn't help wondering if she was still alive. Had it been so, she would have tried to contact them, so it was possible she was held captive, hence not in a position to phone. A vice squeezed his heart at the thought of her being forced into flesh trade in some obscure part of the world, probably drugged into compliance.

His vibrating cell phone brought him back to the present. "She just walked out of Dr Shailesh's room. I'll go in after she leaves the clinic," and excited Adi informed, disconnecting the line.

Gautam kept his eyes glued to the clinic's entrance. Adi was already out of the car, and hovering around a cigarette vendor's kiosk nearby, so Gautam gunned the bike he had borrowed from Hrian for the occasion, as the noise from the exhaust of his bike would attract too much attention.

Priya exited the clinic and turned left; in the direction she had come from. Gautam watched Tony inch his car away from the curb outside the clinic and move forward, so he quickly accelerated his bike, took a U-turn, and went ahead of Tony. Priya turned left at a corner and was walking towards a row of two-wheelers parked at the curb. Noticing Tony's car keeping pace with her, Gautam parked in a vacant spot, killed the engine, and dismounted. He quickly checked his cell phone for the message from Adi. Heaving a sigh of relief, on reading, 'Go ahead, boss, my work's done,' Gautam glanced back at Priya.

She had stopped beside a black gearless scooter and had bent her head as she browsed for probably her key in the oversized shoulder bag.

"Let me help you with that," Gautam suggested, snatching the bag from her shoulders.

"What? Give it back or I'll scream for help," Priya reacted after a fraction of a second. Gautam had deliberately planned the element of surprise because he wanted to take custody of her purse first before he arrested her.

"Go ahead. The police are already on the scene," Gautam urged, flashing his badge.

Priya turned and tried to make a run for it, only to bang into Tony's sturdy body blocking her exit.

"What's going on?" Priya tried to appear bewildered, but Gautam could see the fear in her eyes.

"Dr Shailesh complained you have stolen some money from his office, so we are taking you in for questioning. It will be better if you cooperate and come silently with us," Gautam whispered into her ear. Tony opened the rear door of his car.

There was a fourth person involved in the stakeout, a lady. She stepped out of the car, dressed like Gautam in jeans and a tucked in white pin-striped shirt. Flashing her badge at

Priya, she introduced herself as a detective from the Maninagar crime branch, grabbed Priya's arm and entered the car first, forcing Priya to do so. Gautam followed suit. The lady detective cuffed Priya's wrists together in front of her while Gautam extracted his cell phone, and Tony drove to Maninagar police station.

Gautam dialled Madhav first and instructed curtly, "Please proceed." The second call was made to Kamal, requesting him also to proceed with his part of the plan.

Madhav's undercover operation had paid off as he had been called to Lalitha Towers to sign the forged documents. So had Adi's sleuthing after he had tailed the tout from Hrian's office. The actual forging was happening in the 1000 square feet office in Lalitha Towers, as the tout had gone straight from Hrian's office to Lalitha Towers. There was a third detective from the Ahmedabad police force who was accompanying Madhav that night. A sepecial task force team was waiting outside the office for the detective's signal. They had a warrant issued by Judge Mehra to search the office premises and would do so only after the detective laid eyes on the forged documents.

Another simultaneous raid was about to be executed at Sidanshu's office too. That was what Gautam's second phone call had been about and they had a warrant for that also.

Chapter 75

Lacunae

Beer can in hand, Gautam slinked out of Adi's living room to his balcony and shut the sliding doors behind him. Settling down on the white wicker swing, he stared at the night sky and basked in the peace.

It was a Saturday night. The boisterous party celebrating Adi being reinstated by HR as the ASM of North Gujarat had started at 8 pm after Adi and Trisha picked up Leila and her boyfriend from the airport. Tony was also present with a date, a stylish interior designer who could give both Trisha and Leila a run for their money. Only Hrian and Gautam had been the unattached ones, seemingly contented with their single status.

The party had started with a toast to Gautam, Tony and Hrian, the heroes in Adi's life, as his name wouldn't have been cleared without their help. The simultaneous raids of both Lalitha Towers and Sidanshu's office had provided enough evidence to the bank that even external verification agencies couldn't resist the temptation of fast money, and the bank officials couldn't only hold the sales personnel responsible for fraud.

The documents made for Madhav had provided the classic example. The forgers had access to the serial numbers affixed on IT (Income Tax) returns when they were filed by the public. They used these serial numbers, and the names associated with it to make fake IT returns for potential loan customers. The customer was given the same name, along with a Pan Card whose number was also obtained from the IT return. The external verification agency only checked the serial number with the name on the IT return so they couldn't know it was fake.

Making phony address proofs, bank statements and salary slips were easier. Sheafs of papers with what appeared to be the original logos of several banks, and blank electricity bill formats were seized from the office in Lalitha Towers, so were the banks' stamps that were generally fixed at the end of each bank statement to prove their originality. The forgers had even gone to the extent of leasing out several flats, shops, and offices in different areas of Ahmedabad and forging rent agreements for the customers so that they could be submitted as address proofs.

These flats were generally in the lower middle-class areas, so it was easy to bribe the neighbours into confirming the loan applicants resided there when the FI verification executives questioned them. In some instances, the verification executives had also been bribed. The banks still had a lot of lacunae in their systems.

The real Bonnie and Clyde had turned out to be Priya and Sidanshu. Priya had become an escort during her college days in Mumbai to finance her obsession for expensive clothes and jewellery. When Sidanshu, her senior got wind of her clandestine activities, he convinced her to seduce their friends' fathers, record the rendezvous and blackmail them. It worked till they graduated, then frizzled out when most of their friends had started working or migrated abroad. So, Sidanshu decided to become a loan facilitator with banks, and Priya reverted to being a high-end escort.

She managed to steal the identities of several of her rich customers. Sidanshu used it to get banks to sanction high-value home loans. He would sell the properties after a while, and he and Priya made an obscene amount of money. They fled to Ahmedabad when certain banks started getting suspicious, and purchased the office in Lalitha Towers, from where they ran a new fake documents operation, along with the 'honey trap' scam.

Storming into Sidanshu's office had been the real coup de grâce for Adi, and the doctors and businessmen he was blackmailing. Sidanshu, who had been unaware that Priya had been arrested, had been seated in his plush cabin, looking suave. It had been Gautam who had waived the warrant at him and had promptly seized his laptop, for he knew it might have contained incriminating photos of Adi, Tony, Priyansh, and Surbhi. Well, he had been right, and since it was evidence, he had to present it to the bank's HR team. The senior officials of the bank requested Gautam to be discrete when presenting the evidence in court as the press would have had a field day with this information. Fortunately, Adi and Tony got off with stern warnings.

When the discussions of the scams had died down, the group had toasted Leila as she had refused to withdraw her complaint. Priyansh had tried to defend himself by bringing Adi into the picture, confident that Adi would save his ass, but Adi had denied any unprofessional involvement with Leila. Then Priyansh had tried to rope in Bharat, but Tony had already threatened him not to get involved, so Bharat had clearly stated that Leila had always maintained a professional relationship with him. Realising Priyansh was grasping at straws, HR had politely requested him to resign.

"Leila, Adi tells me you were responsible for transforming him from a country boy to the suave, sophisticated guy he claims to be now. So, what did he look like when you met him for the first time?" Trisha had enquired after they were done hashing out Priyansh.

"Oh, he had been a regular redneck who oiled his hair with that smelly Bring... something," Leila had started to speak, and Gautam had slinked out.

While he was glad things had worked out for Adi and Leila, his mind was on Bipin, who got his exclusive stories regarding the banking scams, especially the sensational 'honey trap'. Karan had panicked when the police had seized his bike and had confessed to injecting Rahul with an overdose of heroin, confident that Uncle Atul, Ahmedabad's infamous criminal lawyer would get him acquitted.

Well, Uncle Atul had openly stated that he had no knowledge of Karan being in love with his daughter and he had cared a lot for his son-in-law, Rahul, because he truly loved his daughter.

Epilogue

Nature's beauty was at its resplendent best. The soft, golden rays of the rising sun, working their way through the grey-black sky served as the perfect background for the nearly 12 feet high sugarcane stalks. The green leaves at the tip of the stalks were swaying gently to the cool breeze.

Adi took a deep breath and waited for the sun to emerge fully from the horizon. This had been his routine for the past four years; wake up at 5.30 am, ride his grandfather's retired thoroughbred *Bahadur* (Hercules' replacement, named by his father!) to his newly acquired fields and watch the sun rise. Then, he used to walk on the paths between his sugarcane crops to examine the newly planted shoots for growth, much like a new father would of his offspring. Of course, he had been a novice farmer then, to assume that farming would be a breeze after his high-pressure job in the bank.

Reality had struck him in the very first week of moving to Bulandshahr after resigning from *TCI*. Wanting to start out on his own, he had insisted on buying his own land. Fortunately, Veer had done the groundwork for him, and five acres of land had been available a kilometre away from his family's lands for a price of Rs 12 lakhs per acre. The farmer who owned the land had gone bankrupt due to his gambling habits, so he was eager to sell the land. Adi had sold his flat in Ahmedabad for a crore of rupees to facilitate the purchase and had used the bulk of the leftover money to acquire the latest technology farming equipment.

Unfortunately, a stay order had been issued a day before the sale deed was to be executed by the farmer's younger brother who claimed his stake in his ancestral land. Three months of formal litigation and an exchange of a couple of lakhs of rupees in bribes had finally resolved the legal case in Adi's favour and he became the proud owner of 5 acres of prime land. Then a social issue raised its ugly head. Most of the farmhands belonged to the lower cast, and they lived in shanties with no amenities like running water and toilets. Soon after the land deal had gone through, Adi had built proper houses for his farm hands with toilets and 24-hour water supply. This enraged some rich landowners, so the living quarters were set on fire one night, resulting in the death of five men and one child.

All the other surviving farm hands had fled from the scene with their families, the next day, leaving Adi stranded when he was supposed to have planted his first crop. Fortunately, his father had stepped in and labourers from his grandfather's fields had ensured the grafting of sugarcane stems had taken place as per schedule. It had been difficult though to get the farm hands to divide their time between the two farms, so his grandfather had used his clout to hire new labourers for Adi's farm and Veer had arranged for 24-hour private security.

Things had been a bit peaceful in the ensuing six months when he had finally married Trisha in a spectacular wedding ceremony in Bihar. Adi's father had been oblivious to the source of the Rs 20 lakh cash dowry Trisha's father had handed him right before Adi had stepped onto the specially constructed and decorated stage for the actual wedding ceremony. It had surreptitiously been provided by Veer who had started to realize such practices were evil. Trisha and Adi had enjoyed a blissful honeymoon in Mauritius before they returned to Bulandshahr and Trisha moved into his ancestral home.

No one, not even his staunch grandfather had objected to Trisha dressing up in jeans and T-shirts when she had started accompanying Adi to his farm each morning, after a family breakfast. Adi had constructed an office adjacent to his farm where he had started share trading to supplement his rapidly dwindling income and Trisha had started teaching the local children in Math, Science and English, in a room specially set aside for her. She had also immersed herself in researching modern farming techniques especially soil nutrients and had arranged for a soil scientist to visit their farm once in six months to test the quality of their soil.

The beads of perspiration dripping down his back snapped Adi back to the present. On realizing it was way past sunrise, he took one last look at his second sugarcane crop and rose from his perch below a Gulmohar Tree. Hurrying up to Bahadur who was contently munching the grass around the tree he had been tied to, Adi mounted the spirited horse and cantered to his office.

A smile lit his face on opening the outer glass door. Trisha was at the blackboard explaining addition to ten children while their six-month-old daughter was seated on the floor in front of them, gnawing on a teething ring as she happily watched her mother.

Life has certainly come a full circle! Adi couldn't help thinking as he tiptoed to his daughter and scooped her up in his arms.

www.ingramcontent.com/pod-product-compliance
Lightning Source LLC
LaVergne TN
LVHW091720070526
838199LV00050B/2472